AN AFFAIR
OF HONOR

Candice Hern

A Regency
Romance

An Affair of Honor

For further information, email
candice@candicehern.com

* * *

Cover art: Detail of "Dinner Dress" from Ackermann's *Repository of Arts*, September 1815. Collection of the author.

Chapter 1

$\mathbf{V}$iscount Sedgewick was dead. He was sure of it.

He had a vague recollection of the sensation of flying as he had been thrown from his curricle. Now, he seemed to be floating in darkness. He could see nothing, hear nothing, feel ... nothing.

Good Lord, he must have killed himself! How the devil had he managed something so stupid?

He had been on his way to ... where? He could not focus his thoughts clearly enough to remember. Was this what happened when you died? Funny. Though he had never actually given it much thought, he had assumed it would be different, somehow—that everything that had in life been a puzzle would suddenly become clear, that a lifetime of forgotten memories would be presented to his mind's eye with the clarity and detail of printed pages in a book. He would never have predicted that thoughts and ideas would become fuzzy and disjointed, as elusive as dandelion seeds scattered in the wind, until they were completely out of reach and could no longer be grasped at all.

Perhaps he had been wrong about death. Perhaps his mind—all he seemed to have left now, no longer having any sensation of a body—would simply fade away until there were no more thoughts at all, nothing whatsoever remaining of Colin Herriot, Viscount Sedgewick, body or mind.

No! I am not ready to go! He struggled to hang on to this one conviction, perhaps his last remaining conscious thought. *I am not ready.*

And all of a sudden, in an almost blinding flash, everything changed. Where moments ago—was it only moments?—there had been nothing, now there was pain. Excruciating pain. Where before Sedgewick had been conscious of no physical sensation whatsoever, he now became aware of his body for the first time, and as far as he could tell, every single part of it hurt.

Now this was more like what he had expected from death, or at least from dying. There had to be suffering, or so he had always assumed. Well, by Jove, he was suffering. The only question now was, how long would it continue? Once dead, one would think it would end. Unless ... unless ...

But no, he couldn't be *there*, could he? He had not done anything that terrible in his lifetime. Or had he? Oh, good Lord. His head, or at least the place where he knew his head to have once been, felt as though it were on fire, so the possibility that he was in fact *there* had to be faced. His poor dead soul was being tortured for his sins. But why?

To be sure, he had led a somewhat capricious life during his thirty-six years. He had enjoyed himself, but what was the harm in that? There had been all those women, of course, but they had all been willing, and often eager. partners. Sedge couldn't help it if they found him irresistible. Besides, he had never knowingly hurt any of them, and they had in most cases remained friends long after the end of an affair. Of course, their husbands might have a complaint or two against him; but even that seemed a bit far-fetched, for, after all, how many of those gentlemen could lay claim to any sort of faithfulness?

So, then, how the hell had he ended up in ... well... hell?

A sharp stab of pain pounded through Sedgewick's head, as if in reply. Dammit, what had gone wrong? How was it he was being judged so harshly?

He had gambled, too, of course, but not to excess, and had never been, as far as he knew, the cause of anyone's ruin. He was prone to be lazy at times, it was true, but for the most part had been conscientious in his duties and obligations. He kept an eye on his investments and tended his estates. Well, to be perfectly honest, he hired excellent solicitors and stewards who ensured that his estates and tenants were well tended, but it amounted to the same thing. He remained close and attentive to his widowed mother and sister, was a loyal friend to many, and generous with his time and money.

Damnation! He did not deserve this. By all accounts he should have ended up someplace altogether different. Some place pleasant and painless and beautiful, with angels strumming harps and singing in perfect harmony. By God, it wasn't fair. It simply was not fair.

Before he could formulate another thought, things got worse. It felt as though his brain had slammed up against the side of his skull. His head seemed to have moved to an awkward angle. Or been moved. *Ohhhhh.* The sound of his own groan echoed in Sedge's head like a clap of thunder. Could a dead person groan? For that matter, could a dead person feel pain like the pounding of Thor's hammer in his head? Thank God he had never committed any truly heinous acts in his lifetime, if this was the punishment handed down for such trivial and common sins as his own.

His present agony was soon increased by the weird, muffled sound of voices rumbling in his head.

Incomprehensible and yet somehow frightening, the odd sounds only intensified the thundering pain so that Sedge thought he might go mad. By God, he was determined to see what it was he faced, despite his helplessness. Frustrated by the stygian blackness, he attempted to open his eyes.

Ohhhhh. It was going to be more difficult than he had thought. He could almost wish he were dead, but, of course, he already was dead, so what was he to do?

He tried again.

His head throbbing mercilessly, Sedge fluttered his eyes slowly open into the merest slits. Blast it all, the light was blinding! Oh, good Lord. Was it fire? The flames of hell?

He groaned and snapped his eyes shut once again. His chest tightened as he breathed heavily, exhausted by the simple effort of opening his eyes. The thought briefly crossed his mind that dead men don't breathe, but he dismissed it as simply a malicious illusion.

Why me? What have I done to deserve this?

He tried again.

This time, after very slowly cracking open one eye and then the other, he steeled himself to withstand the brightness, determined to see how bad the situation really was. Trembling with effort, he strained to keep his eyes open, blinking against the light. Everything was a bit fuzzy, but as he squinted he could make out a dark, looming shape surrounded by a fiery nimbus.

Oh God. This was too much. He quickly closed his eyes again, not yet ready after all to face his own final judgment.

The muffled sound of voices continued to assault his ears. Clamping his eyes tightly shut, he concentrated on the voices. No, not voices. Voice. One voice. Female, slightly musical, somehow soothing. Very, very slowly, he opened his eyes again. Blinking furiously, Sedge tried to bring the dark shape into focus. By God, he would face this thing.

Allowing his eyes a moment to become accustomed to

the almost painful brightness, the dark shape finally coalesced into a face—a hazy countenance only inches away from his own. Sedge forced his eyes to remain open, blinking frequently to ease the pain, and the intense brightness gradually faded into a more normal sort of light that eventually allowed him to see the face more clearly.

It was the face ... of an angel.

Sedge gazed up at a vision of such dreamlike beauty as he had never seen. Before he could notice much more, his eyes fell shut again, this time of their own volition. He could not seem to keep them open. But one thing he knew for sure: that was no demon looking down on him. It was a lovely female face of creamy white skin surrounded by brilliant coppery curls and gazing down at him with huge sherry-colored eyes. She was an angel.

Ha! He had been wrong all along. He was not in hell. He had ended up in heaven after all!

He forced his stinging, uncooperative eyes open, for he must see her again, his angel. Head pounding furiously, he batted his lids against grainy, painful eyes and focused once again on the vision hovering above him, surrounded by light.

* * *

Meg Ashburton gazed down into the bleary eyes of the injured gentleman whose head was cradled gently in her arms. Using an embroidered linen handkerchief quickly retrieved from her reticule, she carefully dabbed at the bleeding gash over his left eye. All at once, his eyes fluttered and a muffled sound escaped his lips. Meg leaned closer.

"Can you hear me, my lord?" she asked, bending low over him. "Can you hear me? Try not to move. We are going to help you."

Lord Sedgewick made another inarticulate sound and

squinted his eyes tightly shut.

"'My lord'? You know him, Meggie?"

Meg looked up as her brother Terrence knelt beside her. When they had come upon the curricle wreckage while traveling home on the Ixworth Road, Terrence had immediately tossed the reins of their gig to Meg. He had jumped down to see to the frightened team of chestnut geldings who were pulling nervously at the steel bar across their backs and dancing skittishly among the tangle of broken traces.

"Yes," Meg replied. She glanced briefly across the road to see that Terrence had freed the horses from the traces and pole, and secured them separately to tree branches with the carriage reins. "It is Lord Sedgewick. I met him once or twice during my Season."

Meg almost laughed at how inadequate the statement sounded, though it was perfectly true. She doubted he would even remember her.

"Ah," Terrence said.

Looking back down in Lord Sedgewick's face, Meg noted a muscle twitching near his right eye and knew he had not completely lost consciousness. He seemed to be working the muscle deliberately. Finally the eyes fluttered open again. Meg watched as he squinted up at her and blinked several times. All at once, his eyes stopped blinking and seemed to fix on hers with a dazed, disoriented look.

"Lord Sedgewick?" She was concerned by his glassy stare. His lips moved slightly as though he wanted to say something. Meg bent her face closer to his. "Lord Sedgewick?"

"An ... gel," he murmured.

Meg looked at her brother in confusion and shrugged her shoulders. Bending her face close to Lord Sedgewick's once again, she studied his dilated eyes, still fixed on hers. "I do not understand, my lord," she said softly. "What is it you are trying to say?"

"An ... gel," he repeated in a slurred, thick voice. "Angel. My ... my angel... speaks." A corner of his mouth twisted briefly into what might have been a grin but immediately became a grimace. His eyes rolled upward and then closed, and his head fell to one side.

Disconcerted by the words for a brief instant, Meg saw Terrence arch a questioning brow. Ignoring her brother, Meg directed all her concentration toward assessing Lord Sedgewick's injuries. She released his head from her hold and carefully laid it down while her eyes scanned his body. He lay on his back with one leg at an unnatural angle, obviously broken. Meg leaned over him, taking care not to jar the injured leg, and quickly attempted to survey the damage. Gently running her hands under his bloodstained greatcoat and jacket, she had not been able to find the source of the blood.

"He might have sustained a broken rib or two," she said. "I cannot be sure. But there is no obvious injury to his body. All this," she said with a sweeping gesture over the muddy, bloodied garment, "must have been from the cut on his head. He has lost a great deal of blood."

"I'll have a look at the leg," Terrence said, moving quickly to the other side of the silent figure.

Meg returned her attention to the head wound. Lord Sedgewick's thick blond hair was heavily matted with blood from the gash over his left eye. Her linen handkerchief was already blood-soaked, so she quickly began to rip the cotton lace from her petticoat, and to tear the plain cotton into strips and squares. She concocted a good-sized padding and pressed it firmly against Lord Sedgewick's bleeding temple, attempting to staunch the flow of blood. Satisfied with the results, she tied the padding tightly into place with the strips of lace. Removing her own cloak, she folded it and gently placed it beneath his head.

Absently wiping her bloodied hands against her skirt, Meg looked toward her brother. He was hunched over the horribly bent leg, and she swallowed the taste of bile at the sight of it. She had seen her share of broken bones, having grown up on a farm, and therefore was not generally given to squeamishness. However, such an unnatural bend could not fail to affect her.

Terrence looked up. "It doesn't look as though the skin has been ruptured," he said, "so we can hope it is a clean break. We won't know for certain, though, until we cut off the boot."

"Now?" Meg exclaimed in alarm. "Here?"

"No," Terrence replied as he stood up. "I do not care to take that chance. We might inadvertently cause further damage."

"Should we try to get him into the gig?" Meg asked.

"No," Terrence replied as he hurried across the road toward the two geldings, "I do not think we should move him. That leg should be set before lifting him. Besides, the gig is too small. We will need a litter." He began to untie the reins of one of the horses. "I'm going to ride to Thornhill for help," he called over his shoulder. "I'll try to locate Garthwaite. You stay with him, Meggie. Try to keep him warm."

Meg watched as Terrence slipped off the harness and tossed it to the ground. He then looped the long carriage reins over and over around his hand and walked the gelding away from the tree. She had no need to ask why he did not take their own horse, understanding at once that the superior strength of one of the beautiful chestnut geldings would serve him better than the older, slower mare they had brought with the gig. Terrence led the dancing, whinnying gelding away from the other horse, all the while stroking his long nose, crooning in his ear, and occasionally blowing gently into his nostrils. Meg watched as her brother expertly calmed the nervous animal before mounting him bare-backed in one graceful, fluid movement. Keeping the carriage reins wrapped tightly around one hand, Terrence turned him toward Thornhill and kneed him into a gallop.

"Hurry!" Meg shouted to her brother's retreating back. *Oh, please hurry*, she thought as she gazed down at the silent figure lying at her side. Gently taking Lord Sedgewick's hand in her own, she closed her eyes and prayed for his recovery. Surely God would not be so cruel as to let him die. Not this man.

She gave in to the sheer pleasure of holding his hand in hers, stroking his long, slender fingers, and tracing the clear lines of his palm. *My angel*, he had called her. Of course, he had been delirious and spouting nonsense, though Meg thought she had seen a flicker of recognition, or something, in his eyes when he spoke. *My angel*. Meg smiled as she hugged those sweet words close to her heart. It mattered not that the man was probably out of his mind. Any endearment from Lord Sedgewick was to be cherished, for she would doubtless never hear such from him again.

She lifted his fingers briefly to her lips, acknowledging at last how cold they were and how precarious his condition was. Meg knew firsthand the dangers of head wounds. Her own father had died of one when he had been thrown from a particularly vicious stallion he had been attempting to train. Recollections of her father's death brought a sick feeling to Meg's stomach.

No, by God, there would be no sad ending this time, if she could help it. Not for this man.

Still holding his hand, Meg kept a careful watch on Lord Sedgewick's face, alert to any sign of change in his condition. Good Lord, but he was pale. And so cold. She gently moved Lord Sedgewick's hands to his sides and tucked his greatcoat more closely around his chin and shoulders to protect him against the chilly March air.

Thank God it was not raining again this afternoon, she

thought as she looked up at the overcast sky. The poor man would probably have died of a chill. She shivered and clutched her arms at the elbows. Looking up at the leaden skies, she hoped their luck would hold out. Meg's eyes followed a cluster of grayish clouds to the line of black poplar trees across the road, their spiky, leafless branches silhouetted against the silvery haze, and then down to the muddy, rutted road below. Catching sight, then, of the gig, an idea occurred to her. She quickly rose and shook out her skirts, dismissing the errant thought that the beautiful blue kerseymere—one of her favorite winter dresses—was now streaked with blood and ruined beyond repair. As she walked across the road, she tried to recall whether or not she had seen a spare horse blanket tucked away in a corner of the gig. Terrence usually kept one handy.

She pushed aside the packages of goods and supplies she and her brother had purchased that morning in Bury St. Edmund's, at last coming upon a worn and stained blanket wrapped into a tight roll. She retrieved the roll, unfurled the scratchy red wool, and shook it out, squinting and coughing against the bits of straw and hay that scattered in the air. She wrinkled her nose as she held the blanket out and examined it. Yes, it was ugly and smelly, but it would do.

Meg hurried to the other side of the road and carefully laid the blanket over Lord Sedgewick's greatcoat. This should at least help to keep him warm, she thought, casting her eyes once again to the threatening skies above.

Meg turned her gaze to the road toward their farm at Thornhill. What was keeping Terrence? Hopefully, her brother would be able to return with Dr. Garthwaite. If Lord Sedgewick had indeed sustained a compound fracture to his leg, the young and compassionate village physician was more likely to attempt a repair than to amputate, as many other doctors would. So, there was little more she could do for now, save keep an eye on the head wound.

Meg knelt once again at Lord Sedgewick's side. At least

he still seemed to be breathing; and her makeshift bandage appeared to have effectively staunched the flow of blood. There did not appear to be anything more she could do, except to feel helpless and wait.

And so she waited. And waited.

She rose occasionally and stood staring down the road toward Thornhill, shielding her eyes against the midday glare. Determining at last that watching the road only made the wait seem longer, she returned to her patient and sat back down on her knees at his side. Her brow furrowed as she looked down at him. Dear, sweet Lord Sedgewick. He looked so helpless and young, though she guessed him to be at least a dozen years her senior. She had never thought to see him again, keeping so close to Thornhill as she did. With wry amusement, she considered the irony of the situation. It was her typical ill luck that when Lord Sedgewick's path finally crossed hers after all these years, it was only to lie half dead at her feet. She shook her head in dismay as she studied his ashen face.

"Do not worry, my lord," she whispered as she brushed back a lock of blond hair from his pale brow, "we will not let you die. We will patch you up and nurse you and send you back on your way."

It was the least she could do, for the only man she had ever loved.

Chapter 2

"**H**e should sleep quietly for some time now," Dr. Garthwaite said. "But he is already slightly feverish. It would be best to have someone watch over him at all times, in case the fever worsens. And when the laudanum wears off, if he is conscious, he will likely be in a great deal of pain, and very uncomfortable." He picked up his medical bag and retrieved a small blue vial. The solemn young man turned toward Meg and handed her the medicine, his eyes earnest behind the glare of his spectacles. "You may give him two more drops of laudanum if he needs it. Just be sure he does not jar the leg too much. Try to keep him as immobile as possible so that the bone can set properly."

Meg nodded, then puckered her brow as she looked down at the bandaged head of their patient. "And the cut on his head? Is there anything special we should do?"

"Ahh," the doctor said, dragging the syllable out as he turned toward the bed. He absently pushed his spectacles up on the bridge of his nose, squinting as he gazed down at Lord Sedgewick's unconscious form. "That is the real concern, is it not? We can never be sure about head injuries."

Meg sucked in her breath and slanted a glance at her

brother. He drew his brows together sharply. Then, looking down, he apparently found something interesting to study on the toe of his boot. His straight auburn hair fell over his eyes so that Meg could no longer see his face. Poor Terrence. He had never forgiven himself for their father's death. He had known the unruly stallion was dangerous and untrainable, but had nevertheless teased his more experienced and very competitive father into trying his hand with the beast. Sir Michael, always pleased to demonstrate his superior skills, had attempted to put the animal through his paces. He had been thrown, struck his head on a rock, and had never recovered.

"My biggest concern," the doctor continued, forcing Meg's attention back to the issue at hand, "is the severity of the fever. If infection cannot be arrested . . . well, I'm afraid I cannot predict the outcome." He turned away from his patient to face Meg and Terrence once again. "Promise you will send for me if the fever worsens."

"Of course, Dr. Garthwaite," Meg said.

"Then I must be off. Sally Maddox is near her time and I should look in on her."

Terrence followed the doctor out of the guest chamber, leaving Meg alone with their patient. Disturbed by the doctor's warnings and the recollections of her father's death, she bent over the unconscious Lord Sedgewick and laid the back of her hand against his cheek.

"How is he, dear?"

Meg turned to find that her grandmother had entered the room. "He seems quiet enough for now, Gram," Meg replied in a soft voice, moving her hand to his other cheek. "His breathing is regular. He is slightly flushed but not overly feverish just yet."

"Thank the Good Lord for that," Gram said. She moved across the room to the seating area near the fire and sank her plump frame into a chair in front of the grate. "Come, my dear," she said, keeping her voice hushed and waving toward the chair next to her. "Sit down and relax. I have asked Mrs. Dillard to bring us a pot of tea while we watch over Lord Sedgewick."

"Thank, you, Gram," Meg said as she checked the tieback on the green damask bed curtain, insuring that the heavy drapery was tightly pulled back to allow easier access to their patient. She then stood straight, pressed her palms against her lower back, and stretched her spine. "I am a bit fagged," she said. "Tea sounds wonderful."

At that moment, the bedchamber door was flung open and the bony bottom of Mrs. Dillard, Thornhill's stalwart housekeeper, backed its way into the room. The old woman, who must have been Gram's age if she was a day, swung around balancing a large, well-laden tea tray in her hands.

Meg went to her side and reached out to help with the tray, but the indomitable woman ignored the offer, as Meg might have known she would, and sailed on toward the far end of the room where a tilt-top tea table was placed in front of the grate. She placed the tray on the table without so much as rattling a dish. Mrs. Dillard was given to making a great show of demonstrating that age had not slowed her down, that she needed no help in running their small household, thank you very much. Meg smiled as she watched the housekeeper arrange the teapot, cups, saucers, and slop dish to her liking, and then uncover a plate of plum cake slices with a subtle flourish. The dear woman deserved a much grander house to manage, Meg thought after thanking Mrs. Dillard and watching her sprightly exit.

"Here you are, dear."

Meg turned at the sound of Gram's voice and reached out to accept the steaming cup of tea she offered. Carefully balancing the cup and saucer, Meg eased her tall frame into the vacant chair. After a long, restorative swallow, she replaced the cup on the tea table, stretched her legs out to their full length, and slid down in the chair so that her head rested on its back. Finally able to relax, exhaustion almost overwhelmed her. Her stiff muscles ached with fatigue and strain.

It had been a stressful afternoon and evening. By the time Terrence had returned to the roadside with Dr. Garthwaite and several grooms, Meg's nerves had been strung as tight as a drum. The doctor had quickly splinted the leg and had had Lord Sedgewick moved to a litter and on to Thornhill. Once the patient had been settled in a guest chamber, the doctor had taken meticulous care in setting the leg, wrapping it tightly in the complex overlapping folds of a multi-tailed bandage, and re-splinting it. He had also tended the gash over Lord Sedgewick's eye with great care—cleaning it, stitching it, and re-bandaging it as best he could. The wound was quite deep, though, and Meg knew the doctor feared the effects of concussion and infection. Though he slept peacefully enough just now, the patient must be closely watched.

Unfortunately, now that she was stretched out so comfortably, Meg did not believe she could keep her eyes open long enough to do much watching. The darkened room only exacerbated her drowsiness. At the doctor's instructions, they had drawn the heavy velvet curtains over the large windows overlooking the stables, and the wood-paneled room would have been pitch dark but for the fire and a few candles. Meg stifled a yawn. Gad, but she needed a brisk ride to work out the tension in her muscles. Knowing she was unlikely to get up and do anything quite that sensible when there was a cozy fire in the grate and a pot of tea at hand, she simply slid down further in the chair, stretched out her feet, kicked off her kid slippers, and flexed her toes.

"Meg!"

The scold, delivered in a stage whisper, elicited no more than a groan in response from Meg, who rolled her head against the chair back to look at her grandmother.

"Sit up straight, my girl." Gram kept her voice low but firm as she glanced across the room toward the four-poster bed. "There is a gentleman present, after all. I will not have Lord Sedgewick thinking you a hoyden!"

"Gram, the man is unconscious. If I stripped naked here and now, he would be none the wiser."

Meg heard her grandmother's sharp intake of breath and watched with some amusement as the old woman's eyes widened in outrage. "Behave yourself, Meg Ashburton!" Gram hissed as her eyes darted to the bed, as though afraid the sleeping Lord Sedgewick might actually have overheard. "He could awaken at any moment. I should hate for him to find you sprawled in your chair in that undignified, unladylike manner. Now, sit up, girl!"

Meg heaved a resigned sigh and pulled herself up straight, tucking her long legs beneath the chair and crossing them at the ankles. She picked up her teacup and saucer, raised the cup ever so delicately to her lips—pinkie finger extended just so— and took a dainty sip. As she replaced the cup in its saucer with the utmost care, she turned toward her grandmother and raised her brows in question.

"Much better, my dear," Gram said with a smile. "You can be such an elegant young lady when you try."

Meg gave a very unladylike snort and took another sip of tea. "I thought you had given up trying to make a lady out of me."

"But, that was before."

"Before what?"

Gram jerked her thumb in the direction of the bed and smiled. "You have another chance with him, Meg."

Meg closed her eyes for a moment and took a deep breath. "Oh, Gram." She put her cup and saucer down and gazed into her grandmother's hopeful, bright eyes. "I never had a first chance. Please do not go getting your hopes up."

"He *danced* with you."

"Yes, he did." Lord Sedgewick had been the only gentleman besides Terrence who had danced with her during that wretched Season, almost six years ago. She had been overly tall and gangly, all straight lines and jutting angles, topped by a mop of unfashionably red hair. Nervous and shy, she had been miserable, wanting nothing more than to go home to Suffolk. To the horses and the grooms and the people who knew her and did not make her feel ridiculous.

But there had been those two dances. Two wonderful dances that had made the whole vile Season worthwhile.

"When he recovers," Gram said, "I am certain he will want to renew his attentions."

"His what?" Meg squealed.

Gram placed her finger to her lips at the sound of Meg's raised voice. "He was obviously taken with you, dear."

"Gram," Meg said in a soft plaintive tone, "he merely danced with me."

"Twice, as I recall."

"Yes, twice. But he must have danced with scores of other young ladies. He was simply being polite to a pitiful wallflower." Meg had always known that to be the truth. He had been kind to her. That was all. But when he had taken her arm that first time and turned the full force of his smile on her, she had fallen in love with him in a moment. Oh, she had known it was a futile emotion, that she was being silly and foolish, but she had been unable to stop herself. By the time he had asked her to dance a second time, some weeks later, she had been well and truly lost.

"Two invitations to dance, my dear," Gram said, "should not be so lightly discounted. I am sure—"

"Ah, Gram, I am glad I have found you."

Meg sent up a silent prayer of thanks at the fortuitous return of her brother at just that moment. She had become quite alarmed at the turn the conversation had taken.

"The doctor gave me some further instructions,"

Terrence continued in a lowered voice as he stood next to the bed and looked down at Lord Sedgewick. Moving toward Meg and Gram, he fumbled in the pocket of his jacket and pulled out a crumpled scrap of foolscap that he held out to his grandmother.

"Some herbal infusion he thought you might be able to make up," he said.

Gram eyed the paper and nodded her head. "Yes, very wise. I believe I have all the ingredients in the stillroom. I will go down in just a bit and check."

Meg watched as Gram studied the receipt, grateful for the distraction it provided. Meg would have to seriously consider what to do about her grandmother's fanciful notions regarding Lord Sedgewick. Before the man regained consciousness, Gram would have to be taken in hand somehow, else the consequences could be embarrassing.

"Will you have some tea, my dear?" Gram asked Terrence.

"No, thank you, Gram," he said as he walked to the clothes- press behind the door and retrieved Lord Sedgewick's greatcoat and jacket.

"What are you doing, Terrence?" Meg asked. "If you are hoping to have those cleaned up, I can assure you they are quite ruined. The bloodstains—"

"No, no," Terrence said absently as he rifled through the pockets of each garment. "I was just hoping to find something to ... Aha! This should be useful." He held up a small printed pasteboard slipcase bearing the familiar words *Peacock's Polite Repository*. "I have been thinking," Terrence said as he pulled the book from the case, "that we ought to notify someone of Lord Sedgewick's accident. You said you recognized him, Meggie, but none of us knows where he lives or where he was going. I was hoping something in his belongings might provide us with his direction, at least. Someone will be missing him, no doubt."

"Yes," Meg said with a sidelong glance at Gram. Biting back a grin, she added, "His wife, perhaps."

"Oh, he is not married," Gram said in the most casual tone before taking another sip of tea.

"How do you know?" The words were echoed by both brother and sister as each turned to look at their grandmother, Terrence with confusion, Meg with wariness.

"Oh, I keep up on such things, you know," Gram replied with a fluttery wave of her hand.

Meg and Terrence shared a look of amusement before Terrence returned his attention to the tiny diary in his hand. A folded letter fell out and Terrence bent to retrieve it. "Well, Meggie, not that I doubted you, but he indeed appears to be Lord Sedgewick." He passed the letter to Meg.

She glanced at the direction, penned in a spidery, feminine hand.

To the Rt. Hon. Lord Viscount Sedgewick
Mount Street, London

The slightest hint of lavender wafted upward from the folded vellum. Wrinkling her nose, Meg handed the letter back to Terrence.

"At least now we know his direction," Terrence said. "I will send a note round to Mount Street." Tucking the letter in the back of the diary, he began flipping pages, finally stopping at one. His brow furrowed as he peered down at the page. "Gad, but the fellow has ghastly handwriting. There is a note scribbled on today's page. 'Travel Bids.' Travel Bids? What on earth could that mean?"

"Give me that," Meg said, reaching out for the diary.

Terrence shrugged and passed it to her. She looked at the page for a moment, and then laughed. "Not 'travel bids,' you idiot. It says 'Trevelian' and then 'Birds.' I do not know what—"

"Trevelian?" Terrence interrupted. "That must be Lord Cosmo Trevelian. We were at Oxford together, though we were never very close. I know that he does have an estate in Norfolk. That must be where Lord Sedgewick was heading."

"And 'birds'?" Meg asked.

"Well, that should be clear enough. Pheasant and partridge are not quite out of season, after all. It must be a hunting party."

"Then, perhaps you should send a message to Lord Trevelian in Norfolk," Meg said, handing the *Peacock's* back to her brother.

"Yes, I shall do that. Still," Terrence added as he accepted the diary back from Meg, "I wish we might contact his family. That head injury worries me." He glanced over at the bed. "If only we knew how to reach them."

"That is easy enough," Gram said as she rose from her chair. She walked briskly from the room without another word, her muslin dress billowing behind her like a sail. Terrence cast a quizzical glance at Meg. She shrugged, and they both chuckled. Since Gram had come to live with them after their mother's death some dozen years ago, they had both become accustomed to her quixotic bursts of energy and enthusiasm. Like the indomitable Mrs. Dillard, age had done little to slow Gram down.

Terrence completed his search of Lord Sedgewick's greatcoat, which yielded a card case, a sovereign purse, a small penknife, and a short length of string, but nothing more that would help him to locate the gentleman's family. Terrence returned the greatcoat to the clothespress while Meg eased back into her chair, stretched her long legs out in front of her once again, and enjoyed her cup of tea. Within moments, Gram burst back into the room with an armload of books. Meg moved aside the tea things to make room for the unwieldy volumes, and Gram deposited them on the table with a look of triumph.

"These should tell us what we need to know," she said, tossing an enigmatic glance at Meg. "Here, my dear, you start with this one." She tapped a finger against the topmost book.

Meg picked it up, noted the title, and gave a soft groan. *Collins Peerage of England.* Gram had even located the correct volume of the set, the one including titles beginning with "S." Good heavens, thought Meg, there will be no stopping the old girl now.

Gram took the next volume, one from the set of *Goddard's Biographical Index to the Present House of Lords*, and Meg let out another groan. If he knew what was good for him, poor Lord Sedgewick would remain unconscious for a long, long time.

Gram began rifling through pages and soon gave a triumphant "Ha!" She stabbed at the page with a plump finger. "Here it is," she said as she read the page before her. "Our guest is no less than the sixth Viscount Sedgewick. The title has been in the Herriot family since Charles II bestowed the patent on Sir Oliver Herriot in 1653. There are—Oh, my goodness, Meg!—three, no four estates in entailment. His primary seat is in Lincolnshire. That's it, Terrence," she said, her voice almost squeaking with excitement. "That's where his family must be. Yes," she said, reading on, "unless his mother has died very recently, she is still in residence in Lincolnshire. At Witham Abbey. He has no wife, you see." This last was said with raised brows and wide eyes directed at Meg, who rolled her own eyes heavenward and tossed the *Collins* back on the table.

"Oh, and his mother was a Howard," Gram continued, undaunted. "And his grandmother a Cavendish. Good heavens, he is related to all the best families!" She turned a beaming smile toward the bed in the corner and heaved a contented sigh. "Take this, my dear," Gram said as she handed the open volume to Terrence. "This will tell you where to write to Lord Sedgewick's mother. Unless you would prefer that I write to her?"

"No, no, Gram," Terrence said as he retrieved the volume, keeping his finger between the appropriate pages. "I must write her myself. I shall do so at once, along with a note to Mount Street, in case someone is there. And one to Trevelian as well."

Gram nodded and turned her attention to Meg. "Oh, Meg, is this not wonderful? A fine old title, excellent connections, several estates ... and no wife!"

"Indeed," Terrence said as he retrieved the stack of books from the tea table and headed toward the bedchamber door. "We must take especial care of such a paragon," he said, grinning over his shoulder at Meg and ducking just in time to miss the spoon she flung at his head.

* * *

Terrence chuckled to himself as he entered the library to return the books. Poor Meg. Gram was likely to be relentless in her pursuit of a match with Lord Sedgewick. And poor Lord Sedgewick, he thought as he reshelved the books. If only he knew what awaited him whenever he regained consciousness.

Terrence thought he ought to have a word with Gram.

He sank into the armchair behind his desk, opened a drawer, and pulled out several sheets of pressed paper. He retrieved a quill from its stand and considered their unconscious noble guest while he absently trimmed the point with a penknife. Terrence almost wished the man was conscious so that might frank the three letters he was about to write. Ha! He was as bad as Gram dreaming up plans to take advantage of the viscount. But at least his own plans, such as they were, could hardly be considered as other than harmless—a bit of franking, a word or two about Thornhill hunters spread amongst the viscount's friends, that sort of thing. But Terrence would be damned if he would get himself tangled up with any scheme of Gram's to encourage a match between Meg and Lord Sedgewick. Besides placing the viscount in an awkward situation, it would no doubt cause great embarrassment to Meg. Terrence was quite fond of his hoydenish sister, and knew she would not appreciate Gram's interference.

He did not think Gram ever really understood Meg's aversion to being trotted out like a young filly at the Marriage Mart. Terrence remembered rather clearly Meg's one and only Season six years before. He had gone up to Town to lend his support, but at the age of three-and-twenty had been distracted by other sorts of amusements, and had spent more time with his cronies from Oxford than he had squiring around his sister.

He began penning an introduction to Lady Sedgewick at Witham Abbey, but his mind wandered before he got much further than "My dear madam." Tapping the quill feather against his cheek, he chuckled as he recalled the ungainly eighteen-year-old Meg, all arms and legs towering over most everyone except her own tall family. Gram, who'd acted as her chaperone, had somehow managed to dress Meg in the most inappropriate styles imaginable—fussy, lacy things, overflowing with ruffles and bows. Poor Meg had looked like a scarecrow. Her bony shoulders had been all turned in and her elbows turned out as she had tried to slouch in hopes of appearing less tall. And her long, almost masculine stride had been completely at odds with the frilly dresses Gram had ordered. He could laugh in retrospect at what a sight she had made, but he knew at the time it had been difficult for Meg. She had been painfully shy and terribly self-conscious about her height. His own friends had teased him, calling him Long Meg's brother. At an age when a young man's friends and their opinions are everything, Terrence had avoided their jibes by accompanying Meg as little as possible.

He knew he should have shown more support, spent more time with her. He ought to have helped ease her into Society more gently. He ought to have tried to bolster her self-confidence somehow. But he had been young and selfish and unconcerned with his sister's plight.

When she had returned to Thornhill and announced to their father that she did not want a second Season, Terrence had not missed the relief in her eyes when their father had agreed. It was clear that she was much more comfortable in familiar surroundings, with familiar people. From that day on, Meg had never expressed the slightest interest in men or marriage, even though gentlemen paraded in and out of Thornhill with some regularity, on the lookout for prime horseflesh. She seemed to be completely at ease with herself and her situation, and Terrence could not imagine that even so fine a catch as Lord Sedgewick would tempt her to change her mind.

He returned his attention to the letter to Lady Sedgewick, but before long his thoughts drifted once again to Gram's notion that the viscount might actually show an interest in Meg. He supposed it was not such a far-fetched idea. It was true, Meg was no longer the skinny, awkward young girl she had once been. Terrence was not blind to his sister's beauty, though he suspected she was. Meg appeared to be completely indifferent to, or perhaps even unaware of, the admiring looks she received from the grooms and stable boys—especially when she was wearing a pair of his breeches. Meg had grown into a beautiful woman. He was not sure when it had happened, or when he had first noticed it. Somewhere along the way she had grown from gangly to statuesque. She also seemed to have become more complacent about her height, for she never slouched anymore. Rather, she walked straight and proud, just as she sat on a horse, displaying her full height for all the world to see.

All six feet of her.

Despite her regal beauty, however, she was still more at home in the stables than the drawing room, more comfortable in breeches than a ball gown, and he had difficulty imagining his sister involved in even so much as a light flirtation.

A knock on the library door jerked Terrence from his reverie. He returned the quill to its stand. "Come in."

Gittings, the butler, entered and announced that Mr. Coogan would like a word with him. At Terrence's nod, Seamus Coogan, Thornhill's head groom, was shown into the library.

"What is it, Seamus?" he asked. The fellow seldom stepped foot inside the house, unless it was something urgent. "Is that new foal in trouble?"

"No, sir." Seamus shuffled his feet and looked thoroughly uneasy. "T'ain't the young'un. He be just fine, he is. But somethin' else mighty queer I thought you should know about"

"Go on, Seamus. What is it, then?"

"Well, that gen'lman's curricle ..."

"Lord Sedgewick's, you mean?"

"Ah, so he's a lord, is he?" Seamus's black brows disappeared behind the unruly salt-and-pepper curls that hung over his forehead. "Well, it looks like his lordship's got hisself in a bit of trouble, you might say. I had the boys bring in the pieces of the curricle. Oh, and a beautiful thing it is, too, sir. A terrible shame it got so cracked up. Can be fixed, though. It needs only—" he stopped as Terrence glared at him through narrowed eyes. "Yes, well, the thing of it is, the axle was split. Clean in two."

"So, that's what caused the accident?"

"Well," Seamus hesitated, twisting his hat in his hands, "not to put too fine a point on it, sir, but it weren't no accident."

Terrence leaned forward on his elbows. "What do you mean, no accident?"

"I mean the axle was cut, sawed almost clear through, it was. Deliberate, like. That rig was bound to break apart at the first deep pothole. 'Twas meant to break apart, if you git my meanin', sir."

Terrence blew out a breath through puffed cheeks. "Good Lord."

Chapter 3

"**W**ake up, you ungrateful cur. After such tender ministrations, the least you can do is crack open an eye."

Meg mopped Lord Sedgewick's face and neck with a cool, damp cloth. She had been performing this ritual with increasing frequency for two days. She and Gram and even Terrence had taken their turns in watching over the sick man. His continued unconsciousness, not to mention the dangerously high fever that had begun the day before, frightened her more than she could say. To combat her own fear and frustration, she had begun to talk to him, to cajole him, to admonish him, to berate him. It made her feel better somehow to blame him, for she could not bear to think that his life might be in her hands. Perhaps she could shame him into consciousness, if any of her reproachful words actually penetrated his brain.

More likely her chatter would bore him into a sounder sleep.

Meg dipped the cloth into the basin of cold water, wrung it out, and proceeded to bathe his hands. "Here you are, almost a perfect stranger," she muttered, taking his left hand and covering it with the damp cloth, "and yet we have all sat with you round the clock, helping you to fight this wretched fever." She stroked the cool cloth over his warm hand, very slowly, from wrist to fingertips. She then began to gently massage each long finger from base to tip as she continued to scold.

"We even put you in the best bedchamber, for heaven's sake," she said as she absently surveyed the large, comfortable room. The dark wood-paneled walls, highly polished and gleaming in the candlelight, were hung with several old family portraits, and over the intricately carved fireplace hung a large painting of Blue Blazes, the Arabian stallion who had been the pride of Thornhill's stables for some years. "And with the most comfortable bed," she added as she eyed the beautifully carved bedposts of the Portuguese bed purchased only a few years ago by her father. He had discovered that ships used to transport troops to the Peninsula often returned loaded with items of furniture as ballast. He had traded a prime hunter for many pieces, including this bed, which was the newest and most elegant in the house.

"And what thanks do we get?" Meg turned his hand over and gently stroked the palm with the cool cloth. "You just lie there," she said, massaging the soft mound at the base of his thumb. "Like a pile of dirty linen. Hmph! Not even the tiniest sign that you know we are here." She drew the damp cloth slowly between each of his long fingers. "That we care." She laid his hand carefully at his side, covered it with the counterpane, and picked up the right hand. "That I care. That I don't want you to die."

She cradled his hand in her own, gently bathing and massaging it ever so slowly, as though memorizing every part of it: the long, tapering fingers, the nails neatly trimmed, the square palm with its clearly marked lines, the fine, soft texture of the skin. An aristocrat's hands, no doubt about it. Not the blunt, broad, rough hands of a laborer. These hands had seen little labor. A sprinkling of coarse blond hair over the tops of his hands and the base of his fingers saved them from appearing effeminate. That, and their size. Hands that large could hardly be mistaken for a woman's

Except, perhaps, for her own. Pressing her left hand against his right, Meg stretched out his limp fingers to their full length against her own. His fingertips reached fully half an inch or more above hers. How extraordinary. "Your hands are even bigger than mine, Lord Sedgewick." She smiled, finding an odd source of pleasure at this small discovery. "Imagine that," she said as she studied their hands, noting that his was slightly broader than hers as well. Good heavens, she felt almost dainty! Slowly, she curled her fingers between his, gently wrapping them around his hand. His fingers naturally bent so that they were entwined with hers. Meg stared at their joined hands for a moment. She chewed on her lower lip as a tight knot formed in her chest.

Finally, she dropped his hand and quickly turned to rinse the cloth in the basin once again. "That bit about being a perfect stranger," she said, "well... that's not true, of course. Gram and I remembered you." After wringing the cloth out, she folded it and draped it over the matching ewer. "Yes, I remembered you."

Meg glanced at the mantel clock and saw that it was not yet time for another dose of laudanum, so she dropped into a chair pulled close to the bed. She gazed over at her patient. Dr. Garthwaite had instructed that his head be kept raised, so Lord Sedgewick was propped on a large stack of pillows, his head tilted to one side against the linen pillow slip. His blond hair above the bandage was rumpled from sleep, lending him an endearing boyish quality which brought to mind the times Meg had seen him in the past, always so cheerful and charming. His face, though, sporting several days' growth of dark blond beard, did not appear boyish at the moment as he scowled in his sleep. Meg studied his high cheekbones and long, straight nose, and the series of parallel lines at the corners of his mouth—lines that hinted at the huge, wonderfully attractive smile he so often wore.

"Yes, I remember you," she whispered. Having once had that famous smile turned upon her, how could any woman forget it?

Meg reached across the bed and laid the back of her hand against his flushed cheek. My God, his skin was blazing hot! She wondered for a moment if she would ever see that smile again.

"If you dare to die on me, my lord," she scolded, "I swear I will wring your neck."

* * *

"Try to keep his arms down!" Dr. Garthwaite shouted. "I don't want to have to reset this leg."

Terrence and Meg were struggling to hold the delirious Lord Sedgewick still while the doctor attempted to secure the leg splint. It was the third night of fever, and during that time the patient had alternated between total unconsciousness and feverish delirium. Just now, his violent thrashing had pulled some of the leather straps loose from the wooden splint, and the doctor's carefully woven bandage was also coming loose.

"Blast!" Dr. Garthwaite exclaimed as he tried to save his meticulous handiwork from ruin. "Hold him, dammit! This bone might not be so easily reset. And watch his head, Meg! Don't let him flail so. It will only encourage further infection if those stitches come loose."

Meg held tightly on to Lord Sedgewick's left arm, trying to keep it immobilized while Terrence held the right. Though taller and stronger than most women, Meg was no match for Lord Sedgewick's superior strength as he continued to thrash against her grip.

"Damn!" she muttered, heartsick with frustration and

fatigue as she tried to hold on. "Hold still, my lord! Please. Hold still!" Her words went unheard as the delirious man continued to toss himself about. Undaunted, she climbed right onto the bed and pressed her full weight against his torso, pinning one arm beneath her knees. Thank God she was wearing breeches. Dr. Garthwaite, having known Meg for some time, expressed not the least shock at her unladylike pose. In fact, she could have sworn she heard a muttered, "Good girl," from the other end of the bed. Her weight on Lord Sedgewick's chest seemed to knock the wind out of him momentarily.

"Quickly," she shouted to Terrence, "the laudanum."

With some difficulty she held Lord Sedgewick down while Terrence forced his mouth open and trickled a few drops of the liquid medicine down his throat.

The undiluted drug seemed to take effect almost at once. Lord Sedgewick's body relaxed slightly, and his breathing gradually slowed from a pant to something more normal. Meg threw her own head back and heaved a great sigh. She closed her eyes in exhaustion as she heard Terrence move to the foot of the bed to help the doctor with the straps.

"It's all right, now, Meg," she heard the doctor say. "He's all right. You did beautifully, Meg. He's all right."

Meg opened her eyes and felt a tear roll down her cheek. God, but she was tired. She had had almost no sleep during the past three days while she tended to Lord Sedgewick. How much longer could this go on? The wretched man was going to wear himself out, despite their efforts to keep him alive. She slowly climbed off the bed and sank into an adjacent chair. She propped her elbows on her knees and dropped her head into her hands. How much longer? *How much longer are you going to put us through this, you hateful rogue?* How much longer could he hold on? For that matter, how much longer could she hold on?

As long as it takes, Meg scolded herself as she raised

her head and wiped the back of her hand across her eyes. She reached over to the table next to the bed and, with what little energy she could muster, dipped a cloth in the basin of cool water. She applied the cloth briefly to her own cheeks before bathing Lord Sedgewick's face.

"Good Lord, he's still so hot," she murmured.

"Yes," said the doctor, suddenly at her side and bending over his patient. "All my good efforts with his leg will be for naught if the fever does not break soon."

"What more can we do, Doctor?" she asked.

"You are doing everything you can do, Meg," he replied, taking the cloth from her hands. "Your stamina and compassion are no less than admirable, especially as the gentleman is completely unknown to you. You are to be commended. I could not have asked for any better assistance. I thank you, Meg. And Sir Terrence and your grandmother as well. You have all been a great help to me." Dr. Garthwaite ran the back of his hand gently over Lord Sedgewick's brow, cheeks, and neck, then tilted his head to one side to examine the bandage over the eye. "He is such a large man," the doctor muttered absently, "in height if not in frame, that I could not have worked without your help."

He returned the damp cloth to Meg and nudged her drooping chin with his knuckle. Meg looked up at the young doctor and found encouragement and hope in his soft brown eyes. She gave him a weak smile, and he smiled in return. He was such a gentle man, and not much older than Terrence. At one time Meg thought he might have had a serious interest in her, and she would have welcomed it, for she was fond of him. No one else at Thornhill, except Gram on occasion, had ever considered her in that way, considered that she might want the same things other women wanted. But even Gram would have regarded a country doctor as beneath Meg's notice. It did not matter anyway, since Dr. Garthwaite had never actually shown an interest after all. He was simply being polite. Just as Lord

Sedgewick had been polite six years ago.

"Keep him as cool and comfortable as possible," the doctor told her. Turning to Terrence, he added, "And hold him down as best you can when he becomes delirious. There's little more to be done. If only there were still snow on the ground, we could pack it around him. We cannot even immerse him in a cold bath without disturbing the leg. We will just have to wait this one out, I'm afraid."

"We will continue to bathe his face and neck with damp cloths," Meg said. "That should help keep him cool."

"His hands, too," Dr. Garthwaite said. "It seems to help."

"His hands, too," Meg repeated. "I have not forgotten."

"And no more laudanum until morning. Such a large man could probably tolerate a higher dosage, but I would prefer to be conservative. Opiates offer relief, to be sure, but can also mask other problems. No more laudanum tonight."

"Yes, Doctor," Meg said before dropping her head into her hands and massaging her temples.

"And see if you can force some nourishment down him when he is quiet," the doctor added.

Meg's head jerked up in surprise, thinking she must have heard wrong. "Feed him?" She studied the doctor with a furrowed brow. "But he has such a fever. Do you not mean—"

"Yes, I meant feed him," the doctor said, turning away from his patient to look at Meg. "I have been reading some interesting papers from a physician in Bristol who has had very good luck with fever patients he fed rather than starved. His results have been very impressive. So, yes, Meg, I would like our patient to be fed." He smiled and turned away and began to pack his bag. "And I would like him to begin taking your grandmother's herbal infusion as soon as possible. The comfrey mixture will help both his wounds to heal quickly."

Meg dropped her head back into her hands. She sincerely hoped Terrence was paying attention to Dr. Garthwaite's instructions—laudanum, food, herbals, what else?—for she was so tired she did not believe she would be able to recall his words an hour from now.

* * *

Lord Sedgewick's fever continued through the night. After a few hours fitful sleep, Meg relieved Gram in the sickroom once again.

"No change, I am afraid," Gram said in a weary tone. "He is quiet, though, thank the good Lord."

"Go on to your own bed, Gram," Meg said, putting an arm around her grandmother's shoulders and ushering her out the door. "I'll ring for help if he becomes delirious again."

And so Meg sat and watched Lord Sedgewick through the rest of the night, scolding him softly now and then about being such a stubborn, disagreeable houseguest.

"Horrid man!" she chided. "Just see if you are ever invited back to Thornhill after such thoughtless, ill-mannered behavior. Wretch!"

Between scolds, she bathed his face and hands and even dozed a bit in a chair beside the bed. Just after dawn she rose, walked to the window, and pulled aside the heavy curtains. It was a beautiful, clear morning, sparkling with wintry brilliance. Good Lord, but she was tired of this dark, dreary sickroom. She yearned for sunshine and a brisk ride.

Meg tied back the curtains and allowed the sunlight to pour into the bedchamber. It was so much more comforting than the prescribed darkness, that surely it would—

A faint groan arrested her thoughts, and she turned quickly toward the sickbed. A sunbeam fell directly over the bed and onto the face of their patient. His eyes seemed to squint slightly in reaction. A pang of guilt stabbed Meg as she dashed back to the window and drew the curtains closed. But he had groaned. She was sure of it. He had groaned. He was not dead.

She moved to the other side of the bed and dipped the cloth into the basin of water, movements so often repeated that she did them now almost without thinking. As she reached down to bathe Lord Sedgewick's face, her hand froze in midair. Could it be? Had she seen what she thought she saw?

"Do not tease me, you beastly man. Do not dare."

She dropped the cloth and reached frantically for the candle holder on the night table. Her hand shook slightly so that the candlelight flickered over Lord Sedgewick's face, but there was no mistaking what she saw.

His face was bathed in a sheen of perspiration. Beads of moisture had formed on his upper lip. His head bandage and nightshirt were drenched. The fever had broken.

Meg's hand flew to her mouth as she choked on a sob.

"Thank God. Oh, thank God."

Another faint groan escaped Lord Sedgewick's lips. Meg wiped the back of her hand across her eyes and bent closer. His eyes flickered open briefly, locked with hers, and then as quickly snapped shut, as though even the light of the candle was too irritating. His lips moved and he mumbled something unintelligible. Meg bent closer.

"Still dead," he muttered so softly Meg was not sure if she had understood him. "Angels."

His head dropped to the side as he fell asleep once again.

Chapter 4

"**A**h, you're coming round at last. Good! Good!"

Sedge came awake slowly, struggling to force his eyes open. Finally, lifting his lashes to let in only the tiniest crack of light, he squinted against the pain at the unfamiliar surroundings as he tried to sit up. Good God, his head was pounding like a thousand drums! He fell back against the pillows, his eyes clamping shut against the pain. Someone must have driven a steel spike through his head while he slept. His hand moved instinctively to his head. My God, he felt so weak that even such a simple movement seemed an impossible effort. His limp hand came in contact with an unexpected obstacle. Cloth? No, bandaging. Bandaging?

"What the..."

"Here you are, my lord. Try and drink a bit of this. It will help ease the pain."

Before he could wonder who belonged to the unfamiliar voice, he felt a cup being pressed to his mouth. Suddenly aware of a terrible parched dryness, he opened his lips without thinking, and a tepid brew was trickled down his throat.

Good Lord, what poison was this? He almost gagged on the foul-tasting liquid. The shock of it caused his eyes to pop open of their own volition. He blinked against the scratchy sting of full light in order to see just who was this soft-voiced tormentor.

A round-faced, elderly woman in a white lace cap bent close to his face, smiling benevolently as she held a cup near his lips.

"I know it tastes nasty, my lord," she said, "but you really must drink it if you ever want to regain your strength. It is full of good, healing herbs. Not the tastiest, to be sure, but the best there are for your condition." She put the cup to his lips once again. "Here, try to swallow just a bit more."

Sedge had no strength to object, and reluctantly allowed more of the horrid brew to be poured down his throat. God's teeth, but it was ghastly! When one more tiny swallow left him hacking and sputtering, the old woman relented and took the cup away. He heard the rustle of her skirts and the clink of glass or porcelain, but did not turn to watch what she did. He was too busy trying to keep the hellish brew down without embarrassing himself in front of this stranger. Finally, he collapsed once again against the pillows.

"Where am I?" he asked in a hoarse whisper.

"You are at Thornhill Farm, my lord," the woman said, standing close to the bed with her hands clasped at her waist. "In Suffolk. It is the home of Sir Terrence Ashburton. I am Mrs. Lattimer, his grandmother."

Sedge attempted a weak smile. "I am pleased to meet you, Mrs. Lattimer. Despite your dreadful concoction. I am Lord—"

"Sedgewick. Yes, we know who you are, my lord."

Sedge lifted a brow at that comment and instantly felt as if his head might explode. He reached for his brow and once again encountered the bandage. "What happened?" he asked. "Why am I—"

"You had a terrible accident, my lord. You were thrown from your curricle not far from Thornhill."

"Ah, yes." He seemed to recall the odd sensation of flying through the air. "I remember a little." He paused and attempted another smile. "I thought I had died."

"We feared you might, if you don't mind my saying so. I am afraid you have a broken leg as well as the gash on your head."

"Broken—?" Sedge leaned slightly forward to see his right leg, above the counterpane, splinted and strapped and bandaged. "Oh, God," he groaned as he sank back into the pillows. "Any other damage?"

"Well," Mrs. Lattimer said, "that nasty gash over your left eye gave you a concussion. But our Dr. Garthwaite stitched it up nice and neat." She grinned at him and added, "It will make a very dashing scar, I am sure."

"Wonderful. A limp and a scar. Dashing indeed." Sedge closed his eyes and considered that this was no doubt one of the larger messes into which he had ever landed. "I am almost afraid to ask," he said without opening his eyes, "but is there anything else?"

"Just that you have been fighting a dangerously high fever the last few days," she said. "You have been quite delirious, off and on. But now the worst is over, and you will be on the mend in a trice. Especially if you continue to drink my herbal infusion. It is Dr. Garthwaite's recipe, with a bit extra of my own thrown in."

Sedge opened his eyes and twitched his lips into what he sincerely hoped was a smile for the kindly woman at his side. "I suppose it is but a small sacrifice compared to what you have done on my behalf. How long have I been here?"

"Four days."

"Four days! Good Lord." Sedge shook his head slightly before realizing the movement only intensified the throbbing. He leaned back into the mountain of pillows and stared at Mrs. Lattimer in astonishment. He had lost four days. Four whole days! It was incredible. Such a thing had never before happened to him.

"I was ... on my way to ... to Trevelian's," he muttered as he tried to recollect what days he had lost. "Yes, Trevelian's hunting box. He invited me for a shooting party. Partridge, I think."

"Yes," Mrs. Lattimer said, "we discovered that. I hope you will not mind, but my grandson, Sir Terrence, went through your things. You were so badly injured, you see, that we wanted to notify someone. He found your *Peacock's* and saw the note about Lord Trevelian. He sent a note to Norfolk, informing his lordship of your accident."

"No, no, of course I do not mind," Sedge said. "I appreciate all your help. My valet may have already arrived at Trevelian's. He had taken ill and remained behind at Hawstead. And my cousin was to join me at Trevelian's, as well. They will all be wondering where I have got to, no doubt."

"Terrence also sent a note to Mount Street, and one to your mother in Lincolnshire as well."

"That was most kind of him," Sedge said. "Of all of you."

He offered another smile, which was feeling much more natural by now, though still slightly jarring to the constant throbbing of his left temple. "I am afraid I have put you and your family to a great deal of trouble. I cannot thank you enough for all you have done."

Mrs. Lattimer gave a dismissive wave accompanied by a dainty sniff. "Anyone would have done as much, my lord. Now, you say you remember where you were going. Do you recall much else? What might have caused the accident?"

"I have only the recollection of flying through the air," Sedge said. "Not much else beyond that. Very little, anyway. I do recall... but, no. I must have been dreaming." He chuckled softly. "You will think it foolish, but I dreamed I had died and gone to heaven. I even recall a beautiful, red-haired angel bending over me and calling my name."

All at once, Mrs. Lattimer's face lit up like a candle. Her eyes widened and a broad smile stretched from ear to ear. "That was no dream, my lord," she said in an excited tone. "That was my granddaughter, Meg. Miss Margaret Ashburton, that is. She has been tending you valiantly throughout your fever."

"Then, I am most grateful to her," Sedge said, too weary to puzzle over the woman's sudden burst of enthusiasm.

"She was the one who first recognized you, you see," Mrs. Lattimer continued. "She remembered you from her Season, a few years back. No doubt you recall her. I believe you danced with her... more than once."

"Miss Ashburton?" Sedge attempted, without success, to place the name, to link it with the beautiful red-haired angel of his dreams. "You must forgive me, please. My head is ... I am still somewhat muddled, I suppose. But I cannot seem to—"

At that moment, the bedchamber door flew open. Sedge turned his head toward the door ... and beheld a vision. Not just any vision. It was his angel.

One of the tallest women he had ever seen glided into the room with a long, purposeful stride. She wore a dark green velvet habit that hugged her shapely curves in such a way as to cause his breath to catch in his throat. She was in the process of removing a jaunty black beaver hat with a green plume, to reveal hair of a remarkable shade of russet, and eyes of almost the exact same color. Her red hair was pulled back in a knot at her neck, but several wayward tendrils refused to be confined and softly framed her face. She had high cheekbones, luminous skin, and an unexpected and thoroughly delightful sprinkling of freckles across the bridge of her nose.

All this was noted in the space of a breath—the one caught in Sedge's throat—as the elegant beauty glided into the room. She was his angel, there was no doubt of it. But she was more than an angel. She was as regal and elegant as any queen—a Celtic goddess, an Amazon, a warrior queen. She was Boadicea herself.

She was glorious.

He could not tear his eyes from her as she moved to stand beside Mrs. Lattimer. An uncharacteristic pang of embarrassment shot through him, that such a woman should meet him just now, when he was at his worst, helpless and weak as a kitten.

Boadicea placed an arm around Mrs. Lattimer's shoulder in a fond gesture. "Your herbal seems to have done the trick. Gram. Welcome back to the Land of the Living, my lord."

"Th-thank you." Curse it all, he was stammering and gawking like a schoolboy.

* * *

Gram pressed a hand in the small of Meg's back and pushed her closer to the bed.

"This is my granddaughter, my lord," Gram said, edging Meg forward. "Miss Ashburton. The one I was telling you about, who nursed you so tirelessly these last few days."

Meg wanted to throttle Gram, but first she silently damned all her red-haired, fair-skinned ancestors when she felt the heat of a blush color her cheeks. She had no doubt her face was as bright as a strawberry. She turned away slightly, allowing the blush to subside. She would not—*she would not*—allow Gram to further humiliate her in front of Lord Sedgewick. Turning back, she raised a hand to interrupt Gram's continued approbations of her heroic nursing, when her eyes met Lord Sedgewick's.

He stared up at her with an odd, blank look. She feared for a moment that his mind must still be addled by the effects of the fever. Then, all at once, his face shifted and transformed itself into the most endearing, most boyishly charming, most devastatingly attractive smile she had ever seen. And had feared she might never see again. His lips stretched into a broad grin that revealed even, white teeth. The flat planes of his face had been rearranged into a series of deep creases that fanned out like pairs of parentheses from the corners of his mouth, almost to the edges of his ears. These lines were echoed by matching creases spreading out from the corners of his eyes, which had crinkled up into tiny slits.

Meg had watched Lord Sedgewick's face so often in repose, or occasionally in pain, over the last four days that she had almost forgotten the power of that smile. Oh, she had never truly forgotten it, of course. It was the one thing about Lord Sedgewick she recalled most vividly. But to have it turned on her again just now almost caused her knees to buckle.

Meg's hand was still raised, to quiet Gram's chattering, and the room had fallen silent while she and Lord Sedgewick shared a smile—for it was almost impossible not to smile in return. In that instant, while they smiled at one another, all Meg's uneasiness flew out the window.

"Please, Gram," she said, still grinning like a fool, "you will tire our patient. You must forgive her, my lord, but I am her only granddaughter and she dotes on me, I am afraid. You are, unfortunately, a captive audience and will no doubt be forced to suffer endless exaltations of my charms and accomplishments. And those of Terrence, my brother, for she loves us both. She is shameless, you see. But, alas, we cannot muzzle her, for she is our grandmother, so what can we do?"

Lord Sedgewick's smile broadened slightly, if that was possible.

"But tell me," Meg continued, "how are you feeling? Has Gram forced her herbal on you, yet?"

The smile became a grimace, and Meg laughed.

"I thought she meant to poison me," Lord Sedgewick said with a shudder. "Awful stuff!"

"But you must listen to her, nevertheless, my lord," Meg said. "She is one of the most knowledgeable herbalists in the county. In some other age, she might have been known as the local witch." Meg grinned at her grandmother and placed her arm around her shoulder once again, hugging her close. "But most folks around here take her advice quite seriously. As should you, my lord, if you know what's best for you."

"I place myself in your capable hands, ladies." Looking down at his leg, he grinned again. "It seems I have no choice, in any case."

"Do not fret too much over the leg, my lord," Meg said. "It was a simple fracture, easily reset. It should heal nicely, without a limp."

"Another bit of good news," he said. "Things seem to be looking up, indeed. I have never broken a leg, though I did break my arm once as a boy. Is this"—he nodded toward the leather straps that tied the splint to the bed frame—"normal?"

Meg looked at Gram, uncertain how much to reveal about his delirium.

"I am afraid you thrashed about a great deal during your fever," Gram told him. "The doctor simply wanted to immobilize the leg as much as possible so the bone would set properly. I am sure he would have no objection to removing them now."

"Thrashing about, was I?" Lord Sedgewick looked thoroughly embarrassed. "Good heavens, I have been a poor houseguest, have I not?"

"Your conversation has left something to be desired, my lord," Meg said with a teasing grin, "but otherwise you have been fairly well behaved. Better than many other Thornhill guests, to be sure."

"What sort of farm is Thornhill?" he asked.

"A horse farm," Gram replied. "Terrence and his father and his grandfather before him have all raised horses at Thornhill."

"Hunters, mostly," Meg added as she watched Lord Sedgewick's eyes widen.

"My God. *That* Thornhill? Why, some of the finest bits of blood I've ever seen came from Thornhill's stables. By Jove, don't you have that spectacular black stallion—"

"Blue Blazes?" Meg smiled to think their prime stud might be that well known. "Yes, he is our pride and joy, a purebred Arab. He sired the majority of our present stock."

Lord Sedgewick groaned. "Just my luck. Here I am, housed at one of the finest stud farms in Suffolk and confined to this wretched bed! Blue Blazes. Gad, but I'd love to see that horse."

"You will, my lord, you will," Meg said. "In time. But for now, you may satisfy yourself with his portrait, just there across the room, over the mantel."

Lord Sedgewick craned his neck and squinted, then smiled as he found the painting. "Ah, but he's a beauty," he said, and then heaved a resigned sigh.

"Never fear," Meg added, chuckling lightly at his frustration, "you will be able to see him in the flesh soon enough. When you're able to walk again."

"Mrs. Lattimer, hand me another dose of that foul-tasting brew," he said. "I wish to be up and about—soon!"

"Good man!" Gram said, reaching for the cup on the night- stand. "Meg, dear, you help Lord Sedgewick to drink this. I must see to mixing up another batch in my stillroom."

"Gram, I—"

"I shall return shortly," she said. "Meg, do keep Lord Sedgewick company for a bit. He will need to sleep soon, though. You mustn't tire him."

With that, Gram swept out of the room without a

backward glance. Oh, Gram! How could you be so obvious? Meg felt another blush heat her face. Blast those fair-skinned ancestors, anyway. Her easily flushed skin revealed far too much for her liking. She kept her head bowed and slightly turned toward the door, too embarrassed to meet Lord Sedgewick's eye.

"Miss Ashburton?" he said in a soft voice. "Miss Ashburton, please do not hide your blushes. I find them most charming."

Meg jerked her head up to find the devastating smile turned on her once again.

Chapter 5

Sedge did indeed find Miss Ashburton's blushes charming.

Another incongruity, along with the freckles, in such an elegant-looking woman. She turned at his words, and he captured her with his smile. Thank God his face had not been injured, for he was quite aware of the effect his smile had on people. Especially women. Though he never quite understood why his smile was any different from anyone else's, he nevertheless recognized its power, and had used it to win many a friend and woo many a lover. He used it now to beguile the Amazonian beauty at his bedside. The blush faded, but she still looked charmingly embarrassed.

"You must forgive my grandmother, Lord Sedgewick. It is just that she ... well, she thinks I... Oh!" She gave an exasperated shake of her shoulders. "You know exactly what she was about. She could not have been more obvious."

"She is fond of you," he said. "That is only natural."

"Yes, she is, but she also believes me to be at my last prayers. So, when fate dropped an unmarried viscount on our doorstep ... well, you can imagine what she has been plotting and planning during your illness."

"Surely not your *last* prayers?" he teased. "Are the gentlemen of East Anglia so blind? Or merely stupid?"

She shrugged and looked embarrassed again, though she did not blush. "I spend a lot of time with horses," she said. "I am afraid I have never been the lady Gram would like me to be."

This elegant beauty, not a lady? Impossible.

"Mrs. Lattimer tells me you and I have met before," he said. "I confess I—"

"Do not worry yourself, my lord. I would not expect you to remember me. We only met twice, and very briefly."

Not remember her? How could he fail to remember this glorious creature?

"And yet, you remembered me?" he said.

Miss Ashburton threw back her head and laughed—a lilting, musical laugh.

The laugh nailed it. Sedge was thoroughly smitten.

"How could I forget," she said, grinning, "the only gentleman taller than me in all of London?"

"How, indeed? I am told we danced together. When ..."

"Good heavens, my lord. It was six years ago. Of course you do not remember."

Sedge furrowed his brow as he tried to bring to mind the spring of 1808. Each Season consisted of a similar round of balls, routs, card parties, and other endless and repetitive social events, so that there was almost no distinguishing between one year and the next. But there was always something, some event or other, that set apart one Season from another. Sedge began counting backward.

Last year had been the Season his friend Jack, Marquess of Pemerton, had come to Town looking for a rich bride and had become engaged to Lady Mary Haviland. The year before that was when his other good friend, Lord Bradleigh, had broken off a miserable engagement at the last minute so that he could marry Emily Townsend, a young woman Sedge had actually been courting himself. That was also the spring the Prime Minister had been assassinated. Sedge recalled. The year before that had been the year the Prince of Wales was declared Regent, and had given that outrageous grand fete. Sedge kept counting backward, but his mind went blank when he reached the spring of 1808. He beetled his brows until his head throbbed, when, finally, it came to him.

"Ah," he said, speaking his thoughts aloud. "That was the year everyone was agog about what was happening in Spain. King Ferdinand had been abducted and forced to abdicate."

"And that scoundrel, Bonaparte," Miss Ashburton said, "put his brother on the throne. Yes, I remember. It was the talk of the Town."

"And I danced with you twice amidst all that buzz?"

"You were only being polite to a tall, skinny wallflower, my lord."

"You? A wallflower?"

The musical laugh tantalized him once again. "Oh, to be sure," she said. "Not many gentlemen care to dance with a young woman whose eyes are at a level several inches above their own."

Sedge tried to conjure up an image of a tall, red-haired beauty but came up blank. He could try to recall all the wallflowers he had danced with, but that would be a monumental task. Sedge was every hostess's dream, for he never failed to give all the wallflowers at least one dance.

This particular practice, which kept him in the good graces of every hostess or patroness in Town, was not based on any manner of calculation on Sedge's part, but rather on a deeply felt personal commitment. He had never forgotten the day his younger sister Georgiana, in Town for her first Season, had sobbed in his arms begging his intervention with their mother in allowing her to return to their home in Lincolnshire. Georgiana, plain and shy, was miserable at having spent yet another ball seated among the dowagers and chaperones, without a single partner during the entire evening. She knew she would never take, but her mother was determined to keep trying. Sedge's heart had almost broken at his sister's obvious unhappiness, and he had in fact talked their mother into returning to Witham Abbey. But he had never let go of his anger over the shallow stupidity of the gentlemen of the ton who could not see beyond Georgie's physical imperfections to appreciate her sweet nature and gentle spirit.

Georgiana had eventually married, though the memory of her shame and humiliation had never faded. From that time on, Sedge had made it a point to seek out the plain-Janes and wallflowers at each ball or assembly, to offer them at least one opportunity to dance. And, more often than not, his cheerful attempts to draw them out had been so successful that others began to take notice. Many a young lady found herself with a much more respectable dance card once Sedge had made the first offer.

Could Miss Ashburton have been one of his wallflowers? Tall women were often overlooked, gentlemen of the ton generally preferring small, dainty women who made them feel protective. He squeezed his eyes shut as he tried to bring to mind various tall girls he may have danced with. He conjured up a vague recollection of a gawky redhead in an abundance of unfashionable ruffles. He opened his eyes and found it hard to reconcile that memory of gangly awkwardness with the statuesque beauty before him.

"Could it have been at Lady Sefton's ball?" he asked.

"Good heavens!" she said. "You *do* remember."

"I seem to recall a very thin, very shy, very tall young woman, in lots of ruffles."

Miss Ashburton laughed. "That was me. Gram dressed me up like a wedding cake, hoping to make me appear more ladylike."

"But," he said, his eyes narrowing as he studied her,

"you do not seem overly shy, despite those charming blushes. And you are certainly not... well, as thin as I recall."

As expected, that comment elicited yet another blush, but at least this time she did not turn away. "I have filled out... that is, I have put on some weight over the last six years." She looked up to meet his eyes, and he turned the full force of the famous smile upon her once again. "Besides," she continued, more at ease, "I have never really been shy in familiar surroundings. It was only the strict rules of the Season that intimidated me, not to mention the frequent disdainful looks from so many people who saw me as an awkward country miss. I rather hated it all, in fact."

"Have you never been back?" he asked.

"Good heavens, no."

"You should," he said, stifling a yawn.

"I beg your pardon, my lord, you must be exhausted. Oh, I completely forgot about Gram's herbal. Here, take a bit more before you go back to sleep."

"Must I?"

She chuckled. "I am afraid you must." She held the cup for him and he shamelessly wrapped his fingers around hers and brought it to his lips. He grimaced after one swallow, but eventually drained the cup. Another yawn overtook him while she replaced the cup on the nightstand.

"I am sorry," he mumbled through his fingers. "But I cannot seem to keep my eyes open."

"You will continue to feel weak for the next few days, I am sure," she said as she fluffed the pillows behind his head. "A fever like that wreaks havoc on a body, and it will take time to regain your strength."

"Yes, I suppose so." His voice sounded fuzzy as the herbal took effect. "You will come back, won't you?" He blinked furiously in an attempt to keep his eyes open.

"Of course," she said. "You will be confined to bed for a few weeks, I should think, and will be bored soon enough. Gram and Terrence and I will take turns keeping you company."

"I. .. look . ... forward ... to .. . it," he said, and then his eyes closed completely.

* * *

Meg left Lord Sedgewick's bedchamber and returned to her own, where she changed out of her habit and into a light woolen dress. Her thoughts were full of the viscount, who was every bit as charming as she remembered, even in his weakened state. More so, in fact, for though she had almost swooned under the effect of that first smile, he had proceeded to put her entirely at ease. And his conversation had been much more flirtatious than she recalled. Of course, it was easier to converse with him in her own home rather than on a dance floor with the disdainful eyes of the *ton* upon her.

But she must be careful not to succumb to that boyish charm and flirtatious nature, not to make too much of that smile. She had watched often enough as he turned it on any number of women to believe that it meant anything special. He would walk out of her life as soon as his leg healed, and that would be the end of it. There was no sense in weaving foolish dreams. Despite Gram's transparent expectations.

Thoughts of Gram led her downstairs toward the stillroom. She needed to put a stop to Gram's interference before she went too far. As expected, Meg found her grandmother at her favorite workbench, grinding dried herbs with a pestle.

Meg walked into the stillroom, breathing in the varied aromas of the hundreds of plants Gram used for her concoctions: sweet, pungent, tangy, peppery, minty, and spicy all mingled together into a pleasant, fragrant whole. Herbs and flowers of every variety hung from the beamed ceiling, and two walls were filled with shelves of stoneware jars and crocks—some with fitted lids, some tied with muslin caps, each carefully labeled with its ingredient.

Above the table at which Gram now sat, narrow shelves were lined with glass vials of every size, filled with concentrated oils and extracts, and smaller crocks of pungent medicinal herbs and roots, for this was where she produced her physics. Another table was lined with baskets of dried flowers, sweet herbs, and orange peels for use in making potpourris, pomanders, and scented waters.

Gram sat with a receipt book propped open before her, listing ingredients and measurements for a specific infusion, written in Gram's own hand. Several other books, including some quite old and rare herbals, were lined up against the wall. Meg pulled over a stool and sat down next to her grandmother. Without a word, Gram handed her a stalk of dried chamomile. Meg grabbed two tiny stoneware bowls from a stack against the wall, and began to crush the stalk between her fingers, depositing crushed flowers in one bowl and crushed leaves in another.

"Did you have a nice chat with the viscount?" Gram asked without looking up, as she continued to grind crushed yarrow leaves into a fine powder.

"Gram, you are an incorrigible old meddler."

"I don't know what you are talking about."

"My dear old love," Meg said as she stripped the chamomile stalk of its last leaves, "your motives are as transparent as gauze. I fear you will send Lord Sedgewick running for his life."

Gram looked up, her eyes wide. "Did he say something?"

"He was quite aware of your reasons for throwing us together like that. You are likely to scare him away, you know."

"Hmph." Gram snorted and returned to her mortar and pestle. "He is confined to bed. Where is he going to go, I'd like to know?"

"He will bolt at the first opportunity if you are not careful."

The two women worked in silence for a moment. Meg was hopeful that her hints had made Gram reconsider her actions, for the last thing the old woman would want would be to have Lord Sedgewick take flight. Once he regained his strength, a broken leg was not such a serious malady to forestall his departure, if he felt the need to escape. Meg must keep reminding Gram of that possibility.

"He is a charming gentleman, though," Gram said at last, "is he not? Such a lovely smile."

"Yes," Meg replied as she took up another stalk and began removing its flowers, "very charming."

"What did you talk about?"

"Oh, this and that," Meg said. "Nothing special."

Another silence fell between them, broken only by the rhythmic grinding of pestle against mortar. After a moment, Gram laid down the pestle and tested the pulverized yarrow. Apparently satisfied, she dumped the contents into a large bowl already filled with sizable amounts of dried betony and comfrey. She glanced at the receipt book and turned to inspect Meg's bowls of chamomile. She picked up a small amount of the crushed flower petals, lifted them to her nose, and nodded in satisfaction. She grabbed another stalk and began crushing the flower heads into the same bowl.

"Did he remember you, after all?"

Meg looked up, startled at the question, but Gram's attention was directed at the chamomile. Meg smiled. Gram had, of course, planted the information in hopes that he would pursue it. "Yes, he did," Meg said. "At least he appeared to do so. No doubt he was only being polite. You may be interested to know that it was those horrid dresses you made me wear that finally jarred his memory."

"Then I was right to have you wear them."

"Gram!" Meg laughed and shook her head. "You are,

indeed, incorrigible."

"I just want you to be happy, my dear." She looked up and smiled. "And he does seem so perfect for you. Why, he must be even taller than you, Meg. The poor man's legs practically hang over the edge of the bed. Tall, and handsome, too. Oh, my dear, I just know that—"

Meg put a finger to her grandmother's lips. "Not another word, Gram. Promise me! Not another word. I tell you, if you persist in pushing this notion of yours, we will see the back of Lord Sedgewick by week's end."

Gram flashed a contrite look, and Meg removed her finger.

"Do you really think so?" Gram asked.

"I do. Gentlemen do not like to feel pressured, Gram. They turn scared and run. Only ask Terrence. So, please, do you promise to give up this campaign?"

Gram heaved a deep sigh. "I promise," she said at last. "But I shall not stop hoping. You are a beautiful young woman, Meg. I saw how he looked at you."

It was Meg's turn to sigh. "Lord Sedgewick is a very friendly, courteous gentleman. Exactly as he was six years ago. But that is all! He will never offer anything more than friendship."

"How can you be so sure?"

"Gram, a rich viscount, even a tall one, would never be interested in a red-haired giantess. He will no doubt prefer a petite, tractable, fragile-looking blonde. All men do. I can never be any of those things, Gram."

"But I saw how he looked at you!"

"He will never be interested in me, Gram. I am merely a novelty. Not the sort of woman to draw serious attention. Not from any man, and certainly not from Lord Sedgewick. You must accept that. Now, remember your promise. Please, do not get your hopes up."

And please, do not get my hopes up, either.

Chapter 6

"That young roan of yours is making splendid progress, Meggie."

"He is, indeed" Meg reached across her brother the jam pot and spread a large dollop of marmalade over her muffin. She and Terrence had shared a brisk gallop before sitting down to breakfast, and her two-year-old blue roan had made a good showing against her brother's more seasoned mount. "I think Bristol Blue may be as fast as his father one day."

"You've done a fine job with him, my dear," Terrence said as he poured himself a second cup of coffee. "You have put Seamus's nose quite out of joint, in fact. He had wanted to train the roan himself, you know."

Meg chuckled, but was gratified by her brother's praise. "Bristol may be ready for higher obstacles, I think. He is very surefooted on the low jumps, with a good strong neck. His equilibrium is sound. I believe he is ready, Terrence. What do you think?"

Before Terrence could answer, the breakfast room door was opened and Gittings entered.

"There is a gentleman to see you, sir. A Mr. Albert Herriot."

"Herriot?"

"Oh, Terrence," Meg said, her voice lifting in interest, "it must be a relative of Lord Sedgewick."

"Of course," Terrence said as he pushed his chair back and rose from the table.

"I have put him in the small drawing room, sir," Gittings said as he turned to lead the way.

"I am coming with you," Meg announced as she quickly rose and followed her brother. She brushed at the skirts of her habit and pushed a stray curl behind her ear in a feeble attempt to make herself more presentable. She knew that neither of them ought to receive a guest in such a fashion, still wearing their riding clothes and muddied boots, and no doubt smelling of horse. But if the gentleman was indeed a relative of Lord Sedgewick's, then he must have learned of the accident and would likely be anxious about his lordship's condition. It would be cruel to keep him waiting.

Meg followed Terrence into the small drawing room, an oak-paneled room dominated by a rather spectacular overmantel of intricately carved classical figures and curling foliage that stretched all the way to the ceiling. A sandy-haired gentleman of average height stood with his back to them as he gazed out the mullioned windows overlooking the gardens. He turned at the sound of their entry, a look of agitated uneasiness on his face.

"I am Sir Terrence Ashburton," her brother said as he extended his hand to the visitor. "And this is my sister, Miss Ashburton."

"Albert Herriot," the gentleman said as he grasped Terrence's hand and absently nodded at Meg. He was a young man, about the same age as Terrence, with a strong, jutting nose, wide mouth, and level gray eyes which, at the moment, were filled with concern. "My cousin, Lord Sedgewick," he said in an anxious voice, "is he—"

"Your cousin is doing well, Mr. Herriot," Terrence said. "There is no cause for alarm."

A look of profound relief passed over Mr. Herriot's face. He threw his head back and swallowed with some difficulty. "Oh, thank God," he said at last. "Thank God."

"Please be seated, Mr. Herriot," Meg said, indicating an armchair near the fireplace. The poor man looked almost ready to collapse. Meg sat in an adjacent settee and watched as he sank into the chair, his face still pale and haggard, as if he had expected the worst and had not quite yet comprehended that his cousin was alive and well. Terrence had walked across the room and returned with a glass of brandy, which he thrust into Mr. Herriot's hands.

The man looked up, nodded, and wrapped his fingers around the glass. "Thank you," he said before taking a swallow. He then looked at Meg and Terrence, who had sat down beside her, and offered a weak smile. "I am sorry," he said. "It is just that I was so concerned. Sedge is ... well, we are very close, you see. I had thought... but you say he is all right?"

"Yes, Mr. Herriot," Meg said. "He has a broken leg, and suffered a concussion and a rather violent fever. But the worst is over and he is doing much better. He is still quite weak, of course, and will be confined to bed for a while because of the leg. But he seemed in good spirits when I last saw him."

"That is good news," he said, smiling more easily. He was a very pleasant-looking man, with a certain look in his eye which made Meg think he might have a bit of the same sort of charm as his cousin. A family trait, perhaps. "Very good news, indeed," he said.

"How did you hear about the accident?" Terrence asked.

"I was visiting Cosmo Trevelian at Bodley Rise, his hunting box in Norfolk," Mr. Herriot replied. "A shooting party. Sedge was to come as well. In fact, we had met along the way, at Hawstead. We had thought to follow one another to Norfolk, but Sedge was delayed a bit when his valet suddenly took ill. I went on ahead." He took another sip of brandy and continued.

"I became a bit concerned," he said, "when Sedge did not arrive at Bodley Rise by the following day. But I assumed he had stayed behind with poor Pargeter, his valet, or had run into another group of friends, or some such thing." He shrugged and amusement tugged slightly at the corners of his mouth. "Sedge is not always the most reliable of chaps, you see. He can be easily"—he paused and looked directly at Terrence— "distracted."

Terrence and Mr. Herriot shared a significant look, and Meg understood at once that the distractions alluded to were women. So, Lord Sedgewick was something of a rake, was he? Not surprising, she thought, as an image of the famous smile came to mind.

"Then Pargeter showed up a day later, without Sedge," Mr. Herriot continued, drawing Meg's attention back to the matter at hand, "and I confess I began to worry. Pargeter told us that Sedge had left him behind at the inn to recover from his illness, and had gone on to Bodley Rise without him. The same morning I had left."

"I am afraid he did not get very far," Meg said. "We found him on the Ixworth Road, a few miles north of Bury St. Edmunds, just before the toll bar."

"The road just there is badly rutted," Terrence added. "Always has been. It looked as though one of his wheels had become snagged in a deep rut, and Lord Sedgewick was thrown from the curricle."

"Poor old chap," Mr. Herriot said. "Must have been daydreaming instead of paying attention to the road. Might have killed himself."

"Indeed," Terrence said, narrowing his eyes slightly, "he almost did."

Mr. Herriot shook his head back and forth and slowly expelled a deep breath. "Yes, well to answer your original question, just on the heels of Pargeter's arrival, Trevelian received your note, which he shared with me. I came as soon as I could. I brought Pargeter along as well."

"We are very glad you have come," Meg said. "And I hope you will stay as long as you like. Lord Sedgewick will no doubt be glad of your company while he is confined to bed."

"Thank you, Miss Ashburton," Mr. Herriot said. "I would like to stay until he has fully recovered, if that is acceptable. Then I shall see that he is safely conveyed home." He rose from the chair. "May I see him?"

Meg started to rise, but Terrence placed a hand on her arm to forestall her. "If you do not mind, Mr. Herriot," he said, "I would like to discuss something with you first."

"Of course," Mr. Herriot said as he resumed his seat.

Meg gave her brother a quizzical look, but he ignored her, keeping his eyes fixed on their guest.

"Does your cousin," Terrence began very slowly, "have any enemies?"

Mr. Herriot's head jerked back in astonishment. "I beg your pardon?"

Meg furrowed her brow and stared at her brother. What on earth had he meant by such a question?

"Are you aware of anyone," Terrence continued, "who might wish to do your cousin harm?"

"I... I do not... " Mr. Herriot stammered and looked thoroughly confused.

"Terrence?" Meg prompted. "What—"

"Good heavens!" Mr. Herriot said at the same moment. "You do not mean that—"

Terrence held up his hand, and both Meg and Mr. Herriot glared at him. "I am afraid that what happened to Lord Sedgewick was no accident. His curricle had been deliberately tampered with. The axle was cut almost clean through."

Mr. Herriot stared at Terrence in open-mouthed astonishment.

Meg grabbed her brother's arm and squeezed hard. "Terrence! What are you saying? You never mentioned this before."

Terrence laid a hand over hers. "I am sorry, Meggie. I had not wanted to trouble you. But now that his lordship's cousin has arrived, I thought it best to let him know the true situation." He turned to face the wide-eyed Mr. Herriot. "I have said nothing to Lord Sedgewick. He only regained consciousness yesterday, and is still very weak."

"You are saying ..." Mr. Herriot began in a voice so soft it was barely above a whisper, "you are saying that someone tried ... tried to k-kill Sedge?"

Terrence glanced at Meg and then turned again toward their guest. "I am afraid it looks that way." He dropped his eyes and lowered his voice. "I am sorry. I thought you should know."

"My God." Mr. Herriot let out a ragged breath. "My God."

"When did you learn this, Terrence?" Meg asked, still clutching her brother's arm.

"Soon after we brought Lord Sedgewick home," Terrence replied. "Seamus discovered the broken axle and was immediately suspicious. After he reported it to me I examined it myself. There is no question about it. The axle had been sawn. It was no accidental break."

"Who would have done such a thing?" Meg murmured, speaking her thoughts aloud.

"I was hoping Mr. Herriot might be able to help us on that score," Terrence said, turning to their guest and raising his brows in question.

"I don't know. I don't know." Albert Herriot's hands trembled as he brought the glass of brandy to his lips and took a deep swallow. He closed his eyes for a moment and then seemed much more steady when he opened them once again. "Truly, I can think of no one. Sedge has no enemies that I am aware of." He shook his head as he looked down at the glass in his hand. "No, everyone loves Sedge. He is . . . well, he is one of the most amiable men I have ever known."

"He has angered no one that you know of?" Terrence asked. "No—I beg your pardon, Meggie—no jealous husbands, that sort of thing?"

"No, no. Nothing that I know of."

"Well, if it is not over a woman," Terrence said, "then such actions are usually a product of either greed or revenge. I take it your cousin is a rich man?"

Mr. Herriot nodded.

"Who looks to inherit?"

Mr. Herriot sighed. "His title and estates are entailed. I am his heir." In the next breath, he straightened upright with a jerk. His widened eyes glared first at Terrence, then at Meg, then back to Terrence. "Good Lord, you cannot think that *I*—"

"No, no, of course not," Terrence interrupted.

"My God, man. Sedge is like a brother to me."

"I understand, Mr. Herriot, and I am certainly not suggesting that you had anything to do with his accident. I am merely trying to make some sense of what happened."

Mr. Herriot relaxed back into the chair, but his brow remained furrowed with confusion and a hint of anger.

"Are there any other persons," Terrance asked, "who might benefit from Lord Sedgewick's death?"

"I am certain his mother and sister will receive generous settlements," Mr. Herriot said in a chilly voice. "And his sister's son, no doubt. The boy is all of five years old and something of a hellion. A bit young, don't you think, to be plotting against his uncle?"

Terrence ignored Mr. Herriot's angry sarcasm and went on. "What about gambling debts? Does your cousin hold anyone's vowels?"

Mr. Herriot continued to glare at Terrence. Finally, he relaxed back into his chair and sighed. "Not that I know of.

There was one fellow a few months back, Lord Digby, who lost quite a tidy little fortune to Sedge. The man was in his cups and made a bit of a spectacle of himself at White's. Never came right out and accused Sedge of cheating, which would have been ridiculous. But cursed my cousin's run of luck quite loudly."

"What happened to Digby?"

"Paid his shot, as far as I know. Sedge never mentioned it again."

"Anyone else you can think of?" Terrence asked.

Mr. Herriot brought a hand to his temple and squeezed his eyes shut. Shaking his head, he said, "No, no one." After a moment, he looked up once again. "And the business with Digby ... well, the man was drunk. I do not want to give the wrong impression."

"I think we should consider this mystery some other time," Meg said as she rose from the settee. Poor Mr. Herriot looked thoroughly rattled. She did not think it the proper time or place to be analyzing all of Lord Sedgewick's actions and acquaintances. "Mr. Herriot will be wanting to see his cousin."

Both men rose as Meg stepped past them, heading toward the door. "Thank you, Miss Ashburton," Mr. Herriot said. "I would like to see him, if he is up to having visitors."

"We will just have to go and see, will we not?" Meg said.

* * *

"Thank you, Pargeter," Sedge said as he toweled his freshly shaved face. "I feel human again." The valet retrieved the towel and then helped Sedge into a clean nightshirt. "It is good to have you back with me, Pargeter. Although," he said, flashing a grin at the dour man as he rearranged the pillows behind Sedge's back, "I have had the most charming nursemaid during your absence. Are you quite certain you are fully recovered? Perhaps you should return to Mount Street and get your strength back. Take a few weeks off."

"I am quite recovered, my lord," Pargeter replied as he straightened the counterpane. "It was only an attack of a bilious stomach which left as quickly as it came. Besides, you will need a proper manservant while confined to bed. It is not right that you should allow a young lady—"

He was interrupted by a knock on the bedchamber door. "Sedge!"

Pargeter held open the door as Sedge's cousin Albert walked into the room, wearing a broad smile. "What sort of mischief have you got into this time?"

"Bertie! Good to see you, old chap." He reached out to grab the hand offered by his cousin and shook it vigorously. It really was good to see him. Though given to a certain amount of recklessness, he had always been a likable young man and Sedge was quite fond of him. He released his hand and swung it in a sweeping gesture across the bed. "As you see, I have made rather a mess of things. Broke my bloody leg."

He looked beyond Albert to see that Miss Ashburton and Sir Terrence had followed him into the room, and were both smiling broadly. Sedge felt the heat of a blush color his cheeks. "Forgive my language, Miss Ashburton," he said, offering a sheepish grin, "I did not see you."

She continued smiling and gave a wave of dismissal. "I just wanted to see that Mr. Herriot found you awake. I shall leave you two gentlemen to converse in private—without the constricting presence of a lady." She grinned at Sedge and then turned to speak to Albert. "Mr. Herriot, your things have been taken to the bedchamber just across the hall. Please, make yourself at home. We dine rather late, due to stable business, but a cold luncheon is always set out just after noon." With that, she turned and walked away,

Sedge's eyes following her as she left the room. After a few brief words, Sir Terrence followed her, leaving Sedge alone with Albert.

Sedge turned to his young cousin, raised his brows, and grinned. "Well?"

"Sedge, you devil! How on earth did you contrive to be rescued by such a beauty? She is magnificent."

"Isn't she, though? A dashed shame to be immobile at such a time."

"That did not seem to keep you from devouring her with your eyes."

"I shall have to be less obvious," Sedge said. "But what the devil am I supposed to do? She is the only female for miles, as far as I can tell, save for her grandmother and the housekeeper. This is a stud farm, after all. Did you know?"

"Oh, yes," Albert said. "There is no mistaking it. Horses everywhere. The iron gates leading onto the estate are topped with a huge, gilded horse's head. The walls of most of the rooms I've seen are hung with equine portraits and hunting prints. Wooton. Stubbs. That sort of thing."

Sedge smiled and gestured to the portrait of Blue Blazes hung over the fireplace.

Albert nodded and walked around the bed to the windows. Sedge had asked that the curtains be tied back to brighten up the room. Though he could see nothing more than sky from his position on the bed, it nevertheless cheered him up to let a little of the outdoors inside. Albert stood at one of the windows and looked out.

"Besides," he said, tilting his head as though to indicate something below, "I saw the stables as I drove up. Very impressive. You should see them, Sedge."

"Bertie, Bertie," Sedge moaned, "*must* you be so cruel? How can I see them when I'm stuck in this damned bed? Oh, but I cannot wait to be up and about."

* * *

"So, you see, Pargeter, you need not worry about the receipt," Gram said as she removed the muslin cover from the crock of her special infusion ingredients. "The mixture is already combined. You need only measure out the correct amount, then allow it to brew for at least one hour. No less, mind."

"Yes, ma'am," Pargeter said, his brow furrowed in concentration.

"Remember," Gram continued, "keep the pot tightly covered while the infusion steeps. If you can smell the aroma of the tea, then the essential goodness of the herbs is escaping into the air rather than being retained in the liquid."

"Yes, ma'am."

"'Tis a very potent brew, Pargeter." Gram chuckled. "His lordship is not overly fond of it, to be sure. But he must drink it, nevertheless."

"Yes, ma'am. One half cup four times a day."

"That's right," Gram said, smiling. "So, you need only brew enough each morning for one jar. Two large handfuls. Remember that. At least twice the amount you would use for a normal tea. And remember to take the mixture from this particular crock. I will keep it covered with a square of blue muslin, so it should be easy enough to identify."

"Thank you, ma'am," Pargeter said as he eyed the myriad of crocks that filled the room, most covered with white muslin caps tied tightly around the lip. What a somber-faced man he was to be serving such a cheerful gentleman as Lord Sedgewick. "I have no knowledge of herbs myself," he said, "and should hate to make a mistake."

"Do not worry, Pargeter. Just let me know when the mixture runs low so that I can make up another batch."

"Yes, ma'am. Thank you, ma'am."

Gram handed him a muslin pouch containing one day's

worth of the infusion mixture. He nodded and turned to go. Gram turned back to her worktable.

"Ooomph!"

The strange exclamation caused Gram to swivel around in time to see Pargeter recover from an apparent collision with Mr. Albert Herriot.

"I beg your pardon, sir!" the valet said in an astonished voice.

Mr. Herriot laughed. "No harm done, Pargeter. My fault entirely. Please, do not let me interrupt you."

"I am terribly sorry, sir. Please excuse me." The discomfited valet bobbed his head and backed out of the stillroom.

Mr. Herriot chuckled as he stood in the doorway. "I did not mean to cause any distress, Mrs. Lattimer. Poor Pargeter. He is such a Friday-faced old thing. I do not know how Sedge abides the fellow"

"He seems very competent." She grinned and added, "Though he is a bit glum."

"I hope I am not disturbing you," Mr. Herriot said. "I confess I was exploring a bit and heard voices. What a marvelous stillroom!"

Gram beamed a smile at the genial young man as he walked into the room, his gaze traveling from the herbs and flowers hanging above his head to the shelves of jars and crocks lining the walls. "Do you know something of herbs, Mr. Herriot?"

He laughed. "Not a thing, I'm afraid. I cannot tell a dandelion from a pokeweed. But my mother always kept an herb garden and a small stillroom. Nothing like this, mind you," he said as his arm swept the room in an expansive gesture. "She especially enjoyed making potpourris. Every room in our home was redolent of her dried flowers. Good heavens, but she would have loved this." He tilted his head back, closed his eyes, and breathed deeply. "What a delicious combination of fragrances." He opened his eyes and looked all around the room. "By Jove, you have a little bit of everything in here, do you not? You must show me your gardens, Mrs. Lattimer, for I suspect they are impressive indeed."

Gram reached out to pat his arm. "I would be glad to give you a tour, Mr. Herriot. I am rather proud of my herb gardens, though, of course, they are not at their peak of beauty just now. In a few months, though ... well, in any case, they are of only minor significance, after all, compared to the true treasure of Thornhill. The stables are unequaled, you know. A young gentleman like yourself must surely find more of interest in the stables than in the gardens."

Mr. Herriot leaned against the workbench and sighed. He looked down at Gram with such a sweet, self-conscious smile—not so terribly different from his cousin's easy grin— that she completely lost her heart to him. A pity he was not taller. "I am naturally keen to see the stables," he said. "But I must confess, the smells in this room bring back such fond memories of my mother, that just at the moment I believe I would prefer to see an herb garden."

Gram reached behind to untie her apron, and tossed it on the workbench. "Then follow me, Mr. Herriot, and see the finest herb garden in all of Suffolk."

Chapter 7

"I think I might kill for a beefsteak." Sedge forced down yet another spoonful of porridge. "Stop laughing, Bertie. No doubt you polished off a disgustingly hearty breakfast downstairs."

"Well, let me see," his cousin said, raising his eyes to the ceiling and tapping a finger against his chin. "There were eggs and kippers and tongue. Oh, and a bit of ham as well. Then toast and jam. And some lovely muffins."

"Oh, shut up, Bertie."

"Have I covered it, Miss Ashburton?" Albert asked with a sly grin, pretending to ignore Sedge's current misery.

"For shame, Mr. Herriot!" she replied, her eyes dancing with amusement. "You really mustn't tease your cousin so. He is still quite weak, you know."

"Balderdash!" Sedge exclaimed, quickly substituting for the more colorful word he would have preferred. "How am I to regain my strength when I am fed this?" He waved his spoon over the porridge and twisted his mouth in distaste. He had begun to chafe under the good-natured coddling he was receiving at Thornhill.

Miss Ashburton rose from her chair and came to stand closer to the bed. "I am truly sorry, my lord," she said, "but

Dr. Garthwaite has ordered that you have only light, bland food for a few more days. Until the full effects of the concussion and fever have passed. Come on, now. Just a few more spoonsful."

Sedge looked into those eyes the color of rich, dark amber and his irritability somehow melted away. At such times he could almost give in to complete weakness and allow himself to be fussed over and ministered to by his red-haired angel.

But he had quickly learned that she was no meek supplicant, but a firm taskmaster who would not abide malingering. And, if truth be told, Sedge would prefer to impress such a woman with strength rather than appeal to her with weakness. Before he realized it, he had taken two more swallows of the wretched porridge.

"Well done, my lord," she said as he continued to drown in her eyes. "You will be back in the saddle before you know it" She reached to retrieve the tray balanced on his lap. "Here, let me move this."

It was not until she turned to place the tray on a side table that Sedge's gaze left her, and then only to catch Albert biting his lip as he suppressed a snort of laughter. Sedge glared at his cousin, who only seemed to become more amused and who finally had to rise and turn his back to the bed, his shoulders shaking with mirth.

"It is time now for Mrs. Lattimer's herbal infusion, my lord." Pargeter's voice drew Sedge's attention to the other side of the bed where the valet poured a cup of the ghastly brew from a glass jar.

"Oh, please! Not that, too," Sedge groaned as Pargeter thrust the cup in his hands. "I will surely—"

"Do not drink that!"

Sedge looked up to see a wild-eyed Mrs. Lattimer dash into the room, launch herself toward the bed, and bat the cup right out of his hand.

What the devil?

The sound of shattering porcelain as the cup struck the wall was followed by a stunned silence, as the room's occupants each stared in shock at the old woman. Mrs. Lattimer stood ramrod straight, her widened eyes turned on Sedge. Her white lace cap had come loose and sat slightly askew, gray corkscrew curls escaping to frame her round face. Her normal plump-cheeked rosiness had turned to chalk. She had brought a hand to her mouth, and Sedge noticed that her fingers trembled as she stared at him. Finally, she covered her face with her hands, slumped over, and began to cry. Miss Ashburton rushed to her side and wrapped an arm around her shoulders.

"What is it, Gram?" she asked in a soft voice. "What happened?"

"Oh, my lord," the old woman said, raising a distraught face to look at Sedge. "I do not know how such a thing could have happened. I simply do not know. I have always been so careful. Nothing like this has ever happened before. Never." Her gaze drifted off into the distance and her brow knotted as though she tried to recollect something. When she spoke again, her voice had become more agitated, her tone urgent. "Everything is separated and properly labeled. Some look very much alike, of course, but I know what's what. I *know* these things. I do! And I used the blue muslin cap. There was no mistaking it. I am sure I did not move the crock since yesterday morning. And it could not have been in there at that time or else you . . . oh, I do not understand it. I ... I do not know ... I just do not know." Her face crumpled and tears poured down her cheeks.

Sedge wondered if the old woman's wits were wandering. She was not making any sense.

Her granddaughter looked at Sedge, Albert, and Pargeter in turn, then furrowed her brow and shook her head. She tightened her arms around Mrs. Lattimer's shoulder. "Come now. Gram," she said softly, "everything is all right. It is all right." After one more squeeze, she removed her arm and took both her grandmother's hands in her own. "But tell me, my dear. Tell me what happened. Is something wrong in the stillroom?"

"Wrong?" Mrs. Lattimer's eyes widened in fright or confusion, Sedge could not be sure. "Yes," she said at last, "yes, something is wrong. Someone," she said, emphasizing the word as her eyes raked first Pargeter, then Mr. Herriot, and settled at last on her granddaughter, "has been in my stillroom, disturbing my herbs."

"What are you saying, Gram? Who would do such a thing?"

"I do not know," the old woman said. She narrowed her eyes and turned her gaze once again on Pargeter. The poor man looked ready to run for his life.

"I—I was in the stillroom this morning, ma'am," the valet said. "But only to get the mixture for his lordship's infusion, just as you showed me. I assure you, ma'am, I touched nothing else."

Mrs. Lattimer seemed to accept that explanation. Pargeter's shoulders sagged in relief as her gaze shifted to Albert. "Mr. Herriot?"

Albert appeared slightly abashed by her question. "Haven't been near the place, ma'am. Spent the morning with Sir Terrence in the stables."

She turned on Miss Ashburton. "Then who, Meg?" she asked, her voice rising in frustration.

"You know the servants never go in the stillroom without permission, Gram. Please, tell us what has happened."

The old woman took a deep breath and swallowed with difficulty, but then continued with more confidence. "I was working at my bench, as usual, and thought to check on the mixture for his lordship's infusion. Just to discover if I might need to make a new batch, you see."

"Yes. Go on, Gram."

"Well, I untied the cap from the crock," she said, and

then turned to look at Pargeter. "I had used a piece of blue muslin, remember, to easily identify the crock for you?"

"Yes, ma'am," Pargeter replied. "I took two handfuls from that very crock this morning, Just as you told me."

"Oh," the old woman groaned softly. "Thank God I stopped you." She turned to face her granddaughter. "You see, when I uncovered the crock I immediately noticed that something was not right. It was not the same mixture. There was... there was the distinct fragrance of... of monkshood."

"Monkshood?" Miss Ashburton's eyes widened in shock.

"Yes. You know, my dear, that I use the tiniest bit of monkshood in my special liniment." She looked once again at Sedge. "It seems someone or other is always falling off a horse around here. I have developed a special liniment for strained muscles. One of its minor ingredients is monkshood, but only the merest pinch. But this," she said, pausing to take a deep breath, "this was not a small amount. There was ... dear God, there was enough monkshood in the mixture to ... " She paused again and gave Sedge a stricken look. "I am so sorry, my lord. It... it would have ... it would have been fatal."

Pargeter's hand flew to his mouth and the blood drained from his face. "Oh my," he murmured. "Oh my."

Good God, Sedge thought, that odious brew had almost killed him, after all. He turned away from the horrified look on Pargeter's face and caught Albert's eye. The young man was as white as a sheet and his hands were tightly clenched. Sedge watched as his cousin's gaze turned on Mrs. Lattimer in astonished horror. Or perhaps it was fear. Or even anger. He sincerely hoped neither Albert nor anyone else was angry at this sweet old lady who was so devastated by a simple mistake.

"Was anything else disturbed or out of place?" Miss Ashburton asked.

"No," her grandmother replied, her voice almost a wail. "Everything was just as it should be, just as I had left it. Oh, good Lord, if no one was in there, and nothing had been moved, then ... then I... *I* must have ..." Her voice trailed off as sobs overtook her once again.

Miss Ashburton wrapped her arm around the old woman's quivering shoulders and murmured words of comfort. "It's all right, Gram. It's all right."

Mrs. Lattimer composed herself, wiped her eyes, and took a deep breath. She looked at Sedge with an earnest expression, as if willing him to understand, to forgive.

"The receipt for the infusion calls for large amounts of comfrey, hyssop, and chamomile, among other things," Mrs. Lattimer said. She spoke quickly and breathlessly, her eyes still on Sedge. But she seemed to look right through him, as though she were not really speaking to him, but to herself. "The combination results in quite a pungent aroma. Most people find it unpleasant, but I rather like it. Unfortunately, dried chamomile leaves and dried monkshood leaves look very much alike. If it were not for the altered fragrance"— she paused as her eyes focused on his once again—"I might not have noticed."

"Well, thank goodness you did, Mrs. Lattimer," Sedge said, offering a smile to the distressed woman, hoping to put her at her ease. "I am very grateful to you. Although," he said as his smile broadened to a grin, "I must admit I rather suspected that wretched stuff might kill me one day."

Sedge's lighthearted comment seemed to ease the tension in the room. Miss Ashburton smiled and cupped her grandmother's cheek. Albert looked relieved and resumed his chair, and Pargeter moved to retrieve the broken pieces of the teacup.

"I still do not understand it," Mrs. Lattimer said. "I keep the more toxic herbs separated from the rest—monkshood, foxglove, Scotch broom, belladonna, that sort of thing. I am certain there was no monkshood in the mixture when I showed it to Mr. Pargeter yesterday. I would have noticed. I am sure I would have noticed." Her eyes followed Pargeter as he held the stacked pieces of broken cup in one hand while he mopped up the spilled liquid with the other. The valet looked up at the mention of his name.

"I beg your pardon, ma'am," he said, "but I would have no idea if the mixture was incorrect when you showed it to me. I have no knowledge of herbs, either by sight or by smell. I simply took what was in the crock."

"Well," Miss Ashburton said, offering a somewhat strained smile, "I do not believe we should dwell on the hows and whys of the matter. It would be a futile exercise in any case, and serve no purpose. It was simply a mistake, one that was fortunately caught in time." She took her grandmother in a warm embrace, resting her chin on the older woman's head and looking over her at Sedge. Her expression seemed to beg his support. "Do not worry about it any further, Gram. No harm has been done, after all."

"That's right," Sedge said, captured by those sherry eyes once again. "No harm done. I am alive and well, as you see. However," he added as his face broke into another grin, "I do believe a nice rare beefsteak would help me to feel much better."

Miss Ashburton released her grandmother and laughed. That wonderful, musical laugh. "All right, you stubborn man," she said, her eyes flashing. "I will have one sent up, if you insist. But when Dr. Garthwaite scolds you soundly for bringing on an upset stomach, I shall disavow any responsibility." She retrieved the breakfast tray from the side table, cast a lingering look at Sedge that almost took his breath away, and headed toward the door. "Come on, Gram," she said over her shoulder. "I will help you prepare a new batch of your herbal mixture. We mustn't allow his lordship to miss a single dose."

* * *

"Your point, my lord."

"About time." Lord Sedgewick's eyes twinkled at Meg over the fanned tops of his cards. "You've beat me on points and flushes with each hand."

"A run of good luck, that is all."

He snorted and dropped his cards. "Luck? Are you certain, my dear? I rather begin to think you cheat."

"Hush, my lord, or I shall call you out for such an insult."

"Call me out, will you?" He flashed a grin at her. "An invalid in my condition? What a cruel woman you are!"

Meg tried not to let that infectious grin turn her heart upside down, but it was no use. During the week since he had regained consciousness, Meg had spent a great deal of time at Lord Sedgewick's bedside. She knew he chafed at his confinement, and she wanted to help keep him company by reading to him or playing piquet or just talking. Mr. Herriot, a good-natured but somewhat restless young man, had become so enthralled with the stables that he seldom left Terrence in peace. His visits to his cousin's bedside had become less and less frequent. Poor Lord Sedgewick was, she knew, bored to distraction. But that was not the only excuse for the amount of time she spent with him. She could not have stayed away if she tried, for she was drawn to him like a moth to a flame. And once again, she had been singed.

Meg's youthful infatuation had been rekindled and seemed to burn completely out of her control. She tried to ignore it, knowing it was pure foolishness. But the man was so amiable, so engaging, so thoroughly charming that it was useless to even try to resist. She was falling in love with him all over again, despite the benefit of greater maturity, wisdom, and confidence than she had known six years before.

"It is your trick, my lord," Meg said, returning her

concentration to the game.

Lord Sedgewick leaned back against his pillows and sighed. He did not pick up his cards. "Would you mind very much if we called it a game?" he asked.

"I beg your pardon, my lord." Meg removed the lap tray they had used as a card table and placed it on a side chair. "You must be tired. I shall leave you to your rest."

Lord Sedgewick reached out and grabbed her hand just as she turned to leave. "No, no," he said, "I am not in the least tired. It is just that I have played enough piquet to last a lifetime. Don't go, Miss Ashburton. Please."

He squeezed her hand slightly and her heart did a somersault. She really must not allow him to do this to her. She was acting like a schoolgirl. He was just being friendly. Nothing more. She gently removed her hand from his grasp and looked down at him with questioning brows.

"Just sit and talk with me for a while, if you do not mind." His voice was soft and mellow, and his blue eyes darkened and held hers with an odd, intense expression that made her feel warm all over.

She reminded herself that beneath all that boyish charm the man was something of a rake. She must be careful here. She must be very, very careful.

She returned to the chair she had used during their game of piquet, inching it ever so slightly away from the bed. She sat up straight and folded her hands in her lap in a manner that would have made Gram proud. "What would you like to talk about, my lord?"

The intense expression disappeared as his eyes crinkled up with the famous grin. "For one thing," he said, "I think it is time we dispensed with such formalities. After all, it is more than six years since we first met."

Meg chuckled at that absurdity.

"It feels like forever, you know," he continued. "You, and your brother, have been such good friends to me during my time here that I feel as if I had known you all my life. It seems somehow ... well, wrong to hear you call me 'my lord.'"

"What would you like me to call you, then?"

"Ah, let us consider the possibilities," he said. He chewed slightly on his lower lip, but his eyes still crinkled with amusement. "You could call me 'darling.'"

Meg laughed and tried not to look as nonplussed as his words made her feel. He is a rake, she repeated to herself. He is a rake, just having a bit of fun with the only woman under sixty available to him at the moment. "I think not," she said.

"No?" He shook his head in mock disappointment. "Well, my name is Colin, you know. But no one, except m'mother, ever calls me that. Most people just call me Sedge."

"Sedge? Why not Colin?"

"I inherited my father's title when still a young boy," he said. "At Harrow, the masters insisted that those of us with titles be addressed by our titles, you see, and never by our Christian names. So I was to be 'Sedgewick' to my betters or equals, and 'Lord Sedgewick' to everyone else. But it was not long before it had become shortened to 'Sedge.' And so I have been called ever since."

"Then 'Sedge' it shall be," Meg said.

"And what shall I call you, Miss Ashburton?" he asked.

"Ah, let us consider the possibilities." She watched him chuckle at having his words thrown back in his face. "Since my name is Margaret, I have been used to hearing myself called any number of variations on that name over the years. I suppose the most common was 'Long Meg.'"

He let out a crack of laughter. "Indeed?"

"Yes. I reached my present stature at a very young age, you see."

Sedge chuckled softly, and then said, "I trust that sobriquet has been retired?"

"Yes, for the most part. Terrence will occasionally tease

me with it, but no one else. Since I can glare down—
literally down—at most people of my acquaintance, they
are generally too intimidated to risk offending me."

"I can almost promise you," Sedge said, "that when I
am able to stand once again you shall not have to look
down at me."

"Oh, I know that. We danced together, remember."

"Ah, yes," he said, though Meg was fairly certain that
he did not, in fact, remember.

"Anyway," Meg said, not wishing to dwell on that
subject, "I would be pleased if you were to call me Meg."

"Meg it is," he said. "Though, I must confess, I should
prefer to call you 'Angel.'"

"'Angel?'"

"Yes. You see, during a few brief moments of
consciousness right after my accident, I remember you
bending over me." He smiled. "I thought I had died and
gone to heaven, and that you were an angel."

Meg threw back her head and laughed. "Me? An
Angel? Ha! I trust you have since been disabused of that
notion?"

Sedge flashed an enigmatic smile and shrugged.

"Well then, Sedge," Meg went on, "since we have
settled on names, what would you now like to talk about?"

"Why don't you tell me more about your horses?" he
said, knowing that was the one subject that should keep her
at his side for hours. "Since I cannot have the pleasure of
visiting the famous stables—yet—why not paint me word
pictures so that I can at least imagine them."

And so Meg launched into an enthusiastic and very
detailed description of the U-shaped grouping of pink brick
buildings built by her great-grandfather. Those beautiful
eyes lit up as she lovingly described the vaulted
passageways inside, flanked with stalls for more than
seventy horses.

Seventy horses?

Sedge was momentarily distracted from his study of the gold flecks in her eyes as he considered the size of such an operation. But he was soon enough captivated once again by the delicately arched, auburn brows, so mobile and expressive as she explained something about the separation of breeds within the buildings, and the pride of place in the older central building given to the thoroughbreds. His eyes traced the shape of her upper lip with its deep dip in the center between two sharp peaks while she told him of the central exercise yard used to put the horses through their paces for potential buyers. He was so completely spellbound as the tiny point of her tongue flicked out to moisten her soft, full lower lip that he lost much of what she told him of the small fenced pens and larger paddocks, as well as the various pastures and runs.

Time slipped by unnoticed as she regaled him with stories of the many finer horses she had had the privilege to know over the years. Sedge was simultaneously enchanted by her lively and colorful narrative while thoroughly bewitched by her beauty. He could not recall when he had so enjoyed a woman's company.

Sedge interrupted a lengthy discourse on bloodlines to ask about Blue Blazes. He was treated to a verbal re-creation of some of the more significant races the famous stallion had won at Newmarket. Meg even told him about Bristol Blue, a young roan she had trained from a colt, and all the plans she had for his future. Her enthusiasm was contagious. Had he not been confined to bed, he would have dashed outside to the stables with her at once.

In the excitement of discussing her favorite topic, Meg apparently had not noticed that she had unconsciously moved the chair closer and closer to the bed, so that at last she actually leaned her arms right on the counterpane. "I am going to take Bristol over the high jumps this week," she said with undisguised pride and excitement. "And then out to the north fields for some of the more difficult cross-country obstacles."

Sedge smiled and rested his hand lightly over hers. "Tell me more," he said.

And she did.

Chapter 8

Sedge gazed out the windows on the far side of the bedchamber and thought how much he missed his friends. He was lonely. At least that was how he explained to himself the obsession he had developed for Meg Ashburton. A reaction to loneliness. As he stared at a group of clouds looking like meringue puffs against a clear blue sky, he thought of Meg outside, probably riding her little blue roan, her eyes wide with excitement and her red hair coming loose of its ribbon and falling down her back. She was one of the most intriguing women he had ever met.

She was also one of the most beautiful. Just looking at her was a balm to his injuries. But what made Meg so special was that combination of mature, regal beauty with an almost girlish innocence. She was a continual surprise of fascinating incongruities. The curvaceous body and the schoolgirl blushes. The elegant bearing and the language peppered with stable boy cant. The distinctly feminine grace coupled with a strong, almost masculine stride. The quick, sometimes biting, wit and the open affection for the things and people she loved. The generally logical, practical turn of mind and the often impulsive, quixotic burst of ideas.

Meg Ashburton was quite simply the most extraordinary woman he had ever known.

She was completely without artifice, which made her unique among most of the women of Sedge's acquaintance. She had an open and trusting nature, and was thoroughly at ease with him, whether he flirted with her or just talked. Sedge suspected that growing up in the masculine world of the stables had made her less intimidated by men, more comfortable with them than might be true of other unmarried women of her age. He doubted, though, that she had any idea of the effect she had on men. Even Bertie, who was never known to be in the petticoat line, could not keep his eyes off her.

Sedge hesitated to admit that he might have actually fallen in love. He was fascinated, intrigued, charmed, perhaps even infatuated. But love was a condition about which he was ignorant He had never been in love before. And was not really in love now. No, he was not in love. It was just that she was here and he was lonely and missing his friends.

He watched the white clouds inch ever so slowly across the frame of the window, heaved a sigh, and wondered what Meg was doing.

Jack and Robert would adore her, he thought.

Robert, Lord Bradleigh and Jack, Lord Pemerton, were Sedge's closest friends. They had spent the better part of their adult lives together, lives of endless pleasure-seeking and self- indulgence. Each of them had wooed and won enough women between them to populate a small town. Though equally successful with women, Sedge's was not the smooth, seductive style of Robert, nor the cynical hedonism of Jack. Rather, he had always been cheerful and deceptively artless so as to make a woman thoroughly at ease in his company. He could then allow his lanky boyishness to weave its own spell, frequently causing women to want to mother him. Sedge had always been very happy to oblige.

Two years ago, the first of the trio of pleasure-seekers had decided to marry. Until Robert's betrothal, Sedge had never even considered the idea of marriage. If he thought about the future at all, he assumed he would continue in his contented bachelorhood and leave the succession to his cousin. Inspired by Robert's betrothal, however, Sedge began to think it was high time that he settled down as well. Since he had no romantic illusions about marriage, he has set about the thing in the practical, sensible manner in which he approached most aspects of his life. Much taken with the beauty and quiet sensibility of Miss Emily Townsend, the companion of Robert's grandmother, he had determined to court her. He had been on the verge of a formal declaration when Robert had abruptly ended his own betrothal and had married Emily himself.

As it was obviously a love match, Sedge could hardly object, and was in fact pleased to see his friend find such happiness. And since he had made no formal offer himself, there was no particular public embarrassment to endure. Nevertheless, he had experienced an unexpected sensation of relief, as though he had somehow managed a narrow escape. He had put aside any matrimonial plans without another thought.

Sedge had fallen back into his usual carefree ways, but found that he missed the companionship of Robert, who now spent most of his time with his wife in the country. And then poor Jack had suffered a family tragedy, and had removed himself from Society for almost a year. The few times Sedge had seen Jack during his mourning, he had seemed somber and distracted. Sedge began to miss the madcap days he had spent with Robert and Jack, both of whom seemed to have moved on to a more settled way of life, leaving Sedge behind.

Sedge traced the path of a sunbeam from the window to a corner of the bed frame. As he watched dust motes dance in the shaft of light, he realized that it was not long after Robert's marriage that he had first begun to feel lonely. The many casual affairs he had long preferred—variety having always been more appealing than constancy—no longer gave him the same satisfaction.

And recently Jack had, like Robert—though certainly more unexpected in one such as Jack—fallen into a love match and was now happily married to a delightful woman. The fact that Jack's wife was a close friend of Robert's wife meant that the two couples spent a great deal of time together. Sedge felt left out. With Jack's marriage, he had begun to feel even more strongly the emptiness in his own life, and as he watched his friends basking in connubial bliss, he understood the cause of that emptiness.

He wanted what they had.

Both gentlemen teased him often enough about finding the right woman, about how he would know when he found her.

They had both assured him that he should not expect an instantaneous explosion—no fireworks or bells or horns to announce the arrival of his true love. It was a gradual sort of realization, they had said. A quiet sort of thing. But there would be no doubt about it. He would know when he found her and she would change his life forever.

Their women had certainly changed Sedge's life.

He was missing his friends.

Lying in this blasted bed day in and day out left far too much time for such reflection. But watching the clouds roll by was not a very stimulating activity, to be sure. Never a contemplative man by any stretch of the imagination, Sedge was not given to bouts of deep soul-searching. He was uncomfortable with that sort of self-examination. He knew himself to be a basically simple man of no more than average intellect. He suspected that no matter how deeply he probed, there would be little of interest to discover.

Nevertheless, he thought as he drummed his fingers

restlessly on the counterpane, there was nothing much else to do while stuck in this bed. He supposed he might read a book. But he had never been much of a reader. He needed company. He wished Meg would come by. He wished anyone would come by. Albert. Terrence. Even Pargeter would be welcome.

His mind drifted along with the clouds.

He was too old, at thirty-six, to continue in the selfish, carefree ways of his youth. The days of carousing with Robert and Jack were long past. He had begun to notice that his companions of late were more often than not some ten years his junior. Young men, like Cosmo Trevelian.

Was he afraid to face the maturity of his years? Afraid to face up to the responsibilities of age? Was he simply afraid to grow up?

Before he could give much consideration to such uncharacteristically sobering thoughts, a knock sounded on the bedchamber door.

"Come in," he said, hoping and hoping that it was Meg.

"Here you are, my lord," Mrs. Lattimer said as she walked into the room, followed by the housekeeper. "A nice bit of nuncheon for you."

Sedge sat up straight and allowed the housekeeper to place a tray on his lap, laden with cold meats, pickles, cheese, and bread, as well as a good-sized apple tart and a tankard of ale. Thankfully, the bland diet had long since been discarded. Sedge now suspected the ladies of Thornhill were out to fatten him up.

Mrs. Lattimer took a chair after the housekeeper left, determined to keep him company during his meal. Sedge was in fact grateful for her company. She was a very sweet lady, and though she never mentioned it, he knew she had never quite forgiven herself for the mix-up with the herbs.

"How are you feeling today, my lord?"

"Fit as a fiddle," he replied, "except for the damned— excuse me, ma'am—darned leg. Can't do much to speed it along, I expect" He took a bit of pickle and followed it with a hearty swallow of ale. Meg had told him that Thornhill had its own brewhouse, almost a necessity with the number of men required to run the stables. Sedge looked forward each day to another taste of the special home brew.

All things considered, there were worse places to recuperate from a broken leg.

"Your head seems to be healing nicely," Mrs. Lattimer said.

"I am glad finally to be free of that wretched bandage," he said with a shake of his head that caused his too-long hair to flop over his forehead. "What do you think, ma'am? Is the scar going to be as dashing as you promised? I could perhaps add an eyepatch and earring for a better effect."

"If you keep your hair that long," she replied with a smile, "no one will ever see the scar. I can barely see it now. But you needn't worry. Dr. Garthwaite did a fine job, so it will at least be a good, clean scar. Not ragged or puckered."

Sedge smiled and continued his meal. Mrs. Lattimer entertained him with local gossip—long, involved tales of people completely unknown to him. But he was thankful for the diversion.

Just as he bit into the apple tart, Meg swept in the open door with her usual long stride, and Sedge almost lost the ability to swallow. Quickly choking the tart down before he disgraced himself, Sedge stared open-mouthed at the young woman chattering away and bending down to kiss her grandmother's cheek. She wore a pair of tight buckskin breeches and high, black riding boots that displayed the shapeliest hips and longest legs he thought he had ever laid eyes on. She wore a green woolen jacket buttoned tight over a thin lawn shirt. Her hair was pulled back into its usual knot at the back of her neck, but enough unruly locks had come loose so that her face was framed in soft red curls. But his eyes kept returning to those breeches and all the delights they did little to disguise.

"Really, Meg!" Mrs. Lattimer scolded after accepting her granddaughter's kiss. "What will Lord Sedgewick think of you? Must you come in wearing those horrible breeches?"

Yes, he thought, she must. She must.

"I am sorry," Meg said, "but I was too excited to take the time to change." She turned to Sedge with a huge smile. "He did it, Sedge! I took Bristol over the most difficult stretch of the north field, and he did not falter once! Not once! He handled the high ground with ease, took all the hedges and fences. He even jumped a ditch—a ditch with flowing water—without the least skittishness. Oh, I am so proud of him!" She practically bounced with enthusiasm.

"You should be proud of yourself, Meg," Sedge said. "It is your own good training that has made him so surefooted."

"And he is so fast," she continued. "I felt as though I were flying. It was so wonderful, I tell you it quite took my breath away."

Her eyes flashed and her cheeks were still pink from exertion, and excitement. He watched through the tightly stretched jacket as the swell of her bosom rose and fell with her rapid breathing. It was indeed wonderful, and she quite took *his* breath away.

She chattered on about the successful ride, oblivious to the fact that Mrs. Lattimer had quietly left the room. Sedge smiled to think that the old woman's tactics were not necessary to help him notice and appreciate her granddaughter. In fact, Meg needed no help from anyone at all in that respect. She did it all by herself.

Meg took the chair her grandmother had vacated and dragged it close to the bed. She swung it around and straddled it backward, perching her elbows on its top rail. The glorious, long legs wrapped around the chair in a manner that would have given her grandmother forty fits, and almost did the same for Sedge, for very different reasons.

"I cannot wait to show you Bristol," she said, reaching for his tray and breaking off a piece of apple tart. "I am going to train him to race, you know. And if you are a betting man, my lord, I tell you now that he is going to be a formidable competitor. Goodness, I am starving." She popped the piece of tart in her mouth and then looked up at him sheepishly as she licked the sticky syrup off her fingers. The slow, sensual strokes of her tongue caused Sedge's groin to tighten in a most uncomfortable manner. He was grateful his lap was covered with the tray.

And suddenly his mind was filled with a vision of Meg's beautiful white body, naked beneath his own. He thought she might be the one woman in the world he could actually look in the eye while he made love to her, instead of having her face buried somewhere in the middle of his chest. Or contorting himself into a knot to reach her face. He was used to women who were some twelve inches or more shorter than his own six feet three inches. But he and Meg could look into each other's eyes. A perfect fit. There were all sorts of advantages to that beautiful, tall, long-legged body. But if he thought of them all just now, he might truly embarrass himself.

She was a gently bred, innocent young woman, after all. She was not a woman to be casually seduced. He should not even be having such improper thoughts about her. Unless ...

"Thank you. Sedge, for allowing me to rattle on and on like this," she said, offering a puckish smile. "I know you are a captive audience, so to speak, but you are such a good listener. I have so enjoyed the times we have spent together."

He reached for her hand and brought it to his lips. "It has been my pleasure, ma'am."

She dropped her eyes, and her long, auburn lashes cast

shadows on her cheeks. Cheeks tinted with a faint pink blush. She kept her fingers curved slightly over his for a moment, and then slowly—reluctantly?—pulled them away. When she looked up again, it was to reward him with a smile of such warmth that Sedge was singed all the way to his toes.

"It is just that..." She paused and flashed a self-conscious grin. "Well, you are so easy to talk to. I feel like I can talk to you about anything. I can, and frequently do, tell you all my thoughts and feelings. And you never dismiss them or belittle them or make me feel silly. You listen. I... I just wanted you to know how much I appreciate that."

His friends had been right, after all. There were no fireworks. It was indeed a quiet sort of thing.

Chapter 9

"So, cuz, tomorrow is the big day?"

Sedge looked over at his cousin, who stood with an arm propped against the wide window embrasure, looking out at something below. "Yes," he replied to Albert's back, "the doctor wants me to try my hand at crutches tomorrow." And he could not wait to get even as far as that window. He had studied every inch of this room from his position on the bed— every chair, every table, every painting, every cushion. He had memorized the patterns in the curtains, in the rugs, in the bed hangings. He had traced the shapes carved into the paneling, the chair legs, the picture frames, the bedposts. He could describe every detail of the room with his eyes closed.

If he could only get as far as the window, he could at least expand his world beyond these four walls.

"At first," he continued, wondering what Albert found so fascinating outside, "I will probably only be allowed to hobble across the room and back. But you can be sure that I will be stumbling all over Thornhill before you know it. I cannot wait!"

Albert turned and smiled at Sedge's excitement "You must be simply itching to get out of that bed."

"Indeed, I am ready to climb these walls. I am anxious to be up and about again."

"And then," Albert said, "you can be on your way. You must be wanting to get back home."

Sedge shrugged and grinned. "Oh, I don't know," he said enigmatically, eliciting a deep chortle from Albert. "But I tell you, I am more than ready to get out of this bed. You cannot imagine how stiff I am. Not just the leg, but all over. I fear my body may have completely forgotten how to move properly. I am desperate for some exercise."

"Did you have any particular type of exercise in mind?" Albert asked with a sly grin.

"Why, Bertie, what can you mean?"

Albert chuckled and moved to stand next to the bed, his arms folded across his chest. "It has not escaped my notice, Sedge, how taken you are with Miss Ashburton. I thought perhaps you might be considering a bit of diversion while here in the country. She is quite beautiful."

"So she is," Sedge said.

"Were you really thinking of a dalliance with our host's sister?" Albert shook his head in disapproval. "Not like you to court danger, Sedge."

"Breaking my leg is more than enough danger for me, Bertie. Do not worry. I am not planning anything foolish." Wasn't he? He had thought he might actually begin a real courtship of Meg, once he was on his feet again. But perhaps that was indeed a foolish notion. The ultimate goal of a courtship, after all, was marriage. Is that what he really wanted? He had toyed with the idea of marriage to Meg. There were advantages, to be sure. But the very idea of marriage still tended to strike terror in his bachelor's heart. He had not quite settled in his mind if he really wanted to go through with it, if he was ready to go through with it. And he was confused by these new feelings she inspired in him. He still had much to consider.

"I am glad to hear it," Albert said as he reached for a

chair and pulled it closer to the bed. He sat down and crossed one leg languidly over the other. "Could have been awkward. Sir Terrence might have insisted on a formal offer." He chuckled softly. "And we both know that you would run screaming from such a situation. *If* you could run, that is."

Sedge laughed, but did not respond.

"You had better be careful, cuz," Albert continued, "since you are in no condition to flee. Don't allow yourself to be lured into any traps."

"Don't worry, Bertie. I have said I will do nothing foolish."

"Yes, but I remember a certain conversation we had at Witham Abbey during your mother's Christmas party. Do you recall? You were in your cups and bemoaning the loss of your friends—Bradleigh and Pemerton."

"I do have a vague recollection of polishing off several bottles of the Abbey's best claret with you one night. Got a bit maudlin, did I?"

"You could say that," Albert replied, amusement tugging at the corners of his mouth. "Mostly, you talked about marriage."

"I did?"

Albert laughed. "You did. Talked about how it might be time to settle down and fill up your nursery. The most confirmed old bachelor I know actually speaking of marriage! You had me laughing for hours."

"I am pleased to have amused you, Bertie, I am sure."

"Well, you must admit, old man, that it is certainly unlike you even to consider such a subject." Albert slid further down in the chair, leaned his head against the back rail, and laughed at such an absurd notion. "But you will never marry. You know that you will not. You have said so often enough. That sort of settled, routine way of life is not in your nature. Never could be."

"No doubt you are right, Bertie," Sedge replied as he

considered the truth of his cousin's words.

"You were simply mourning the loss of your close friends to the bonds of matrimony," Albert continued. "Feeling left out, I suppose. And I can understand that, Sedge. I know how close you and Bradleigh and Pemerton had been all those years. But things change, you know. Their lives have taken a different turn from yours, that is all. I should hate to think that you were considering marriage simply as a means to reclaim those old friendships."

Is that what he was thinking of doing? Using a wife to get back into the circle of friendship he had so missed? To make himself a part of a couple so that he was no longer the odd man out? Was he that desperate to bring things back to the way they had once been?

"Besides, you cannot turn back the clock, you know," Albert said, as if he had read Sedge's mind. "Things can never be the same again. Life moves on. Didn't Bradleigh's wife have a child recently?"

"Yes," Sedge replied. "Last fall. A little girl."

"Ah," Albert said with a lift of his brows, "then you can be sure there will be other children until Bradleigh has a son. No, cuz, once children enter the picture, there is no looking back. The past is in the past."

"I know that, Bertie. I know that."

Albert hunched a shoulder and flashed a sheepish grin. "Sorry, Sedge. Didn't mean to lecture. I just wanted to make sure you weren't allowing your confinement to warp your judgment where Miss Ashburton is concerned."

Sedge heaved a weary sigh and sank back against the pillows. Perhaps he *was* spinning foolish dreams about Meg. Perhaps when his leg had healed and he had resumed his active life in Town, Meg Ashburton would no longer seem so extraordinary. Perhaps.

"I appreciate your words of advice, Bertie," he said. "But I promise you, I will not do anything foolish. And, as you say, once I have thrown off this wretched confinement, I shall be moving on. And believe me, I would not for the world do anything to hurt Miss Ashburton. She is much too delightful a young woman to be trifled with."

"Well, then," Albert said, "we must think about getting you back to Town soon, old chap, where there are plenty of women willing to be trifled with."

Sedge threw back his head and laughed.

Albert changed the subject and launched into a ribald tale of one of their mutual friends, whose two mistresses, each unaware of the other, happened to meet and compare notes. The man had been forced to leave Town to escape their dual wrath.

Sedge listened to Albert with only half an ear. His mind was still full of questions about Meg, his feelings for her, his motivations, his plans for her. This was all so new for him, this swelling of emotion he felt for her. And despite what he had told Albert, he was certain it had nothing to do with his confinement to bed. Had he met her in any other circumstance, he would have felt the same.

He had come to recognize her step in the hallway as she approached the door to his bedchamber, and his heart quickened at the very sound. Each time she entered his room, with a radiant smile as if nothing pleased her more than just to see him, he was filled with a sudden rush of longing. It was as though there had been an empty place in his heart, and she had somehow slipped in to fill it.

His friends had told him he would know when the right woman came along. Well, he knew it. At least, he thought he knew it. He was fairly certain that he knew it. In thirty-six years, no other woman had affected him so. She *must* be the one.

But he would not rush his fences. He wanted to court her properly, once he was up and about. He wanted to do things right.

And he would not tell Albert or anyone else. He wanted

to be absolutely sure of his own feelings, and he wanted to attempt to determine her feelings as well. He was fairly certain she was attracted to him. She occasionally gave him a look that seared him to the bone, though he suspected she was unaware of the desire written so clearly on her face. She had admitted how much she enjoyed being with him, and talking with him. If nothing else, they had developed a wonderful friendship. But he must be certain that she might be interested in more than friendship before making any decisions.

After all, Meg was well past the age when most women married. Perhaps she was not interested in marriage. He could not imagine that in all these years no other man had shown an interest in her. In fact, he had more than once caught a certain look in Dr. Garthwaite's eye as he glanced at Meg. His eyes often followed her across the room when he thought she was not looking. Sedge wondered if there were any expectations from that quarter? But he had never seen Meg look at the doctor with anything like desire.

Perhaps his own vanity clouded his judgment. Most women of his acquaintance were fairly open in their desire for him.

But Meg Ashburton was not most women.

He wanted to know how she felt, to know what she wanted. And once he had made his decision, he did not want to make any mistakes. He wanted to do things right.

He wanted to court Meg properly.

* * *

Meg ran the stiff-bristled dandy brush over Bristol Blue's back in long, firm, sweeping strokes. It was an activity she had been doing since she was a child, and she performed the task almost absently as her mind wandered from stable matters, to minor household crises, to Gram's problem in the stillroom, to Sedge. It always came back to

Sedge. Her mind was full of him. And so was her heart.

Brushing backward and downward over the roan's flanks, she wondered how Sedge was progressing with the crutches. She had spoken to Dr. Garthwaite as he left earlier that morning, and he had encouraged Meg to leave the viscount alone with his valet for a few hours so that he could practice in private.

"Several weeks in bed can make a body stiff and uncooperative," the doctor had said. "His use of the crutches is still somewhat feeble and awkward." He gave her a knowing glance. "I am sure you would not want to embarrass him by being witness to his weakness, Meg. Give him a little time."

Meg had turned away, conscious of her heightened color. But then the doctor had confirmed that Sedge was impatient to be mobile once again, and knew that with practice he would soon manage the crutches with steadiness and skill.

"He should not be allowed to hobble beyond the bedchamber for a day or two," the doctor had told Meg. "And when he finally does, he will require assistance on the stairs. But let him wander a bit. He needs the exercise."

"Is there anything further we need to do for him?" Meg had asked.

"I have adjusted the splint," he replied, "and tied it slightly differently to make it easier to walk. I gave several extra sets of bandages to his valet and showed him how to replace them, how to braid the tails to keep the splint tight. He seems a competent man. Lord Sedgewick is in good hands, Meg. He will be just fine."

Meg had been anxious to go to him, anxious to see him walking again. But she had taken the doctor's advice and left him alone with Pargeter for the entire morning, while she took Bristol Blue for a long run.

She flipped Bristol's dark gray mane to the other side of his neck, then began to bring it back again with the brush, one lock at a time. She no longer bothered to deny her feelings for Sedge. They had grown stronger and stronger with each hour she spent by his side. She had never before felt this way about a man, except for the brief infatuation with this same man six years ago. But it was different now. Then, she had been captivated by his smile and a few moments of kindness. Now, she knew him as a person.

During the hours she had spent with him she had discovered that the charm and affability went beyond the smile. He was a genuinely kind, sweet-natured, generous, compassionate man. She loved talking with him. It was as easy and comfortable as talking to Terrence. But she had discussed subjects with Sedge that she had never broached with Terrence. Or even with Gram. Somehow, he put her so at ease that she shamelessly and effortlessly bared her soul to him.

He was also incredibly handsome, Meg thought, smiling to herself as she continued to brush Bristol's mane right out from the roots, to make it shine like gun metal. She held the silky mane in her hands and thought of Sedge's hair. She adored his long blond hair, which was mostly the color of honey, but also contained several lighter streaks, especially in the front. She hoped he would keep it rakishly long, as it was now, but suspected he would cut it short when he returned to Town for the Season. And she loved his brilliant blue eyes, even when they almost disappeared from sight as they crinkled into slits as he grinned. Often, they flashed with shared amusement or mischief or enthusiasm. But occasionally she had noticed them darken as they locked with hers, and at such times the air seemed to tremble between them.

Meg did not misunderstand the desire in his eyes. She had been around men long enough to recognize it for what it was. She had discovered at a young age that men could be lustful creatures—as randy as Thornhill stallions—and Meg had been ignoring such looks for years. But with this particular man, she wanted to believe it was real, to believe there was some real feeling behind the physical desire.

But she knew him to be a rake, she reminded herself as she began to brush Bristol's tail. An accomplished womanizer must necessarily be very good at that sort of thing, at making a woman feel desirable. She grasped the end of roan's dock and held it out straight, then let down one gray lock at a time, brushing out the ends first and working up to the roots. It was what rakes did, after all—convince women to capitulate to their seduction. But she did not expect Sedge would ever go any further than seducing her with his eyes. He was a gentleman, after all. He would not make any sort of improper offer.

But neither did she expect any more respectable offer from him. She could never forget that she was a six-foot tall, red- haired Amazon. And a hoyden to boot, to hear Gram tell it. Such a woman could not expect any serious interest from a man like Lord Sedgewick. Oh, he had been friendly and kind, and had shown a real interest in her work in the stables. But then, what man was not interested in horses? As much as she would love to believe otherwise, she knew there was nothing special in Sedge's feelings toward her.

After finishing Bristol's grooming so that he gleamed like Birmingham silver from head to foot, Meg returned to the house to change her clothes and have a leisurely bath. This day, when Sedge was able to walk for the first time, she had no wish to go to him smelling of horse. She dressed with care, selecting a turquoise muslin dress with long, full sleeves and an open V-neck filled in with a cambric chemisette. Her maid styled Meg's hair in a variation of its usual low knot in the back, with more curls artfully arranged around her face.

Meg finally dismissed the maid and surveyed herself in the cheval glass. Standing with her shoulders back and her head high, she was pleased with the overall effect of what she saw. She had long ago given up the foolishness of slouching and bending her knees in order to appear less tall. What was the point? Short of lopping off her legs at the knees, there was nothing she could do about it, after all. So she had grown to accept her height, even to be proud of it. She found, too, that when she walked tall and proud, others generally treated her with more respect.

With one last adjustment to the chemisette, Meg strode from her room and down the hall to the guest chamber used by Sedge. She knocked softly.

"Come in, Meg."

She opened the door to find Sedge standing at the window, a huge smile splitting his face. He was dressed in a white cambric shirt, a blue pin-striped waistcoat, and doeskin breeches. He wore white stockings and a black kid slipper on his left foot. He wore no jacket or cravat, and his shirt was open at the neck. He looked incredibly handsome, and thoroughly masculine, and Meg found herself staring open-mouthed. She gathered her scattered wits and smiled in return.

"Do you know how I have longed to look out this window?" he said. "Simply to look outside and see the world again. 'Tis a wonderful thing, Meg."

She started to walk toward him, but he held up his hand to stop her.

"Do not move," he said. "Let me come to you."

Meg felt a chill of apprehension as she assessed the distance between them. He would have to take a diagonal path from the window in the far corner to the door where she stood. They were about as far apart as they could be, and this was one of the largest bedchambers in the house, with its spacious sitting area at one end and the bed at the other.

He reached for the wooden crutches propped against the window embrasure, lifted himself onto them, and somewhat shakily positioned himself to face Meg. "You are looking particularly beautiful today, my dear. A special incentive to make it across the room."

Meg felt the heat of a blush color her cheeks, but ignored it as she watched Sedge swing his splinted right leg forward, keeping it bent and not allowing it to touch the ground. Leaning heavily on the crutches, he dragged his left foot forward.

"Well done, my lord!" Meg beamed at him, though her heart constricted at the effort she saw in his furrowed brows and the tight line of his mouth.

"'Tis only one step, my dear," he said in a slightly breathless voice. "At this rate, it may take all day to reach you."

"It is but a beginning," she said. "You can do it, Sedge. Come to me."

He gazed into her eyes for a moment with an expression that caused her breath to catch. But he quickly returned his concentration to the task of walking. He made slow progress, but seemed to gain confidence with each step. He began to maneuver the crutches with more assurance, and appeared to become more comfortable with using his left foot to push off and cover greater distance.

As he neared her, he looked up briefly and Meg reached out her hand toward him. "Come on, Sedge," she said. "You are almost here."

After what seemed an eternity, he finally stood directly in front of her, breathing heavily but flashing a broad, triumphant smile. She still reached out for him, and he allowed his left crutch to clatter noisily to the floor as he grasped her hand.

"Oh, Sedge!" she said. "You did it! You did it. I am so proud of you."

Leaning on one crutch, he held her hand tightly and pierced her with his bright blue eyes. Eyes almost level with her own. How extraordinary. Her heart pounded as his gaze held hers and his smile softened. She believed—she truly believed—that she detected something more than the need for support in the way he held on to her hand. A rush of warmth from his touch tingled all the way up her arm.

Meg dropped her eyes to their joined hands. An image came to mind of Sedge lying feverish and unconscious while she bathed his hands. While she measured her own hand against his larger one. While she allowed their fingers to entwine, just as they did now.

"Ah, Meg," he said finally, breaking the profound silence that had fallen between them. She raised her eyes to meet his. "It is a pleasure to see you at last from this vantage." He lifted her hand slowly toward his lips. "I knew we would see eye to eye," he whispered before placing a warm kiss on her fingertips.

Chapter 10

The stables were teeming with activity. Representatives for the Duke of York were scheduled to arrive later that day to view Thornhill's thoroughbreds. It would be a large feather in Terrence's cap if the duke were to add Thornhill horses to his own stable. Meg's brother had set every groom and stable boy to cleaning stalls and grooming horses. Even the lesser breeds must look in top form to insure the reputation of Thornhill quality.

In the midst of all the excitement, Meg was taking care of her own horse. She did not want to leave Bristol to one of the grooms. She wanted to see to it herself that he looked and behaved perfectly, even though he was not for sale.

She recognized the voice of Mr. Herriot as he hailed Terrence in a hearty greeting. Meg peeked over the top of the wooden stall door and saw the two gentlemen heading in her direction. She ducked quickly back inside the stall, hoping they would pass by without noticing her. She did not wish to engage in conversation with Sedge's cousin while she was clad in breeches. He had come upon her once before when she was in her working clothes, and he had looked at her in a way that made her very uncomfortable. Despite the fact that he was Sedge's cousin and that Gram had been thoroughly charmed by him, Meg simply could not warm up to him. He generally wore a broad, congenial smile, and although it was similar to his cousin's engaging grin, it did not quite reach his eyes. And it was Sedge's eyes, after all, and the way they became a part of the whole expression, that made his smile so special.

"Do you mind if we have a brief word in private, Sir Terrence?" His voice carried clearly, even amidst all the noise of stable activity.

"If you do not mind using one of the empty stalls," Terrence replied. "I am afraid I cannot return to the house just now."

"This will do just fine," Mr. Herriot said, and Meg heard the hinge creak as the door to a nearby stall was opened.

She peeked out again and just caught Mr. Herriot's profile as he followed Terrence into the stall across and one over from Bristol's. It was the stall used by Cartimandua, a bay mare who was currently being exercised in the main courtyard. Mr. Herriot's eyes had flicked in her direction for an instant. Meg thought he might have seen her, but she quickly ducked back inside the stall and could not be certain.

"What did you wish to speak to me about, Herriot?" her brother asked, his clear voice carrying easily, as did all sound in these vaulted halls.

Meg was situated to hear every word, but had no wish to eavesdrop. They would probably speak of stable business, Mr. Herriot no doubt wanting to bargain for a bit of prime horseflesh. Whenever anyone asked for a private word with Terrence, it was bound to be awkward. She had no desire to be a witness to what would likely be an embarrassing transaction— an offer well below value, a request for credit, an unequal trade, or some such thing. Poor Terrence was frequently faced with that sort of business proposition from gentlemen who claimed they absolutely must have such-and-such a horse, but were temporarily without funds.

Meg never ceased to be amazed at how people seemed to forget that the Thornhill stables were a business. A very successful business, but a business nonetheless. If Terrence happened to raise sheep, no one would suggest that he give away the wool. But since he raised horses, many gentlemen who called themselves friends expected all sorts of special favors. The true gentleman, though, recognized the value of a horse and paid what it was worth.

Meg ignored the conversation of the two gentlemen and returned to Bristol to continue with his grooming. Now, here was a horse whose value one day would be something to be reckoned with. She held his bent leg gently with one hand as she scrubbed his hoof with a stiff brush to remove dirt and straw.

"This is a bit embarrassing, Sir Terrence, but it is about Miss Ashburton."

Meg's head jerked up at her name. *Me?*

"My sister?"

"Yes," Mr. Herriot continued. "And my cousin. You see, it is just that I have noticed that the two of them spend a great deal of time together. Especially now that Sedge is up on crutches. I have often noticed him exploring the stables or other parts of Thornhill with Miss Ashburton at his side."

"She is no doubt acting as his guide, Herriot. She knows this place as well as I do."

"Of course, you are probably right. It is just that..." Mr. Herriot's voice trailed off, and Meg shamelessly scurried to the front of the stall, almost tripping over the grain tub in her haste. She did not want to miss this. "Oh, dash it all," he continued, "this is deuced awkward. He is my cousin, after all. Like a brother to me. But the fact is, Sedge is a trifle loose where women are concerned."

"Indeed?"

"I would hate to see your sister hurt, Sir Terrence. I... I simply thought I should warn you."

No, you thought to warn me. He must have seen her after all. He had wanted her to overhear.

"You believe your cousin to be trifling with my sister's affections?" her brother asked in a steely voice.

"Not intentionally, no. Sedge is a gentleman, after all. It is just that they have spent so much time together, and I have once or twice caught a certain look between them. I just would not like for Miss Ashburton to get the wrong idea."

"What wrong idea would that be?"

Mr. Herriot sighed loudly. "I just hope she does not believe he is ... well, that he is courting her, that he means to make her an offer. He will not, Sir Terrence. I can assure you of that. Sedge enjoys the company of women. But he does not marry them. He will only make one sort of offer to a woman, and it is not of a proper nature, if you take my meaning."

"Are you telling me Lord Sedgewick is likely to offer Meg a slip on the shoulder?"

"Good God, no," Mr. Herriot replied in a horrified tone. "I only meant that neither you nor your sister should expect that he will make any kind of offer at all."

A strained silence followed that pronouncement while Meg tried to calm her breathing. It was what she knew to be true, but to hear the words spoken so bluntly had the effect of being punched in the stomach. She was being made, by Mr. Herriot's deliberately overheard words, to face the truth.

"I do not think you need worry about Meg," her brother said at last "Never in all her life has she shown an interest in any particular gentleman. And God knows she has met more than her share here at Thornhill." He chuckled softly. "Meg is not like other young women. As far as I can tell, she does not care for men in the usual way, and probably would not have the least notion how to go on if she did. She is fairly naive in that respect But I do not suppose that, at her age, she is likely to change. As you may have noticed, she traipses around Thornhill in breeches as though she were one of the stable hands. She has a much greater interest in horses than in romance, Herriot"

Meg covered her mouth to stifle a groan. Is that how Terrence viewed her? A hoyden with no interest in the opposite sex?

Not like other young women.

"Why, in the last few weeks," her brother continued, "she has spoken more of her blue roan than she has of the viscount. She will yammer on for hours about that young horse. As far as Lord Sedgewick is concerned, I can only ever recall her commenting on the progress of his recovery."

"But they do spend a great deal of time together," Mr. Herriot persisted.

"I think she simply enjoys his company," Terrence said. "He is a very friendly, easygoing sort of fellow."

"He is too charming by half," Mr. Herriot said with a laugh. "That is what concerns me. I would not want Miss Ashburton to misinterpret that engaging manner of his. It is just his way. He uses that smile to charm everyone he knows, from the sternest dowager to the most stiff-rumped old nob. I just don't want your sister to get her hopes up."

Get my hopes up? What hopes? I have no hopes.

Not like other young women.

Terrence laughed. "I think the only one around here with the sort of hopes you are implying is my grandmother. I believe she has decided Lord Sedgewick is the right man for Meg simply because he is taller than she is." Meg could almost see her brother grinning and shaking his head in resignation. "Poor Gram. She only wants to be helpful, but she really does not understand. Even Meg has been embarrassed by Gram's obvious tactics. That may be one of the problems, actually. The old girl leaves Meg alone with the viscount at every opportunity."

"Good God," Mr. Herriot exclaimed, "she is not trying to trap Sedge into some sort of compromising situation, is she?"

Oh, Lord.

Once again, Terrence laughed. "No, no, Herriot. Do not get yourself in a pucker. Gram only wants to leave them alone together so that Lord Sedgewick will get to know Meg better and, naturally, fall in love with her. The old girl's a romantic at heart, but she means no harm."

"I hate to disillusion your sweet grandmother," Mr. Herriot said, "but Sedge ain't the falling-in-love sort."

"I know," Terrence said. "But it is only Gram's notion, not Meg's. I do not believe you have to worry about any misunderstandings on Meg's part. But if you'd like, I will have a word with her."

"It might be a good idea," Mr. Herriot said. "Just in case."

Just in case what? In case I did not overhear every single word?

"By the way, Herriot," Terrence said over the sound of the creaking hinge, "did you ever tell your cousin about his carriage? About the cut axle?"

"As a matter of fact, I did," Mr. Herriot replied, his voice along with his footsteps moving away. "He will not accept that it was deliberate. He prefers to believe that it was some kind of accidental break that happened while at the inn at Hawstead. Some freak slip of an axe, or some such thing. He refuses to believe it may have been intentional. He has dismissed the whole incident as a simple accident."

"Hmm," her brother said as they walked farther away from Bristol's stall. "And what do you think, Herriot?" They were out the stable door before Meg could hear a reply.

But she was much more interested in what had been said before. She leaned up against Bristol and gently stroked his lower neck and withers. The one good thing she had learned was that her own infatuation with Sedge was not apparent to Terrence. Of course, he did not believe she was capable of the same feelings and desires as other women. He probably did not think of her as a woman at all. Besides, he had always told her that her every thought or emotion was written clearly on her face. He teased her that she should never take up gambling, for there was no way she could ever bluff anyone. And her father had always said she was a terrible liar. That blasted fair skin!

So, if Terrence did not know she was head over heels in love with Sedge, then she must have at last learned to school her features. "Have I done that, Bristol?" she murmured as she continued to stroke the horse's neck. "Are you able to read my heart in my face?" Bristol shook his head and snorted, his ears pricking forward in interest. "Well, if you can, then perhaps Terrence simply is not looking anymore. Or perhaps he just does not recognize such an unexpected emotion in his heartless hoyden of a sister."

Bristol snorted again, and Meg reached up to stroke his ears, blinking furiously to clear her suddenly watery vision.

As for what she had learned about Sedge, it was nothing she had not already known in her heart. And though she could no longer control her feelings for him, she had never really had any expectations of an offer from him. Despite what Mr. Herriot may think, she had known all along that there was no hope for her as far as Sedge was concerned. His cousin's words only hardened her resolve against any such hopes.

It galled her that Mr. Herriot must think her such a green girl. Hearing his words—which she had no doubt she was meant to hear, and which rankled, despite the kindness and concern she knew to be behind them—made her realize how her actions might be misconstrued by others. Perhaps even by Sedge? It was true that she spent a great deal of time with him. She knew he would leave Thornhill soon enough, and she only wanted to be with him as much as possible.

Appearances aside, however, she was only making it more difficult for herself, more difficult to face their eventual parting. The solution, of course, was simply to spend less time with him. He had become very adept at getting about on crutches, wielding them with great aplomb and agility. He had even learned to negotiate the stairs without much difficulty. He no longer needed Meg to help him get around, if he ever had.

She gave Bristol one more affectionate pat and stood back, hands on hips, and considered the situation. Sedge would simply have to find other company as he hobbled about Thornhill. Gram or Terrence, or even Mr. Herriot. He did not need her. Not to get around the farm, or for anything else. She would remember— yes, Mr. Herriot, she would remember—not to harbor false hopes.

"I would never be so foolish as to hope, now would I, Bristol?" Meg walked around to the front of the stall, reached in her jacket pocket, and pulled out several pieces of carrot. She held the carrots out on the flat of her hand, and Bristol took them eagerly. "No, I would never be so foolish."

Bristol Blue nudged her with his nose and responded with a soft whicker.

* * *

"Much obliged, Pargeter," Sedge said as his valet helped him on with his coat.

Thank God for Pargeter. Now that Sedge was up and about once again, he was required to dress appropriately. Balancing on one leg, he would not have been able to manage on his own. But with Pargeter's able assistance, he felt reasonably presentable. Except for the wooden splint on the right leg, he looked every inch the country gentleman: buckskin breeches, bottle green coat, russet-colored waistcoat with thin gold stripes, crisp white shirt and cravat, gleaming top boots. Top boot, that is.

Damn, but he would be glad to finally be rid of the splint and wear two boots again. Ha! Just a little over a week ago, he was wishing he could get out of bed at all. Now that he had passed that milestone, he dreamed of wearing two boots. The doctor explained that he would be required to use the splint for a few more weeks. It helped keep the leg immobile so the fracture could heal more quickly and cleanly. He had threatened Sedge with a permanent limp if he did not keep the splint in place.

Sedge took the crutches handed to him by Pargeter and hauled himself up onto them. The valet scowled at the resulting destruction of the coat's perfect lines. While Sedge adjusted his position, Pargeter adjusted the coat. With a final nod of approval from his valet. Sedge hobbled across the room. Pargeter held the bedchamber door open and made one last survey of Sedge's appearance. As Sedge made his slow navigation of the hallway, he heard the bedchamber door close softly behind him.

He had become rather good at moving about on crutches. The rhythm of pushing off with his left foot and swinging the splinted right leg had become almost second nature. Thump, slide. Thump, slide. Thump, slide. As he made his way toward the landing at the top of the stairs, the gentle aromas of breakfast wafted upstairs to tease him. Gad, but he was hungry.

He hoped to see Meg at the breakfast table this morning. He had not seen her for days. He missed her. Until a few days ago, his so-called courtship had been progressing nicely. To a point, that is. They had spent even more time together, now that he was mobile. Her pride in

Thornhill was obvious as he toured the stables and grounds with her. It was every bit as beautiful as the word pictures she had painted for him while he was confined to bed. He had enjoyed their necessarily moderate pace—thump, slide, thump, slide—as well as Meg's animated commentary. As they had strolled about Thornhill, they had talked and talked, but they had often drifted into long silences that were equally comfortable.

And even though they talked and laughed and joked and were quiet together with ease, whenever Sedge flirted with her, flattered her, or touched her in any way, he felt her draw back slightly.

Meg never said anything to discourage him. Nevertheless, Sedge felt her shrink away from him, or saw her posture stiffen at his side, or heard a momentary tightening of her voice. Small things, but noticeable. He was not sure what it all meant, but he did know that he was becoming more and more besotted with her, and so he would not give up just yet

Sedge pushed forward for the final step on the landing before beginning the arduous negotiation of the stairs.

And his left foot went flying out from under him.

What the devil?

The crutches wobbled as he fell forward. Instinctively, his arms flew out to the side for balance, and the crutches fell to the floor, one of them bouncing noisily down the stairs. Swinging his arms like windmills, he teetered over the edge of the landing. His heart pounded wildly in his chest as he realized he was about to follow his crutch down to the bottom. Damnation!

"Sedge!" The feminine shriek came almost at the same moment that he was grabbed roughly from behind. Meg's arms wrapped around his waist with surprising strength and tugged him back to safety.

Sweet heaven, but that was a close call.

Sweet heaven, but Meg was holding him in her arms.

"Are you all right, Sedge?"

He could barely hear her over the sound of his racing pulse. Good Lord, that had been close. He had nearly killed himself. And she had saved his life. Again. Ah, sweet Meg. He closed his eyes and tried to calm his breathing. He could feel her breasts pressed against his back as she continued to hold him tightly. He leaned back against her and drank in the fragrance of wild violets that always seemed to linger about her in the mornings.

"Sedge? Are you all right? Are you hurt?"

He could feel her warm breath against his ear as she spoke. She pulled him closer as she rested her chin on his shoulder, pushing forward as though trying to see his face. Her skin against his cheek was soft and smooth as satin.

"Did you hurt your leg? Oh, please, Sedge, tell me! Are you all right?"

"I am fine," he murmured as he brought his own arms up to cover hers, basking in the feel of her, the scent of her. "I am fine." In fact, he had never been finer. He did not care if he never moved again from this spot, with this woman's arms around him.

"But, what happened? Did you trip on something? Did you lose your balance? Are you sure you are not hurt? Why did you not ask for help? Oh, we should never have allowed you to attempt the stairs on your own. Good Lord, do you realize you might have broken your neck?"

Ignoring her frantic entreaties, Sedge awkwardly turned himself in her arms until he faced her. Oh, this was even better. Wrapping his own arms around her shoulders and pulling her close, he locked eyes with Meg's as she chattered on.

"Are you sure you are not..." Her voice faded and she seemed momentarily captivated as he continued to hold her eyes. Sedge had no doubt that his own smoldered with desire.

He inched his face closer to hers, intoxicated by those

sherry eyes. And by the look in those eyes. Beneath the wide-eyed surprise lurked an expression of undisguised longing. This was the moment he had waited for, when she looked at him with desire equal to his own. When he knew she wanted what he wanted.

He did not move for what seemed a long moment, allowing the unspoken tension to build between them. Then, very slowly, he lowered his lips to hers.

And Meg wrenched away from his grasp.

Chapter 11

Meg turned quickly away from the danger of the viscount's arms, and the dangerous look in his eye, and bent to retrieve one of the fallen crutches. She must not succumb to foolishness. She must not. She could still feel the warmth of his arms as they wrapped around her shoulders and pulled her close. It would have been so easy to give in to the comfort of his embrace, to lay her head on his shoulder and her heart at his feet. But if she allowed him to kiss her—and oh, how she had wanted him to kiss her—she would be setting herself up for disappointment

For she knew—now more than ever, after what his cousin had told Terrence—that he meant nothing serious in his attentions toward her. He likely had nothing more than seduction in mind.

But—oh!—how he had looked at her!

Could the charming gentleman she had come to know so well truly be so callous in his regard for her? Would he really attempt to seduce her without any serious intentions? She must remember Mr. Herriot's words.

He does not marry them.

And the alternative was not to be considered. Yes, she would repeat Mr. Herriot's words like a litany, until she got over this foolish infatuation.

Handing the crutch to Sedge, without meeting his eye, she wrenched her attention back to the situation at hand.

"You have not yet told me what happened, my lord."

His brows rose slightly at the use of his title. "I am not certain," he said. "My foot just seemed to slide out from under me. Just clumsy, I suppose."

Meg's eyes surveyed the hallway and landing. There were no rugs or other objects that might have caused him to trip. Perhaps he was less steady on the crutches than she had believed. Perhaps it was as he said, just a moment of clumsiness. In that case, she should dismiss the matter, change the subject, and help him downstairs to breakfast. She would not wish to embarrass him by dwelling on the incident.

"I will lend you my arm," she said, "to assist you down the stairs. Your other crutch—" She stopped as something odd caught her eye. "Hold on a moment," she said, retrieving her arm and leaving Sedge where he stood, half propped against the corridor wall.

Meg bent down and examined the floor just at the very edge of the landing. A dark patch of a thick, oily residue of some kind coated the dry-scrubbed wooden floorboards.

"No wonder you slipped," she said, looking up at Sedge, meeting his eye for the first time since pulling herself from his embrace. "Someone has spilled something, just here, at the top of the stairs." She turned back to examine the stain and shook her head. "Good heavens. Anyone could have slipped and fallen down these stairs." A shiver ran down her spine at the thought of what might have happened. She would have a harsh word or two with Mrs. Dillard.

"Since no bodies are piled up at the foot of the stairs," Sedge said, "I gather I am the first to have encountered this hazard?"

Meg smiled to think that he could joke after such a near

escape. Her heart was still pounding, though perhaps for other reasons. She could vividly recall, however, the racing of Sedge's heart as she had grabbed him from behind. No, he was not as unaffected as he seemed. He merely masked his anxiety well. She remembered the same lightheartedness after Gram's mix-up with the monkshood. He had sliced through the tension in the room with a single quip.

"It seems you are the first, my lord," she said. "Gram has taken a bedchamber downstairs since the trouble with her knees last year. And Terrence, I believe, was up all night in the stables. One of his favorite mares was ready to foal, and he expected a difficult time. I do not believe Mr. Herriot has gone down yet. So, it appears you are the earliest bird after all."

"Well, thank goodness you were not too far behind, my dear, or you would have found me in a heap at the bottom of the stairs. With another broken leg, no doubt."

Meg shuddered as she considered that it would more likely have been his neck that had broken. She ran her fingers over the oily stain and lifted them to her nose. "How odd," she said. She repeated the procedure and sniffed harder. "Oil of vitriol." She rose to her feet, still holding her fingers under her nose. Speaking almost to herself, she said, "Who on earth would have spilled oil of vitriol?"

She turned at the sound of Sedge's laughter. "I believe I can answer that question," he said. "You see, Pargeter— and you must swear never to repeat this, my dear—Pargeter uses oil of vitriol as a part of his 'secret' blacking receipt. Only see how my boot gleams."

"Pargeter? But what business would he have spilling the stuff here, at the top of the stairs?"

"I am sure I do not know," Sedge replied.

"Is he still in your bedchamber?"

"Yes, I believe so."

"Then I shall ask him myself." Meg turned and marched down the hallway, leaving Sedge to balance on his single crutch. It was unconscionable that the man should be so careless. She knocked loudly on the bedchamber door. When Pargeter opened it, he quickly masked a look of surprise.

"May I help, you, Miss Ashburton?"

"I believe you may," she replied, unable to keep the sharpness from her tone. "Have you recently had an accident with oil of vitriol?"

The valet reddened from his neck to his ears. His eyes dropped to the floor. "Yes, ma'am," he said in a quiet voice. "I am that sorry, ma'am, but I did spill a bit last evening."

"And did you not think to clean it up?"

His head jerked up. "Of course I cleaned it up!" His eyes widened with outrage at such a suggestion. He shook a finger at the floor, pointing just in front of the spot where Meg stood. "See there," he said in an agitated tone. "Not a spot remains. I sanded and scrubbed and sanded and scrubbed until the stain had disappeared. Only look at my hands!" He held both hands up to display their reddened, raw tips. He then seemed to think better of such impertinence and clasped his hands behind his back. "As you see," he said, nodding toward the floor, "it is as white as the rest of the corridor, though still a bit damp."

Meg looked down at her toes, and indeed there was a freshly dry-scrubbed area. At least he was telling the truth about working hard to remove the stain. "But what of the other spill?" she asked. "Why did you not sand it as well?"

"Other spill? What other spill?"

"The spill at the top of the stairs," Meg replied with impatience. "The one that almost sent your employer tumbling to his death."

Pargeter blanched and followed Meg's eyes to the end of the corridor, where Sedge waited, leaning on his single crutch. "Oh my," the valet said before dashing down the hall to Sedge's side. Meg followed.

"Are you all right, my lord?" Pargeter asked in a frantic voice. "Can I help you, my lord?"

Sedge chuckled and laid his hand briefly on Pargeter's shoulder. "I am fine, Pargeter. As you see. No harm done."

"Look here, Pargeter," Meg said, pointing to the stain. "See how this spill was not cleaned up. His lordship slipped on it and almost fell headlong down the stairs."

"Oh my."

"I am still waiting for an explanation, Pargeter," Meg said. "Why did you not clean up this spill as well as the other?"

"I swear to you ma'am, my lord, that I knew nothing of this spill."

"But you admit to causing the other spill?" Meg asked.

"Yes," he replied in a slightly hesitant voice. "I had been mixing up a batch of blacking. It is a receipt I devised myself."

"A big secret it is, too," Sedge added with a grin.

"No, no," Pargeter said, his chest puffing out a bit. "Not a very big secret. The proportions I prefer to keep to myself, but I don't mind revealing the ingredients. Porter, a bit of ivory black, molasses, gum arabic, and oil of vitriol. A few other minor ingredients as well, but that is the main part."

Meg bit back a smile to think that it was likely those other minor ingredients that were the true secret to the receipt. "Go on, Pargeter," she said.

"Yes. Well, as I said, I was mixing up a new batch when there was a knock on the bedchamber door. I am afraid I had a small bottle of the oil of vitriol in my hand when I went to open the door. I should have put it down, of course, but in my haste, I am afraid I forgot." He turned to look at Sedge as he continued. "It was Mr. Herriot, my lord, asking for you. I told him you had not yet come upstairs. He said he would look for you downstairs and left. As I turned to shut the door, I accidentally bumped the handle against the bottle I carried. I regret to admit that it fell to the floor and shattered. Made a terrible mess, it did. But, as I told Miss Ashburton, I sanded and scrubbed the floor to remove the stain."

"Nothing to worry about, Pargeter," Sedge said. "I am sorry about the broken bottle, though." He grinned at the valet. "I trust you have a spare to keep my solitary boot shining like jet?"

"Of course, my lord."

"Good. Good. Then, you had better be about cleaning this bit of oil up as well. Dangerous stuff."

"But, my lord, I assure you, I did not—"

"No need to worry, Pargeter. It was only an accident. But you had better clean it up before someone else slips and falls."

"Yes, my lord." The valet's lips were drawn in a tight line as he hurried back down the corridor.

"Well, then," Meg said, "I will offer my arm once again to help you downstairs. We must both take care to step around the oil stain."

Then perhaps we should cling to each other very tightly, Sedge thought wickedly as he accepted the support of Meg's arm. But he doubted she would appreciate any further clinging on his part. His mind was still reeling with disappointment that she had fled his last embrace.

He had been so sure she was willing to accept his kiss—and oh, how he had wanted to kiss her. He could not believe he had misread the look in her eye. She had wanted him. He was sure of it.

But she had pulled away. Why?

Sedge was forced to relinquish Meg's arm in the long run, as he found it easier to use the banister and one crutch to best negotiate the stairs. Once they had reached the bottom, Meg retrieved the second crutch and helped him onto it. He looked up at the sound of vigorous scraping to see Pargeter sanding the stain at the top of the stairs, an irritated scowl on his face.

Sedge hobbled along in Meg's wake as she led the way to the breakfast room.

Meg insisted that Sedge remain seated while she served him. He did not argue. The notion of being served by Meg quite appealed to him. He watched her graceful movements as she moved from serving dish to serving dish, her blue muslin skirts alternately swinging and clinging. At last, she laid a plate in front of him piled with a bit of everything from the sideboard. She also served him a cup of coffee before seating herself opposite him with a plate laden as high as his own.

"And so, my lord," she said as she reached for the jam pot, "you have cheated death once again."

"What's that?" Sedge was thoroughly distracted by the crossed blue ribbons over the bodice of her muslin dress. He could almost still feel the imprint of her breasts crushed against his back while she had held him close.

"In the short time I have known you, Sedge"—oh, good, she had finally dropped 'my lord' and was back to 'Sedge'— "you have had three close encounters with death. You must feel very powerful, indeed. Or very righteous."

"Three times, you say?" Sedge speared a piece of ham and brought it to his mouth as he watched her drop a large dollop of blackberry jam onto her plate.

"The carriage accident," Meg said as she slathered a piece of toast with the jam, "Gram's monkshood, and now the stairs. Are you like the proverbial cat, with six lives remaining?"

"Good Lord, I hope so!"

"Have you always been so... so accident-prone?"

Sedge laughed and then took a long swallow of coffee. "Not that I can recall, my dear. Seems to be a recent phenomenon."

"How recent?"

Sedge gave her a quizzical look. What was she getting at? Finally, he shrugged and said, "The curricle accident was the first time I have so much as fallen off a horse since I was a boy. But such things do happen. No one is to blame, Meg."

"I know that, Sedge. It is just that—"

"Surely, you would not accuse your own grandmother of deliberately trying to poison me?"

"Of course not!" She began to chew on her full lower lip, and Sedge tried not to think of what those lips might have felt like beneath his own.

"And you cannot possibly mean to accuse poor Pargeter of intentionally spilling the oil?" he said. "The man was white as a sheet when he saw what had almost happened."

"No, no." Meg shook her head, but her brows were still furrowed. "I do not blame Pargeter for a moment of carelessness."

"And there you have it, then. All accidents. No one to blame. And no harm done." He punctuated this last with stabs of his fork in the air. "Just a patch of bad luck, that is all."

"If you say so."

"I do say so." Sedge wrenched his eyes from the creamy white skin of her throat and took a few bites of egg. He then turned his attention to the sausages.

"By the way," Meg said, "Pargeter seems a very resourceful man. That blacking receipt was fascinating."

Sedge laughed around a mouthful of sausage. "Yes, I am quite pleased with him. Despite what you may have thought this morning, he is generally an excellent valet. Don't know what I ever did without him."

"How long has he been with you?" she asked as she diced a piece of ham into small bits and mixed them with her eggs.

"Only about six months."

Meg's head jerked up. "Six months?"

"Yes," he said. "My former valet, Bassett, had been with me for donkey's years. Suddenly one day, he announced that some relative had left him a small inheritance. Said he had an eye on a farm in Sussex. A farm! Well, you could have knocked me over with a feather. Had no idea the man dreamed of farming. Seems he had been saving for it all along, but the inheritance meant that he had enough money to buy the thing now. Gave his notice, married one of the housemaids, and took off to plow fields in Sussex."

Sedge shook his head in fond recollection of Bassett. He must remember to write to him and see how he was doing.

"And so that is when you hired Pargeter?" Meg asked.

"Not right away, no. You see, Bassett had been with me since my school days. I was at sixes and sevens without him. Had no idea how to replace him. Used a footman for a time, while I made inquiries."

"I know how it is to become attached to family retainers," Meg said. "Mrs. Dillard, for example, has been at Thornhill since before I was born. I cannot imagine life without her."

"Fact is," Sedge said, "we take them for granted. Don't appreciate them enough. Learned that with Bassett."

"And how did you find Pargeter, then?"

"Oh, he was recommended to me by a friend," Sedge replied after taking another sip of coffee. "Lord Digby. Pargeter had apparently been with Digby's brother for some years before the young man was thrown from his horse and broke his neck. Digby put it about that if anyone had use for a valet, he knew of a good one. I said I'd give Pargeter a try, and I have been pleased so far. Plan to keep him."

"Lord Digby?" Meg said. "The name is familiar, but I cannot place him. Perhaps he is an acquaintance of Terrence."

"Speak of the devil," Sedge said as Sir Terrence walked

into the breakfast room, looking, in fact, like the very devil. He was unshaven, his hair tousled, and dark circles hung beneath his eyes. It was obvious the man had had no sleep.

"Terrence!" Meg exclaimed, her face lighting up. "How is Zenobia? Did she foal?"

"Yes, Meggie, she did. Finally." Terrence poured himself a cup of coffee and took a long swallow before sinking into a chair. He sighed deeply, then turned to an anxious Meg. A slow, lazy smile creased his face. "A beautiful little filly."

Chapter 12

Sedge stood beside Bertie in the stable courtyard and knew the young man was right. He just wished he could turn away from his cousin's advice and ignore it.

"You know I am right, Sedge."

"I wish you would stop doing that, Bertie."

"Doing what?"

"Reading my mind. You echo my own thoughts more often than is entirely comfortable."

Albert laughed. "Shared blood, and all that, I suppose." He walked next to Sedge along the gravel path leading from the central courtyard of the stables back to the main house, slowing his pace to match his cousin's awkward hobble. "But I am glad you agree," he continued. "I know it is pleasant here—for a variety of reasons." He slanted a significant look at Sedge. "But it is past time that we took our leave."

Sedge nodded his agreement, but said nothing. The stable path met the main drive, and as they approached the house, he gazed up at the eccentric structure he was so loath to abandon. Though of relatively modest size, Thomhill's irregular gray stone facade showed additions and renovations from every period over the last four hundred years. What could have been a hodgepodge of disparate styles, however, somehow blended into a single harmonious whole.

The oldest section, as Meg had proudly pointed out, was the medieval crenellated tower and great hall. Flanking those were gabled Elizabethan and Jacobean wings. To the south, marching toward the brewhouse, was the newest wing, from the middle of the last century. It was all very unique and wonderful, and Sedge would miss it.

Of course, the charming house had nothing at all to do with his reluctance to leave.

"I do not believe it is necessary to remain at Thornhill until your splint can be removed," Albert said. "That would be stretching the bounds of hospitality, would it not? You can hobble along in your own house just as well, and have your own doctor look after your leg."

"I am sure you are right," Sedge said in an irritated tone. He had heard all this sound reasoning time and again.

"Might be a good idea, in any case," Albert continued. "This Garthwaite fellow could be a country quack, for all we know."

"He seems exceedingly competent to me."

"As well he may be," Albert said. "But that is neither here nor there. The point is—"

"The point is that it is time to leave. Yes, Bertie. I know. I know."

The two men did not speak as they continued along the drive, with only the crunch of gravel beneath their feet to break the silence. Sedge's mood blackened as he considered his cousin's words. Albert was right. It was time to leave Thornhill. His peaceful countryside idyll had come to an end.

But what was he to do about Meg?

They approached the front of the house with its rows of large stone urns flanking the entrance, each sporting bursts of early spring flowers. Sedge paused before the entry stairs and cleared his throat.

His cousin turned around and raised his brows in question.

"All right, Bertie," Sedge said. "We shall leave as soon as it can be arranged."

Albert's face broke into a smile and he clapped Sedge on the back. "I will accompany you, of course," he said. "Just to make certain that you arrive home in one piece, you understand."

"Thank you, Bertie."

"We can use my traveling carriage. The good doctor would have apoplexy if you were to set foot in a curricle just yet. I haven't detached the driver's box, as you know how I hate postillions, so you will not have the forward view you are accustomed to. But, even though it is only a small chariot, it will be more comfortable for you than the curricle. Less likely to jar your leg so much."

"I appreciate that, cousin." Sedge smiled at Albert's cheerful enthusiasm. He really was a very good sort of fellow. "You know, Sir Terrence's men did a fine job of repairing my poor curricle. Looks like new. Perhaps he will lend me a groom to drive it home for me."

"I am sure he will oblige."

"You mean he will be that anxious for our departure?"

Albert laughed. "No, nothing of the kind. I just meant that he is a most accommodating chap, and all that. Good fellow. Pleased to have made his acquaintance."

"Yes," Sedge said, "so am I. In fact, I shall miss the whole family."

"Anyone in particular?" Albert asked, flashing a wicked grin.

"Let us make plans to leave in the morning," Sedge said, ignoring his cousin's jibe. "I will have a messenger send word to Mount Street so that Mrs. Verney can prepare for my return. Can you be ready by tomorrow?"

"Of course," Albert replied. "I will let my coachman

know. In fact, I should probably return to the stables and speak to him at once. Do you mind if I abandon you here? Can you manage the stairs on your own?"

"Yes, I can manage, thank you. Oh, and, Bertie?" he called out as his cousin had begun to walk away. Albert turned and looked at Sedge. "Thank you for making me face the fact that it is time to go. I should hate to overstay my welcome, which surely would have happened without you to give me a bit of a push."

Albert grinned and gave a jaunty salute, then went on his way back down the gravel path.

Sedge hopped up the short flight of stairs to the simple, large wooden door. After readjusting his balance, he rang the bell. While he waited, his gaze took in the medieval stonework surrounding the door and the small mullioned window above. Everything he saw at Thornhill reminded him of Meg and her spirited chatter as she had been first to show it all to him. She was so proud of the history of the house, which had been in her family for over four hundred years. This area was apparently the only remnant of the original grim medieval structure. Sedge remembered Meg telling him of the ancestor who had built it. While she spoke, she had run her hand lovingly over the old stonework just here. Sedge reached out to touch the spot she had caressed so gently.

What was he going to do about Meg?

The door opened and Sedge quickly drew his hand away from the wall. A footman held the door while Sedge hobbled into the Great Hall. Despite its name, the hall was not terribly great in size, especially compared to the Great Hall in his own home at Witham Abbey. But this was Meg's home, the home she loved, and he suddenly felt the need to memorize every aspect of it as he prepared to leave it, as if it were a part of Meg herself.

Though the exterior walls were medieval, the interior of the hall was distinctly Elizabethan. Handsome oak paneling climbed the walls to about the level of Sedge's eyes. The remaining third of the walls, as well as the ceiling, were covered with elaborate plasterwork. Sunlight streaming in from the mullioned windows glistened off pieces of armor hung over the huge fireplace, and several sets of antlers graced the woodwork on either side.

Sedge paused a moment to admire the armor. He smiled as he recalled Meg's proud tale of her father discovering it in an old storage room in the tower. It was from the days of the Civil War, during which the Ashburtons, along with most of East Anglia, had been staunchly Royalist. Young Meg and her mother had spent weeks polishing and shining the breastplates and helmets, restoring them to their original luster and then hanging them in this place of honor, for all the world to admire. If a footman had not been hovering nearby. Sedge might have run his hands along their smooth surfaces, just as he had been drawn to do at the entrance—to touch the things Meg had touched, the things Meg loved.

Sedge made his awkward way upstairs to his bedchamber and rang for Pargeter. He would want to begin packing right away. He dragged a chair to the alcove made by the deep window embrasure, tossed his crutches aside, and fell rather ungracefully into the chair.

His thoughts were still full of Meg. Ever since he had capitulated to Albert's insistence on leaving Thornhill, he had been trying to decide what to do about her. The notion of never seeing her again made him feel empty and hollow with loneliness. He had never before felt that way about a woman. For Sedge, parting with a woman had seldom been anything more than a moment of regret—if that—for there had always been others ready and eager to take her place. Those brief moments of regret had never caused the almost physical ache he now felt at the prospect of parting with Meg.

There was no other woman to take her place.

After a moment, he sat bolt upright, slapped his thigh, and let out a crack of laughter. Of course! *There was no other woman to take her place.* Because no other woman could. Because Meg was the one. He had known that for some time now. It was her own feelings that were still a mystery to him. He had wanted to make sure she returned his regard before proceeding to a more formal courtship. But there was no time for courtship now. He was leaving tomorrow.

A knock on the door was followed by the appearance of Pargeter. "You sent for me, my lord?"

"Yes, Pargeter. We will be leaving in the morning. I need you to start organizing the packing."

"Yes, my lord."

And I will start preparing what to say to Sir Terrence when I ask for permission to marry his sister.

* * *

Meg sat at her brother's desk in the library, her head bent over pages and pages of Thornhill's breeding charts. Several mares had begun their breeding cycle, and Terrence had asked her to review the bloodlines in anticipation of the best pairings.

A knock at the door intruded on her concentration. "Yes? Come in."

She looked up in surprise to see Sedge trudge into the room. He stopped short when he saw her.

"Oh!" he exclaimed. "I—I was looking for Sir Terrence." He sounded uncharacteristically sheepish and Meg was surprised to hear him stammer. It was not like the gregarious viscount.

"I am sorry, Sedge, but he went out early to exercise Blue Blazes. He should be back within the hour. Can I help you with anything?"

If she did not know better, she would have said Sedge

actually blushed. But it must be just a trick of the morning light. The central pane in each window included a colored depiction of the Ashburton coat of arms. A bit of red glass no doubt reflected off his face.

"Uh, no, no. I will w-wait for him to return." He looked down at the Turkey carpet and did not meet her eyes.

Why was he suddenly so shy and awkward with her? Was he perhaps remembering that incident on the landing, when he had almost kissed her?

She felt the heat of a blush color her own cheeks.

"I must speak with him," Sedge continued. "I wanted to do so last night, but with his friend Mr. Hawksworthy present... well, it just did not seem the right time."

"Mr. Hawksworthy is a neighbor, as you know," Meg said. "He often takes dinner with us. I am sure he would have understood if you wanted to be private with Terrence."

"Yes. Well, now it seems I must wait." Sedge took another step further into the room. "You see, my cousin and I are leaving this morning."

Oh, God. It was true, then. He was leaving. She had heard several of the servants whispering of furious packing and organizing, and so knew he must be planning to depart Thornhill. But she had not expected it to be so soon. Not today. Not this very morning.

"I wanted to thank your brother for his hospitality," Sedge continued. "And all of you for your kindness and generosity." He took another step closer. "Especially you, Meg."

She found herself captivated once more by those blue eyes, and almost without realizing what she did, she rose from her chair to stand in front of him.

He was leaving. He was really leaving.

"You saved my life, Meg," he said. "More than once. I wanted to thank you, and your grandmother, for nursing me back to health, and for being such good companions during my convalescence." He chuckled softly. "I am sure I would have been bored to pieces without your company, Meg."

She took a step toward Sedge. Good Lord, how was she to endure this? "No need for thanks," she said, for she had to say something, even if she could not say what was in her heart. "Anyone would have done as much."

"No," Sedge said as he took a step closer. "You, and your family, have done more than anyone has a right to expect from virtual strangers."

He was saying good-bye. She might never see him again. She did not know if she could bear it

"You never seemed a stranger," she said.

"Nor did you," he said.

"Are you returning to London?"

"Yes." He smiled softly—not the usual broad grin, but something more intimate. "Do you think you might like to come to Town for the Season this year?"

Meg laughed at such an absurd notion. "I have not been to Town for six years. I do not believe I care to subject myself to that kind of scorn and ridicule again."

"Oh, I think I can assure you that things would be different for you this time, Meg." He smiled into her eyes, and Meg's knees felt as if they had turned to jelly. "After all, you are no longer the skinny, shy schoolgirl of six years ago." He took another step closer. "You are a stunningly beautiful woman, Meg. You will set the *ton* on its ear."

Yet another blush warmed her face. But she could not turn away. She could not tear her eyes from his, now only inches away. "I wish I had your confidence, my lord."

"Will you come to Town, Meg?"

"I don't know."

"Please."

"But I know so few people in Town."

"I will be there," he said, his voice barely above a whisper.

"Yes. You."

Meg was only vaguely aware of the sound of his crutches crashing to the floor as he gathered her in his arms.

Without waiting like before, without teasing her with desire, without giving her a chance to refuse, he captured her lips with his own.

Oh, Good Lord!

His lips were gentle and light as they moved over hers in that first touch of discovery. This was not her first kiss, but it might as well have been for all the new feelings it aroused in her. His lips were so incredibly soft. She had not expected a man's lips to be so soft. How could such a light touch ignite such a fire in her? Meg leaned into him, wanting more somehow. She wrapped her arms around his shoulders, and he responded by lowering one hand to the small of her back and pressing her closer.

Ah, but he felt good. She inched one hand up the back of his neck, and threaded her fingers through the long, blond locks. Oh, God.

Sedge lifted his mouth slightly and Meg opened her eyes to find him gazing at her with a look of such longing, she thought she might die. Terrence was wrong. She was not different. She was not without feeling. She did, after all, have desires like other women. More so. For no other woman could have ever wanted anyone as much as she wanted Sedge.

"Meg," he whispered against her lips. "Ah, Meg."

He pulled her against him more tightly as his lips descended again, this time with a crushing force that astonished Meg momentarily, before she responded with a surprising passion of her own. Opening his mouth, his tongue teased the seam of her lips. Meg shuddered slightly as she realized his mouth was compelling hers to open for him. Unfamiliar with this sort of kiss, she hesitated only briefly before shyly parting her lips. His tongue plunged in to meet hers, boldly probing her mouth with a fire and urgency totally unexpected. She followed his lead, exploring and tasting him in a way she had never imagined.

Meg knew she should stop him before he got the wrong impression, before he thought her a perfect wanton. But she completely lacked the will to do so. Perhaps she meant to prove to herself that she was not so different from other women after all. Even if she was only now discovering it for the first time.

She did not know how long they clung to one another, exploring each other's mouths, when his lips finally left hers and began to trace a fiery path down her throat and neck. She tilted her head back, encouraging his exploration, and gave an involuntary moan of pleasure. Oh, God, she had no idea it could be like this.

Something this good had to be real. It had to be. Surely he would not kiss her like this, set her body on fire like this, if he did not care for her. When his lips traveled back up to her jaw, her temple, her eyes, she ceased to doubt his feelings. He cared. He loved her. He must.

When he reclaimed her mouth, it was with a sweet gentleness flavored with such promise that Meg thought she might collapse with joy. At last, he lifted his head and looked again into her eyes. And his eyes crinkled up into a smile.

Chapter 13

"Meg, Meg. Do you know how long I have wanted to do that?"

He smiled into her eyes and rested his forehead against hers. "You have no idea, my dear, how pleasant it is to kiss a woman without having to twist my spine down to her level. It's as though you were made just for me." He kissed her softly at each corner of her mouth. "Tall and beautiful, with the most delicious lips. And eyes I can look right into as I kiss you like this. We are perfect together, Meg. Absolutely perfect."

She gave him the most dazzling smile, and his heart soared. God, how he wanted this woman. He pulled her closer, cradling her head against his neck. The clean smell of soap and wild violets tantalized him as he buried his nose in her luxurious red hair. Soon enough, he was kissing her neck, savoring the taste of her. He found a pulse point at the base of her throat and teased it with his tongue. Her racing pulse told him how much she wanted him, and even though she had not spoken a word, it was enough. He knew.

Sedge kissed her again and marveled once more at her uninhibited response as her body melted against his. Her lips were moist and parted, inviting.

He kept his weight on his good leg as best he could, but also needed the right leg for balance. The doctor would scold at his disregard for the splinted limb. But Sedge did not care. Not now. He was damned if he was going to move now.

He clasped her to his chest again and simply held her, his hand against the back of her head. He thought of all the things he wanted to say, and how to say them. He had not meant to rush his fences. He had wanted to speak to her brother first, to state his intentions formally, before saying anything to Meg.

He had planned to declare his serious and honorable interest in Meg, ask Sir Terrence's permission to pay his formal addresses, and suggest that Meg come to Town for the Season to celebrate their betrothal. He wanted to show her off, to show all of society what a treasure they had so casually overlooked.

He had been foiled in his plans last night, with Sir Terrence so obviously enjoying the company of his friend Mr. Hawksworthy. When he unexpectedly found Meg in the library this morning instead of her brother, he had been momentarily rattled.

She had looked so beautiful sitting there, with the morning sun streaming in and burnishing her coppery curls. He wished he had already spoken to Sir Terrence, for he had desired nothing more at that moment than to tell her how much he wanted her. But it wasn't right And more than anything, he wanted to do this right.

He had tried to keep to his noble plan, to speak briefly of inconsequential matters and then back out of the room and await her brother. But she was completely and utterly irresistible. Instead of backing away, he had been drawn to her as inexorably as she had been drawn to him. And he did not regret it. Oh no, he thought as he held her close, he did not regret it.

But now that he had overstepped the bounds of propriety, it no longer seemed important to speak to her brother first. That would come later. Just now, he wanted to tell her how he felt, how he loved her, how he wanted a life together with her. She must surely realize some of this already, after those kisses that had sparked a blaze of passion between them such as he had never known before. But it was important to put it all into words for her.

Only, he did not know how. He did not know how to tell her what was in his heart. He did not know how to put it into words. Women, he knew, set great store on words. Look at how they idolized that Byron fellow. But Sedge was no poet. He was a simple man, with simple feelings. And he did not know how to put them into words.

He nudged his shoulder and she lifted her head to look at him. He wished she would say something. It might make it easier. But he knew in his heart that she waited for him to speak, that it was up to him to speak first. And he wanted to do it right.

Sedge took her face in both hands and looked deep into her eyes, willing her to believe him, to trust him. He opened his mouth to speak, but the only sound to come out was her name, over and over, like a prayer. "Meg. Meg." The words he wanted were all racing around in his head, as fast as the beating of his heart. Words of desire and love and passion and need. Disjointed and chaotic, his mind could not seem to organize them into any sort of order. When he spoke again, they came spilling out, uncontrollably.

"I want you, Meg," he said as he searched her eyes for understanding. "I want you. You obsess me. You are so beautiful. Everything about you is so beautiful." His thumbs caressed the sides of her face. "I want to let your glorious hair down and bury my face in it. I want to hold your magnificent body naked in my arms. I want to make love to you, morning and night."

Sedge watched in dismay as Meg's eyes widened in shock and confusion. Damnation. He was doing this all wrong. "Ah, Meg." He pulled her head back down on his shoulder and held her tight. "I am not very good at this, am I?" he said softly, close to her ear. "It is just that... that I want you so much! I want us to be together. I want to be with you, Meg. More than I've ever wanted to be with any other woman. I know I could make you happy. I know I could. I can give you everything you ever dreamed of. And more. I am a rich man, you know."

He thought she flinched slightly, but perhaps it was just surprise. From low in her throat came a single strained word. "Rich?"

"Oh, yes," he said, nuzzling her neck. "You need not worry about that. I can give you anything you have ever wanted. I can make you happy. I can. I know I can. I said you were perfect for me, and I meant it. More than any other woman, Meg." He rained soft kisses along her neck and ear. "We could be so good together, make such beautiful love together. I know we could. You have such a passionate nature, so much fire. Ah, Meg, my angel. I want so much for us to be together. Put me out of my misery. Say you will have me. Please, Meg."

* * *

Meg dragged her head out of the clouds and fell back to earth with a thud. Oh, dear God. Mr. Herriot had been right, after all.

He does not marry them.

She had been so happy. She had been flying, soaring with the shared passion of Sedge's kisses. She had been so lost to him that she had wanted to melt right into him. And, as always, she had been entranced by his smile. By his eyes.

He will only make one sort of offer to a woman.

What a fool she had been!

With a firm resolve to maintain her composure, Meg gently pulled away and stepped back slightly within the circle of Sedge's arms, her hands resting lightly on his chest. She steeled herself against those eyes still burning with passion, determined not to show him how much his words had affected her.

"Let me be certain I understand," she said, in a calm voice. "You want us to be together. To make love together. Morning and night, I believe you said."

He flashed his most seductive grin. "Oh, yes, Meg. I have never wanted anything so much in my life."

"And you would put your wealth at my disposal?" she continued. "Give me anything I wanted?"

"Of course."

"Jewels, for instance?"

"The best, the brightest, the biggest money can buy," he said with enthusiasm.

"And carriages? Horses?"

"Anything, my love." He was positively beaming. "The best from Thornhill or Tattersall's or any other stable you wish. And carriages to make you the envy of every woman in London."

"And a house in Town, no doubt?"

"Naturally," he said. "It only awaits your special touch to make it your own."

"Naturally," she said through clenched teeth. So, he had the house already. Had probably used it for all his past mistresses. And now he expected her to move in and take their place. If she were not so angry, she might have died on the spot of mortification. How dare he! Meg dropped her hands to Sedge's shoulders, and gently pushed away.

"Meg?"

Sedge allowed her to extricate herself from his embrace, and she turned away from his imploring gaze. She held her hands tightly clasped in front of her in an attempt to still their trembling. How could he have asked such a thing of her? A knot of anger began to twist like a knife in her chest—anger at Sedge for daring to so insult her, and anger at herself for allowing him to believe he could do so.

She kept her back to him. "I am sorry, my lord," she said, trying to keep her voice level, "but I cannot accept your offer. I think it is best that you leave Thornhill at once."

Meg heard Sedge catch his breath, as though startled. Had he been so sure of her, then? He did not speak, and Meg turned and headed toward the library door. She no longer wanted to be in the same room with him. She had to get away.

"But, Meg ...," Sedge said in a choked, plaintive voice. He caught her by the arm, but she wrenched away and stormed out of the room. She did not stay to hear what further insults he might hurl at her and neither did she turn around to look at him. If she looked at him again, she might feel obliged to strike him. She had to get away.

She hurried through the corridor, slowing her pace when she encountered one of the housemaids and not wishing to appear anything other than normal. Besides, she need not hurry. He could hardly run after her with his broken leg. And if he so much as tried, she might be inclined to break the other for him. Holding her head high, she slowly walked up the stairs. As she neared her bedchamber, however, her pace became faster until she almost ran when she finally reached her own room. She flung open the door, slammed it behind her, and threw herself headlong on the bed.

What a fool she had been!

Taking deep gulps of air in hopes of calming her racing heart, she considered her own stupidity. Mr. Herriot had tried to warn her. But the moment Sedge kissed her, she forgot all about those warnings and twisted the whole situation to suit her own notions. But Sedge's notions were very different. He wanted her for his mistress. He could not have been more plain. He wanted her body and was willing to pay for it.

What a fool she had been!

Despite her attempts to remain calm, Meg could no longer hold back her tears. She buried her face in a pillow and wept for her broken heart. Her entire body was wracked with uncontrollable sobs as she replayed in her mind all that had taken place, all the words spoken, and tried to make some sense of it

She still did not fully understand all that had happened in the library. Terrence was right about one thing: she was very naive where men were concerned. She should never have let him kiss her. Even knowing that Sedge was a rake and remembering all that his cousin had said, she had not pulled away from his kiss. Not like she had done before. Why had she let him kiss her when she knew how dangerous it would be?

No, that was not entirely true. Meg had not in fact, known how dangerous it could be. She had been kissed a few times in the past. Young men had more than once tried to steal a kiss behind the stables or in the gardens, for which she generally had boxed their ears. But even when she had allowed it out of sheer curiosity, it had never been more than a simple meeting of lips. No sparks. No fire. Not at all dangerous.

She had not been even remotely prepared for what Sedge had done to her. Though his first kiss had begun not all that differently from the others, it had ignited a spark between them almost instantly, and her body had caught fire. That was the only way she could define how she had felt with him, as though she were on fire. And the only difference between Sedge and all those other young men was that she loved him, so she had assigned all her own passion to love. She had been certain that two people who shared such a fiery moment must also share deep feelings for one another. For Meg could not imagine that it was the mere touching of lips and tongues that had caused her body to react so. It was because it was Sedge. It was all wrapped up in her love for him. It was a part of the expression of her love for him. It only followed, did it not that his passion also sprung from love? As hers had?

And it was that perfect blending of love and desire that had caused her to allow him to do those other things, to put his tongue in her mouth and press their bodies together in that intimate manner. She had no experience of such things, but she had wanted it. Oh, how she had wanted it He had made her want it

And like the naive idiot that she was, she thought he made her want it because he loved her. Because that's what people in love did.

What a fool she had been.

Just when Meg was certain that he loved her, he had thrown those awful words at her. Though surprised at first by the boldness of his declaration, she thought he might simply be overcome with the ardor of the moment. That words of love, even words of marriage, would soon follow. If they had followed, the rest would have been acceptable. For if Sedge had loved her and wanted to marry her, she would be pleased that he also desired her body. It would be right.

But those words had never come. He only wanted her body. And he would use his wealth to tempt her, to give her anything she wanted in return.

Meg sobbed and sobbed, pounding her fist into the pillow until it was flat. She was humiliated that Sedge could even imagine that she would consider such an offer. And she was embarrassed at her own foolish infatuation and how it had allowed her to so badly misjudge him. How could she have loved such a man?

Terrence had said she was naive. Well, she would not be naive any longer. Now she knew what Gram meant when she said all men were lustful creatures. Meg would never again mistake a man's lust for love. She had learned her lesson well.

Her sobbing subsided at last to a gentle cry. She sat up, swung her legs over the side of the bed, and rubbed her eyes with the heels of her hands. Thank God he was leaving. He was leaving this very morning and she would never have to see him again.

It occurred to her that when Sedge and his cousin departed, Terrence and Gram would expect her to be available to say farewell, to send them on their way with kind words and good wishes. Meg did not care to be a party to their leave-taking. She could never look him in the eye again, and Gram and her brother would certainly find her behavior odd. She must get away and stay away until they had left Thornhill.

She began pulling at the tapes of her morning dress. She would take Bristol out for a hard, long gallop.

Chapter 14

Sedge stood in the library for some minutes, without moving, almost without thinking. His thoughts had been scrambled and agitated before, but now it seemed his brain had turned itself off entirely. He felt numb, unable to move or think or speak.

At last, he heard voices in the hall and was obliged to stir himself. He bent to pick up his crutches, lifted himself onto them, and hobbled to the door. He was met by Sir Terrence and Albert.

"Ah, Sedgewick," Sir Terrence said. "I understand you are leaving us this morning."

"Yes."

"I have told him, Sedge, that we will be taking my carriage," Albert said. "It is all packed and stands ready for us. Sir Terrence has agreed to send your curricle along with a groom later."

"If you do not mind the delay of a day or two," Sir Terrence said. "I am afraid there is some pressing business today that does not allow me to spare anyone. But I will certainly have your rig and team driven to Town as soon as possible."

"Fine."

"I was telling Sir Terrence how much we appreciated his hospitality," Albert said with a pointed look at Sedge. "How grateful we are that he came upon your accident, brought you to Thornhill, and had you nursed back to health."

"Yes. Very grateful."

"Why, only yesterday Sedge was lauding the generosity and kindness of you and your family, Sir Terrence."

Albert's eyes kept darting to Sedge in an apparent hope that he would speak for himself. But Sedge was not capable of rational speech just now. Perhaps later.

"He was telling me how he could not have asked for a more comfortable, congenial place to convalesce," Albert continued. "Is that not correct, Sedge?"

"Yes."

"Are you certain you are fit to travel, my lord?" Sir Terrence asked, his eyes narrowing in concern. "You appear quite pale this morning. Are you feeling unwell?"

"I am fine."

"I—I think he is just a bit tired, Sir Terrence," Albert quickly added. "He is wishing to be home, no doubt."

"Well..." Sir Terrence eyed Sedge curiously, and then shrugged. "If you are quite sure." He held out his hand to Sedge. "I hope you will return to Thornhill under more pleasant circumstances one day. You will be most welcome."

Sedge stared at his outstretched hand for a moment—her brother's hand—before putting his own forward to grasp it. He looked up and caught Sir Terrence's glance. He resembled her in many ways. Sedge had never noticed it before. The shape of the mouth, the high cheekbones, the straight nose. The eyes were different, though. His were blue, not like hers at all. Sir Terrence furrowed his brows slightly as he shook Sedge's hand, and Sedge realized he should say something.

"Thank you," he managed in a raspy whisper. "Thank

you for everything. And please thank Mrs. Lattimer as well. And your..."

When it seemed Sedge would not continue, Sir Terrence said, "I will give both Gram and Meg your thanks. But I am sure they will both wish to say their own farewells. I will round them up while you and Mr. Herriot finish your preparations." He turned and headed toward the back of the house.

Albert grabbed Sedge sharply by the shoulder. "What the hell is wrong with you? I know you hate to leave, but you could at least make an effort to be civil. My God, man, you were uncommonly rude to Ashburton."

Sedge roughly shrugged off his cousin's hand and headed toward the Great Hall. "Let's get out of here," he said.

Albert shook his head in resignation. "We should check upstairs to see that everything is in order, nothing left behind."

"Let Pargeter do it."

"But—"

"I do not wish to trudge up those stairs again."

"But—"

"I will await you here in the hall."

"All right," Albert said. After one last curious glance at Sedge, he turned and headed toward the stairs, leaving Sedge alone.

Sedge sank onto an ancient old settle near the entry. He leaned forward, his elbows on his knees, and his hands hanging down limply toward the worn old flagstones of the floor. He kept his head down, no longer anxious to memorize the details of the room as he had done the day before. As he sat there alone, blessedly ignored, he suddenly felt the full extent of Meg's rejection with stunning force.

What on earth had he done wrong? He had thought she must surely love him. By God, she had practically melted in his arms. To be sure, there had been a sweet sort of innocence to her passionate response. Though she was clearly inexperienced, as he gently led her through the escalating steps of desire she had been open and eager and very willing. How could he have misjudged her so?

He might have been able to explain it all away as an awkward misunderstanding, a misinterpretation of simple friendship for something more. But her response to his kisses flew in the face of such an excuse. He did not misinterpret her response.

Sedge reached up one hand and ran it absently through his hair, then kept it there and sank his forehead onto his palm. He ran his thumb over his new rakish scar, and realized his temples had begun to pound with the dull beginnings of a headache. Sedge was miserable with disappointment. The throbbing in his head merely served to punctuate his anguish.

Although he had not been entirely certain of Meg's feelings toward him, he had remained optimistic. And though he had been confused and tongue-tied when he had finally made his offer, he had never truly expected she would reject him. He had been totally unprepared for the look of horrified disbelief in her eyes when he had first asked if she would have him.

Disbelief. As though the very idea that Sedge might think she would want to marry him was somehow unimaginable.

But then she had asked him all those questions about his wealth and what he could give her. He thought he had acquitted himself well in that respect, for he was, after all, a rich man. But, apparently, it was not enough.

And so, he had made a bloody fool of himself. For the first time in his life he thought he had found a woman he might want to spend the rest of that life with, and she had thrown his offer back in his face like so much dirt. Bertie was probably right. He had been confined with this wretched leg for too long, and his imagination had spun dreams out of loneliness and boredom. He was missing his friends and jealous of their marriages, and attached himself to the first available woman in hopes of imitating their new lives.

What a fool he had been.

He had let himself fall in love with Meg, a thing he had never before done in his life. Sedge remembered once telling his friend Bradleigh that he did not believe in love. He had said that the notion of love was nothing more than schoolgirl nonsense fostered by romantical novels and poetry, and that mature, sensible adults should not expect such impassioned relationships, particularly in marriage. At the time, Sedge had believed his own words, despite the evidence of such love between Bradleigh and his wife, and later between Pemerton and his wife. He had believed it for himself. He had always been rather sensible and pragmatic in his approach to all aspects of his life: his home, his finances, his family, his lovers.

Somewhere along the line he had stopped being sensible.

When he had come awake to find a fiery-haired angel bending over him.

What a fool he had been.

He looked up at the sound of voices. Albert was followed by Timms, his valet, Pargeter, and a Thornhill footman. The two valets carried various parcels and the footman hurried past Sedge to open the heavy oak door to the outside. All three bustled out the door and down the front steps to the waiting carriage. Sedge looked up at Albert, who glared down at him and lifted a brow in question.

Sedge uncurled his lanky frame from the settle, stood, and pulled himself onto his crutches. Without a word, he hobbled through the doorway and hopped carefully down the steps to the gravel drive below. He was headed toward the open door of Albert's carriage, with its boxes and portmanteaux strapped to the top, when a voice stopped him.

"Lord Sedgewick!" He turned to find the plump figure of Mrs. Lattimer bouncing down the steps toward him, a look of chagrin on her round face. "You are leaving us? So soon? Are you certain you ought to be traveling just yet? Oh, but of course, you are missing your own home. How foolish of me to wish you to stay." She held out a hand to him, and Sedge tossed his crutches into the carriage and reached out to take her hand in his own. He brought it to his lips and attempted a smile.

"I am most grateful, ma'am, for all you have done for me," he said. Out of the corner of his eye he caught Albert's sigh of relief. He no doubt feared Sedge would continue in his sullen, inarticulate rudeness and further embarrass them. But Sedge had somehow gathered his wits together. He really did wish to thank these good people. They had, after all, saved his life.

He said all that was proper to Mrs. Lattimer, and to Sir Terrence, who had come up behind her.

"I am sure Meg would wish to make her farewells to you, but we cannot seem to locate her," Mrs. Lattimer said with a disappointed frown. "That girl! She is probably out with that horse of hers."

"Not to worry," Sedge said. "She and I.. . spoke earlier. We have said our good-byes."

Mrs. Lattimer's eyebrows disappeared beneath her lace cap as her eyes widened in surprise. "Well, then," she said, "I suppose we must say ours as well. It has been a pleasure, my lord, Mr. Herriot."

More good wishes, thank yous, and farewells were exchanged before Sedge finally hauled himself into the carriage. He slid across the single upholstered bench to make room for Albert. The two valets would ride in the servants' seat perched at the rear of the chariot just above the back wheel. Sedge noted that Pargeter had made his usual meticulous preparations for Sedge's comfort and safety, including several extra cushions on which to prop his leg. At least there were some things in this life he could still count on.

Albert entered the carriage, and Sir Terrence closed the door from the outside, with final good wishes for a safe journey. Albert raised his hand in a parting wave as the carriage at last pulled away along the gravel drive.

They drove through Thornhill's large, elaborate stone entry and Sedge saw for the first time the gilded horse's head atop the iron gates that Albert had told him about some weeks ago. He only glanced at the golden head in passing, wishing more than anything that horses and stables would someday cease to remind him of Meg. To remind him of his foolish attachment to a woman who did not care for him.

* * *

Meg held an anxious Bristol Blue in place on a slight rise near the southern boundary of Thornhill's land. The unusual land ridge, thought to be the remnants of an ancient barrow, overlooked the road below as it wound its way through the wide, flat clay loams on its way to join the Ixworth Road. Just below Meg's position, the road came to a small stone bridge spanning a narrow portion of the Black Bourne. Screened from view by a well-timbered hedgerow and a stand of elm trees, she had a clear prospect of the river and the road. A jackdaw screeched as its gray head swooped down toward the fat clumps of marsh marigolds edging the river, and Bristol danced and nickered in his impatience to be off. Meg stroked his neck to calm him as she watched the black-and-yellow carriage make its way across the stone bridge.

"Good-bye, Sedge," she whispered.

A single tear rolled down her cheek as the carriage disappeared from view into the thick woodlands beyond.

Chapter 15

The jostling and jouncing of the carriage as it rolled along through the rustic Suffolk landscape aggravated both Sedge's headache and his black mood. Whenever Albert attempted to make conversation, Sedge rebuffed him and turned to stare out the window of the carriage. He wished his cousin would just leave him alone.

He kept his gaze firmly out the window as they bounced along through clay farmlands dotted with windmills and enclosed by frameworks of ditches, banks, and hedgerows. Through tiny hamlets of clustered thatched-roof cottages. Through larger villages of timber-framed and jettied houses and gray flint churches. Through market towns crowded with blue-painted wagons. The road swept past budding poplars and rampant nettle, bright lupine and wild poppies, and fenced pastures of new lambs and wobbly-legged foals. Sedge watched it all pass by, and saw nothing. As new life and growth flourished all around him, he felt as if a part of him had died.

His desolation at Meg's rejection increased along with his headache as they traveled through Bury St. Edmunds and Hawstead. He thought of all that might have been and now would never be. He would never ride over the parklands of Witham Abbey with Meg at his side. He would never walk hand-in-hand with her through the abbey ruins in the moonlight. He would never see all eyes turn toward him as he entered a ballroom with Meg proudly on his arm. He would never get the chance to introduce her to his mother and Georgie. His mother would have adored her.

Ah, Meg. Why did you do this to me?

By the time the carriage had passed Sudbury, his misery had gradually transformed itself into full-blown anger. How could he have made such a fool of himself? How could he have embarrassed himself so? With his first ever proposal of marriage? He should have listened to Albert's warnings. He should have left Thornhill earlier. With each bump and jerk of the carriage, his anger at his own stupidity increased.

When the carriage slowed, Sedge's temper flared. "What the devil are we stopping for this time?"

Albert poked his head out the window. "Another herd of sheep," he said, turning a wary eye toward Sedge.

"Confound it, must the world come to a halt because of a few sheep? Why can't they keep the bloody beasts to the roadside?"

"It appears they must cross the road, cuz, to get wherever they are going."

Sedge snorted.

"Are you in such a hurry to get to Town?" Albert asked. "I had thought you were reluctant to leave Thornhill."

"I was not reluctant to leave," Sedge snapped. "In fact, I could not have been more anxious to leave. And now my head aches, my leg is stiff, my backside is sore, and I just want to be finished with this journey. Blasted sheep!"

Sedge shifted his weight on the bench and readjusted the cushion beneath his right foot. What made Albert think this damned chariot was any more comfortable than his curricle? There wasn't enough room to stretch his legs out in front of him, and no bench opposite that he might have propped his feet upon. He should have had his own carriage sent to Thornhill. At least it had been designed with Sedge's long legs in mind and was more comfortable on a long journey. But this one, he thought as he shifted the angle of his legs from left to right, was a bloody nuisance.

Albert watched Sedge's movements in silence and shifted to the far edge of the interior to allow his cousin more room. "I know your leg must be paining you, Sedge," he said. "If you'd like, I can ride up on the box and you can stretch your legs across the bench."

"Thank you, Bertie," Sedge replied, feeling miserably contrite that his cousin should be willing to put his own comfort aside on Sedge's behalf. "I appreciate the offer, but it really is not necessary. I will be fine. It is just that I am feeling particularly disagreeable and have the devil of a headache. I do not mean to take it out on you."

Albert waved his hand in dismissal. "What has you so cross, then? If you don't mind my asking. You have been in a brown study all day. Not like you, cuz."

Sedge beetled his brows as he watched the last of the black- faced sheep reach his side of the road. He did not know how much he wanted to tell Albert. He would as soon no one knew how he had been made a fool by that long-legged, red-haired siren. "Sorry, Bertie," he said at last, just as the carriage lurched forward again, throwing him hard against the seat back. "A few unpleasant words with Miss Ashburton this morning set me off. Nothing important. It is just this wretched headache that has made me so irritable. I am afraid I am not very good company today."

Sedge turned his body away from his cousin and closed his eyes as he rested his head against the window frame, hoping to nap a little. But the bouncing of the carriage caused the barely healed gash over his left temple to bang against the wood frame. Damnation. He twisted back around and threw a cushion behind his head and closed his eyes once again.

He never fully slept—the roads being as bad as they were— but he dozed a bit, on and off. After another hour or so, he was jolted awake when the carriage jerked to a stop so suddenly it almost tipped over. Albert was flung against Sedge with a jarring force that sent stabs of pain through his splinted leg. Damnation. He shifted his leg with a groan. "Now what?"

Albert shot Sedge an apologetic look as he scooted back across the bench. He opened his window in time for them to hear altogether too clearly those words dreaded by all travelers.

"Stand and deliver!"

Bloody hell! This was all that was needed to make the day a complete disaster. At this rate, he would be lucky to make it to Town at all.

Leaning forward, Sedge could see through the window two masked men on horseback. One pointed a pistol at their coachman while the horses whinnied nervously and plunged in their traces. The other waved a pistol in their direction, and Sedge's anger flared.

"Oh, my God." Albert looked as though the blood had drained from his face.

The second rider eased up to the side of the carriage, bent down from the waist to roughly jerk open the door, and sat smugly with a cocked pistol resting across his forearm. "Awright, gents," he said with a sadistic leer. "Let's 'ave yer blunt, then, and no one'll get 'urt. Come on down, now," he said with a wave of the pistol, "both o' yer. An' we'll just 'ave a look through them fat pockets o' yers."

"Damnation!" Sedge muttered.

"We had better do as he says," Albert said in a soft, nervous voice. "I don't like the looks of him."

"Aye, the lad's a smart 'un 'e is, fer a gentry cove. C'm on down, then, boys, and I'll be real nice, like."

Albert made a move to leave the carriage when Sedge's

arm whipped out across him holding a long-nosed flint-lock pistol. "The hell we will," Sedge said through his teeth. With only one shot available, he had to make it count. Within the space of a heartbeat, and almost without conscious thought, he aimed at the horseman, cocked, fired, and landed a bullet in the man's shoulder. The rider screamed and was almost thrown from his horse by the force of the gunshot, but managed somehow to stay in the saddle. The sound of the blast echoed in the carriage and smoke billowed in dark gray swirls around a stunned Albert, whose nose had been a mere inches from the flashpan. The rider's wail of pain was followed by the sound of hoofbeats as his companion galloped in retreat to the woods edging the road. Clasping a hand to his bloodied shoulder, the horseman uttered a curse, turned his mount, and fled into the woods in the wake of his partner.

By God, he had actually foiled an attempt at highway robbery, Sedge thought as a tiny bubble of triumph began to fill his chest. He had even shot a man. He had never done such a thing in all his life.

Albert stared open-mouthed at Sedge, sputtering and coughing as he waved away the smoke. Sedge felt a momentary pang of regret that the spark from the flint had practically exploded in his cousin's unsuspecting face, but there had been no choice.

"What the devil did you do that for?" Albert shouted, looking wide-eyed and pale. "You bloody fool, he might have killed us."

"Precisely why I fired," Sedge replied.

The coachman and both valets had jumped down from their respective perches and huddled in the carriage doorway, each looking slack-jawed with alarm and concern.

"Are you gentlemen all right?" the coachman asked.

"We're fine," Sedge replied as he reached across Albert to hand the pistol to Pargeter. "As you see. Now, may we please continue with this endless journey? I begin to despair of reaching London before the Season ends."

The coachman returned to his seat on the box and Albert's valet climbed back up to the servant's seat. Before resuming his seat, Pargeter, who had disappeared briefly, appeared at the open door once again, and handed a pistol across to Sedge.

"Thank you, Pargeter," Sedge said as he took the gun and tucked it into the empty sword case beneath the window.

Pargeter nodded and closed the door. The carriage bobbed slightly as he took his seat in the back. With a word from the coachman, the carriage lurched forward as the horses took off once again.

Albert turned toward Sedge, his eyes blazing with outrage. "How could you do something so foolhardy? Have you lost your mind? My God, man, those two might have fired back."

"But they did not."

"But you could not have known that!" Albert said, his voice rising with fury. "You might have got us both killed, you bloody fool."

"Oh, for God's sake, Bertie," Sedge said, his own impatience and anger mounting, "those two oafs fled like scared rabbits. Their type is only out for money, not murder. And I was not as willing as you to part with mine."

Albert shook his head in dismay. "I have never known you to act so recklessly."

"Blame it on my black mood."

"And so," Albert persisted in a sarcastic tone, "just because your head ached and you were angry with Miss Ashburton, you rushed headlong into potential danger, putting both our lives at risk? I cannot believe it. I simply cannot believe it!"

"Oh, stubble it, Bertie! You are neither dead nor stripped of your valuables. And all because my bad temper prompted me to action. Seems to me you ought to thank me, not berate me."

Albert crossed his arms and set his mouth in a tight line. He turned away from Sedge and kept his gaze fixed out the window. Blast it all, what was wrong with Albert, anyway? Why couldn't he allow Sedge to enjoy even the smallest moment of triumph in one of the more wretched days of his life? Sedge snorted in disgust, sank back against the squabs, and folded his arms tightly across his chest.

After a few moments, Albert spoke again, spitting his words out like so much venom. "I did not even know you had brought a gun. You might have warned me."

Sedge heaved a sigh and turned to look out his own window. "That's Pargeter's doing," he said. "The man is terrified of his shadow. Always insists I carry a gun when we travel. Places a loaded gun within my reach with every journey."

Albert turned and waved a finger in the direction of the sword case. "So he put it there? Not you?"

"Yes," Sedge replied. "But I saw it as soon as I sat down. He generally tucks it someplace where it is both inconspicuous and handy."

"And that one," Albert said, still pointing, "the one he handed you. Is that one loaded, too?"

"Of course. He simply retrieved the second gun from the traveling case. He has no doubt already reloaded the first one. I told you, the man takes no chances."

"No, you take them all for him."

"Damnation, Bertie!" Sedge's voice rose as he had lost all patience with his cousin's belligerent attitude. "You act as though you would rather those two louts had been successful in robbing us."

"No, I do not," Albert said in a tight voice. "I simply do not appreciate the cavalier way in which you reacted. You might have got us killed."

"Oh, shut up, Bertie!"

And so now not one but two black moods darkened the interior of the carriage as the two cousins turned away from each other and spoke not a word for the rest of the journey.

* * *

Meg walked through the next few days in a listless stupor. Sedge's illicit offer had had a profound effect upon her, causing her emotions to swing wildly between fierce anger and unrequited longing. His offer had been insulting, infuriating, disappointing, confusing, and ultimately heartbreaking. For though she hated him for what he had proposed, there was no denying she had fallen in love with him. The more difficult thing was to fall out of love with him. And so far, that was something she had not been able to accomplish.

She kept remembering how he had touched her, kissed her, looked at her, smiled at her. Even the most fleeting memory of his touch was enough to stir her blood in a most uncomfortable manner. He had awakened her body in ways she had never before imagined. And now the thought of never knowing that touch again made her feel empty, cold, and hollow with longing.

Meg kept to herself as much as possible those first days, with her emotions in turmoil and dangerously near the surface. She found herself close to tears more often than was comfortable. She had a horror of breaking down in front of her family or the staff, a thing she had never done in all her life. Meg was a woman who seldom resorted to tears, and when she did, she did so in private. These days, she seemed to require a great deal of privacy.

So she stayed away as much as possible, making a special effort to avoid Gram and Terrence. Meg was not ready just yet to face her grandmother's inevitable questions or her brother's quizzical looks. She rose early each morning, rode out and stayed out as long as possible, then spent the rest of the day in and around the stables. The constant activity in the stalls, the tackroom, and the exercise paddocks, as well as the sometimes raucous joviality of the grooms and stable boys, helped to keep her mind off the miserable state of her heart. In the evenings she took a tray in her room, claiming fatigue.

This morning Meg had ridden Bristol Blue hard and fast to the farthest reaches of Thornhill property. She slowed as she reached the river, and stopped to let Bristol take a drink. Then she walked him at a leisurely pace along the river's edge so that he could cool down completely and catch his breath. They ambled along past clusters of spiky, leafless coltsfoot. The strange plant sprung almost magically out of the ground each spring, the woolly, scaly shoots each topped with a single flower. It was only after the flowers had withered and gone to seed that its fuzzy, hoof-shaped leaves appeared. Each summer Meg accompanied Gram in long walks beside the river's edge, gathering baskets of coltsfoot leaves for the still room. But just now, their yellow blooms announced the arrival of spring.

Spring. The time of year when the social Season became a backdrop for the Marriage Mart. Meg pulled up sharply on the reins.

Marriage?

Must she forever dream about the offer she had hoped for, rather than the offer she had received? She silently scolded herself for behaving like such a ninny and she angrily swiped at the tears that had begun to trickle down her cheeks. If she did not stop dwelling on what might have been, she would surely go mad with despair. She had to get over this disappointment and get on with her life. Until then, it would be nearly impossible to face her family. They had always known her to be strong, even-tempered, tough-skinned. Hard-hearted, even. Her own brother thought her entirely without feminine sensibilities. She only wished all of their expectations were true. Just now, Meg was none of those things. And until she put this ridiculous little episode out of her mind, she never again would be.

She flicked the reins and Bristol moved on. As they made their way back toward Thornhill, Meg's head continued its battle with her sore heart, scolding that Sedge was a cad and that she was well rid of him. Her heart weakly confessed to still loving him, to dwelling all too often on how it had felt to be in his arms. Her head scoffed that it was unfortunate she had permitted her infatuation for him to develop into something deeper. It was unfortunate that she had not recognized, or perhaps acknowledged, his true colors earlier. It was unfortunate that her own naïveté had allowed him to make a fool of her. The whole ugly situation was merely an unfortunate episode. Nothing more. Not life-threatening. Not earth-shattering. Simply unfortunate. And best forgotten. She could and would survive. She had learned her lesson and would pick up the pieces of her life and move on.

Meg's heart finally conceded defeat to her head in this battle. She repeated the logical admonitions over and over in her mind on the ride back to the stables—he was a cad, she was a fool, the whole thing was best forgotten. She continued to repeat them while she rubbed down Bristol and brushed his coat to a high gloss, while she replenished his grain tub and hay feeder, and while she refilled his water bucket. She kept up her litany of logic as she returned to the house, took a leisurely bath, and changed into a fresh sprigged muslin dress.

When a knock sounded at her bedchamber door, Meg was feeling more confident and ready for the first time in two days to face whoever it might be. She swiveled on her dressing table stool and turned toward the door.

"Come in."

The door opened and Gram entered. "Oh, good," Gram said. "You are dressed. Does that mean you will be joining us for dinner tonight?"

"Yes, Gram. I was planning to come down." Meg turned back to face her mirror and continued to brush out her long hair. "I just need to finish my hair."

"Here, let me do that," Gram said as she reached for the brush. "It's been a long time since I've brushed your hair, Meggie. You used to enjoy it so when you were a girl."

Meg tilted her head forward as Gram's soft hands gently flipped the hair over her shoulders so that it hung down her back. As her grandmother began to pull the brush through the hair in long strokes, starting at the front of her head and continuing all the way to the ends, Meg let out a soft moan. "Ah, Gram. I still enjoy it." She let her head loll backward and closed her eyes. "That feels wonderful."

Gram continued to brush, in long slow strokes, and Meg became more and more relaxed. Just as she thought she might actually fall asleep, Gram spoke. "I have been worried about you, Meggie. I thought you might not be feeling well."

"I feel fine," Meg said in a drowsy voice.

"When you asked for a tray in your room the last two nights, I was concerned that you had taken ill. But then each morning you disappeared with that horse of yours and stayed away all day long." Gram continued the soft brushing. "Then I thought perhaps you were avoiding us."

Meg stiffened slightly, thinking her grandmother was too clever for her own good. But then Gram tugged the brush over her temples and behind her ears and Meg relaxed once again. "Why would I be avoiding you?" Meg asked in her most ingenuous voice.

"I asked myself the same question," Gram said as she tilted Meg's head to one side and began brushing out from her nape. "I thought perhaps ..."

"Perhaps what?"

"Well, I thought it might have to do with Lord Sedgewick's leaving."

Here it comes. The conversation she had been avoiding for days.

"What made you think that?" Meg asked, trying to keep her voice flat, indifferent.

"Well... you did not come to the house to say a proper farewell when he and Mr. Herriot left."

"We had spoken earlier," Meg said, parroting the excuse she had been memorizing for just this occasion. "We had said our good-byes."

"Yes, so he said."

Meg's eyes popped open. "He did?"

"Yes." Gram did not elaborate, much to Meg's regret. She would be very interested to know just exactly what the viscount had said. "But then, ever since he left," Gram went on, "you have kept so much to yourself. I thought perhaps you were missing him. That you felt a bit sad to have him gone."

Meg sighed. "I guess I do miss him a little." A little? What a bouncer. She couldn't get the scoundrel out of her mind. "We spent a lot of time together. We had become good friends." In a softer voice, she added, "Or so I thought."

"Oh, Meg!" Gram wailed as she gathered up Meg's long tresses and began to twist them into a knot. "I had thought—"

"I know what you thought," Meg said. "But it was not meant to be, Gram. I am sorry to have disappointed you."

"Oh, my dear, it is not you who disappointed me, but Lord Sedgewick. He seemed so taken with you. I was sure he would make an offer."

"Oh, Gram!" So, we were both duped by the charming viscount.

"Or at least court you properly, in hopes of making an offer later." Gram's brows furrowed in frustration as she secured the knot with two tortoiseshell combs. "I was so sure of it! Oh, I simply do not understand it. He seemed the most amiable young man I have ever met. And I saw how he looked at you, Meggie. He could not take his eyes off you."

Oh yes, he desired my body. Enough to pay for it.

Gram rested her hands on Meg's shoulders and captured her eyes in the mirror. "I was so sure he was falling in love with you, Meggie. I was so sure of it." She gave Meg's shoulder a gentle squeeze. "Is that what's been troubling you, dear? Were you sure of it, too?"

"Oh, Gram." Meg reached up and covered one of her grandmother's pudgy hands. "I suppose I had hoped a little myself. But remember, I told you more than once that I was not the sort of woman for him." Not for marriage, anyway. She patted Gram's hand and then rose from the stool. She placed an arm around the old woman's shoulders and led her toward the door.

"I do not care what you said, I had high hopes, Meggie. And I am very disappointed in that young man."

So am I, Gram. So am I.

Chapter 16

Sedge tipped the brandy decanter over and poured the last of its contents into his glass. Blast. Empty again. He would have to ring for Wigan to uncork another bottle. He shook the decanter so that its last golden drops trickled into his glass. As he held the bottle, the light from the fireplace shot through its blue glass like a star sapphire, entrancing him momentarily with its intense color. With an unsteady hand, Sedge slowly reached toward the side table to return the decanter to the silver tantalus which held two matching bottles, one labeled Rum, the other Hollands. Each of the same blue glass. Special radiant blue glass for which the city of Bristol was celebrated. Bristol blue glass.

Bristol Blue.

Damnation! Was there nothing that would not remind him of her? Sedge flung the empty decanter wildly, and it crashed to pieces against the iron grate. How was he ever to force her from his memory if even a blasted brandy decanter brought her to mind?

Ever since his return to London almost two weeks ago, he had done his damnedest to expunge the memory of that redheaded hoyden from his mind. Once it was known that he was in Town, friends began to call. Finding him more often than not in a foul mood, they began to drag him out for nights of drink and cards and general revelry. He managed the nuisance of crutches at first. Since graduating to a cane last week after the splint was removed, it had become easier to carouse about Town with his young cronies. He had spent most of his nights at various clubs or at any number of gaming hells, getting blistering drunk and losing small fortunes. He spent most of his days recovering from his nights.

Invitations arrived for a few of the early events of the Season, but Sedge had no stomach for the formality of Society functions just yet. For the first time in his life, the broad smile did not come so easily. He declined all invitations.

Nothing seemed to cheer him. He became more and more belligerent toward his companions, more and more intolerant of their good humor and high spirits. He had come home two nights ago, aggravated with the world at large, and had ripped the knocker off the front door. If he was going to get drunk and wallow in misery, he would as soon do it in the privacy of his own home, alone and undisturbed.

The servants had given him a wide berth; only Pargeter and Wigan, his butler, daring to come near. Wigan had strict orders that he was at home to no one, should anyone be bold enough to ignore the removed knocker. Wigan had defied that order once, when Albert had come to call. Apparently Sedge had not been specific enough to include relatives in the collective ban. Albert had ostensibly called to check on Sedge's leg and general well-being, but before long he had begun once again to berate Sedge's recklessness in having shot the highwayman.

"God's teeth, Bertie, must you continue to sing the same old refrain? I'm bloody tired of it."

"You're bloody drunk," Albert had replied.

"So what if I am?"

"It's the middle of the afternoon, cuz, in case you hadn't noticed."

"So?"

"So, you'd better go easy, old man," Albert had said. "You're becoming more and more reckless. It ain't like you, Sedge."

"Bugger off, Bertie. I'll do as I please."

Albert had departed in a fury that Sedge's clouded wits did not comprehend. What business was it of Albert's if Sedge got quietly foxed in his own house?

Sedge glared down at the blue glass shards littering the grate and thought perhaps he could no longer lay claim to being quiet. In fact, before he could formulate another coherent thought, Wigan entered the study. Damn. He was in for it now, Sedge thought as Wigan turned a gimlet eye toward the broken mess. Might as well have smashed the whole blasted set. Harder to replace just one.

Wigan raised his brows without comment and announced that a visitor waited in the hall.

"Dammit, Wigan! How many times must I tell you that I wish to see no one? And who the hell forces himself into a house with no knocker, anyway?"

"I beg your pardon, my lord," Wigan said. "I thought you might wish to make an exception this time. It is Lord Pemerton."

"Jack? Well, send him in, for God's sake. Don't make the man wait in the hallway." Sedge raised his voice to a shout. "Jack? Jack? Is that you? Come on in."

Wigan rolled his eyes heavenward, and stepped aside to allow the Marquess of Pemerton to enter. Nodding toward the grate, the butler said, "My lord, would you like me to—"

"Leave it, Wigan. You may go. Oh, and bring more brandy, please."

Wigan's eyes strayed briefly to the broken decanter. "Yes, my lord," he said before leaving the room.

Lord Pemerton's eyes had followed Wigan's to the shattered decanter and he now raised his black brows in question. "Heard you were in Town, Sedge," he said. "Heard you'd been drinking quite a lot. Hadn't heard you'd taken to smashing things."

"Sit down, Jack." Sedge waved a slack arm toward a chair.

Jack pulled the chair closer and set it at a right angle to Sedge's chair. Seating himself, he was forced to angle it away a bit in order to make more room, as Sedge was incapable just then of tucking in the long legs stretched out before him. "So," Jack said, settling back into the chair, "what happened?"

"I broke the bloody decanter. So what?"

"That's not what I mean," Jack said.

"What, then?"

"What really happened, Sedge?" his friend asked in a quiet, deep voice. "What's eating away at you?"

"I don't know what you're talking about."

"Give over, Sedge. I've never seen you like this. You've seen me like this more times than I would wish."

"Like what? Drunk, you mean?" He let out a mirthless crack of laughter. "Yeah, I've seen you drunk plenty of times. Plenty of times. You ain't here to preach to me, are you? 'Cause if you are, you can leave right now. I don't need preaching. Mary hasn't turned you up temperate, has she?"

Jack laughed. "Not a chance. Too many years of dissipation to give it all up flat. In fact, if I may ..." He stood, moved to the side table, and gestured toward the row of decanters.

Sedge fluttered a limp hand in a wave of dismissal. "Sorry, old man. Should have offered. Pour yourself a drink. Out of brandy at the moment, I'm afraid."

Jack looked at the broken glass in the grate and nodded. He picked up one of the matching blue bottles and held it up to read the word Hollands written across the front in gold letters. He wrinkled his nose in distaste and replaced it in the silver holder. He then reached for one of the larger, clear etched glass decanters and held it up toward the light. There was no label on this one.

"Claret," Sedge volunteered.

Jack nodded again and poured himself a glass. Just then, Wigan returned with a new decanter of brandy. Sedge held out his glass and Wigan refilled it, his face puckered up in a scowl of disapproval. As the butler left the room, Sedge watched his retreating back with an irritated scowl of his own. Who the devil did the fellow think he was, anyway? Sedge did not have to put up with that sort of insolence. By God, he did not.

Jack had resumed his chair. He took a long swallow of the red wine, and sighed with pleasure.

"You gonna get drunk with me, then?" Sedge asked, grinning at his friend.

"No."

"You gonna preach at me?"

"No." Jack kept his eyes on the shattered glass in the grate. "I was just wondering what got you mad enough to fling that decanter."

Sedge snorted but did not reply.

"Come on, Sedge. I owe you one, you know. Remember how you towed me out of Covent Garden and tried to shake some sense into my drunken head?"

Sedge laughed. "What a mess you were, Jack."

"Don't I know it. I was pretty miserable when Mary left me." He took another swallow of wine. "That's why I realize how you feel right now. Miserable." His brows knotted together as he stared into the fire, then raised slightly in concern as he looked over at Sedge. "I just don't know why."

Sedge turned away, drained his glass, and stared into the fire.

"Thought you might want to talk about it," Jack said. "Perhaps I can help in some way. I owe you that, Sedge."

Sedge remained silent. Why did everyone have to harp at him? Why couldn't they all just leave him alone?

"Tell me why you smashed the decanter, Sedge."

"Because it reminded me of her!" he blurted without thinking.

"Who?"

Sedge shifted his stiff leg and crossed his ankles. Damn Jack, anyway, for poking his nose where it did not belong. "No one," he said.

Jack bent to pick up a piece of broken glass and rubbed the smooth surface between his fingers. "No one, eh?" He turned the shard over and studied it. "No one in particular. No one with eyes the color of'—he paused as he held the blue glass up to the light—"sapphires, perhaps?"

"Sherry."

Jack looked at Sedge's empty glass and raised his brows in question. "You want some sherry?" he asked in an astonished voice.

"No, no," Sedge replied impatiently. "Her eyes."

"What?"

"Her eyes. The color of sherry, not sapphires."

"Ah." Jack leaned back in his chair and smiled. "Sherry- colored eyes. I see." He fingered the blue glass shard, furrowing his brows as he studied it, then looked at Sedge in question. Getting no response, he shrugged, tossed the shard back in the grate, and picked up his wineglass. He took a long swallow, then returned his gaze to the fire. His elbows rested on the arms of his chair and he absently tapped a finger on the rim of his glass. It was several moments before he broke the companionable silence.

"And what about her hair?" he asked.

Sedge had been conjuring up images of those sherry eyes, darkened and heavy-lidded just after he had kissed her. He expanded the image to include her hair. Unruly wisps escaping the severe knot at her nape and framing her face like a soft halo. How could he describe the color of Meg's hair? It was red, of course. But somehow that simple description did not suffice. He thought for a moment. "You know those cliffs down at your Devon estate?" he asked.

"Pemworth? The cliffs at Pemworth?"

"Yes. The red ones. Sort of that color."

"Ah," Jack said. "Terra-cotta."

"Yes, that's it. Like old Tudor brick. Like... like at Hampton Court, or some such place. Or... or maybe more like an October sunset. You know, all sort of fiery and bright?" Sedge's hands fluttered in circles around his own head as he struggled to describe Meg's hair. He caught Jack's eyes, flashing with amusement, and quickly dropped his hands.

"So," Jack said, smiling broadly, "fiery red hair and sherry eyes. I am intrigued. What else?"

Sedge's lips curled up into a grin. "You won't believe this, Jack. She's taller than you. Almost as tall as me."

"Good God!"

"With the longest, most beautiful legs you've ever seen."

Jack threw back his head and laughed. "So, who is this no one in particular with red hair and sherry eyes and legs up to here?"

And so Sedge, his tongue surprisingly loose, told his friend everything. Without having intended to do so, he found himself telling Jack all about his accident, his rescue by the fiery- haired angel, his recovery at Thornhill, and all that had happened with Meg.

"She turned you down flat?" Jack shook his head in astonishment.

"Just like that!" Sedge said as he reached over and snapped his fingers in front of Jack's face. "'I think you had better leave,' she said. Now what's a fellow to think of something like that, I ask you?"

"And you have no idea what could have set her off?" Jack asked.

"None."

"Hmm. And you say that up until that moment she had been very receptive to your... your attentions?"

"So I had thought," Sedge replied, staring into the bottom of his empty glass.

"And you had thought that you ... that she was The One?"

"God help me, I did." Sedge ran his fingers through his hair. "I did. What a bloody fool!"

"Ah, don't be so hard on yourself, old man," Jack said. "Correct me if I am wrong, but I do not recall any other woman ever before affecting you this way. If you think she is The One, then she probably is. In which case, I would advise you not to give up just yet. Let her cool down. Then try again. Perhaps she was just playing coy, and wanted to be chased a bit, wooed a bit longer."

"Not this woman."

"How can you be so sure?"

Sedge slid deeper into his chair and groaned. "That's just it," he wailed. "I can't be! 'Pon my word, Jack, I shall never understand women!"

Jack raised his glass in salute. "I'll drink to that."

* * *

Meg tossed and turned and could not seem to fall asleep. She pounded the pillow again, the thick, muffled sound an echo of her loneliness. How could she be lonely in this busy farm, with people coming and going every day? But the truth was, she was lonely for Sedge. She missed him. How could she have grown so used to him in so short a time? And what business did she have missing someone who had treated her so shabbily?

Her head still told her to forget him, but her heart could

not forget. She rolled to her side and hugged a pillow to her stomach, remembering his kiss. Maybe Terrence had been right after all. Perhaps she had never had the typical feminine sensibilities where men were concerned. But not once in all that time had a man stirred the feelings in her that Sedge had awakened. The memory of those feelings— warm, sensual, breathless, yearning for more—caused her body to relive them all over again. She hugged the pillow tighter and smiled against it. At the ripe old age of twenty-four, she had finally discovered what all the fuss was about.

As quickly as those warm feelings were resurrected, an enormous sense of loss overwhelmed her. She choked on an unexpected sob, and tears began to course down her cheeks. She clutched the pillow more tightly against her breast and sobbed for what could never be. Meg had been shown a glimpse of the secrets of love; but that tantalizing glimpse was all she would ever know. For she had lost Colin Herriot, Viscount Sedgewick, the one man in all the world who could have taught her those secrets.

But how could she lose what she had never possessed?

Ah, but she could have had him. If only she had accepted his offer, she could have had him.

Meg sat bolt upright in bed. Now, where had that notion come from? *If* she had accepted his offer. There was no question about accepting that hateful offer. Was there? No, of course not. She was being ridiculous. She sat back against the headboard, propping a pillow behind her head. To accept an offer such as Sedge had made was unthinkable for a young, gently bred female such as herself. Then, why had he made it? He should have known she could not accept. Shouldn't he? But perhaps such liaisons were more common among his social set. Perhaps she was simply too sheltered here at Thornhill to know how other people, more sophisticated people, went on. Still, it was not the sort of thing that Meg Ashburton could do. She could never live with herself if she agreed to such a tiling. Could she?

That afternoon she had been strolling in the herb garden with her grandmother, and, as usual, Gram had turned the conversation to Lord Sedgewick.

"I still cannot understand that young man," she had said, plucking off a leaf of Spanish lavender and rubbing it between her fingers. "The least he could have done was to make some kind of plans to see you again. I was so certain he was taken with you." She had brought the leaf, now fragrant with released oils, to her nose and sniffed. Smiling, she held it out for Meg. "Did he say nothing about seeing you again?"

Meg held the lavender under her nose and nodded her appreciation. "Well, he did ask if I was coming to London for the Season," she said.

Gram's eyes had lit up like candles. "He did? Well, then, we must go!"

"I think not, Gram. You know how I feel about London. Besides, I told Lord Sedgewick that I would not be going."

"Oh, my dear girl, are you so sure?"

"Yes, Gram. You know I much prefer it here in the country."

"I know, dear," Gram had said. "But Lord Sedgewick—"

"You must get over this obsession with Lord Sedgewick, Gram. He is gone and will not be returning."

Gram had looked at Meg with an expression of resigned sadness in her eyes that had almost broken Meg's heart. "I am sorry, my dear," Gram had said. "You are right, of course. He was a charming gentlemen, but there will be others." She had reached up and gently cupped Meg's cheek. "Someone else will come along."

Gram's words rang in Meg's head as she burrowed herself more deeply into the stack of pillows.

Someone else will come along.

But Meg knew in her heart that no one else would come

along. In twenty-four years no one else had come along. And even if they did, Meg knew that there was only one man she would ever want. Had wanted for over six years. One tall, lanky, blond-haired gentleman with a smile to turn a person's knees to jelly.

And she could have had him. Perhaps she could still have him. If she accepted his terms. But how could she possibly do such a thing? She snuggled close against her pillow, imagining Sedge's arms around her, and wondered how she could not?

She was six feet tall and firmly on the shelf. It was next to impossible to expect that she would ever receive an honorable offer of marriage at this stage of her life. Unless it was from some older, widowed gentleman who needed a nursemaid, or a mother for his children. How was that to be preferred to a less honorable but more passionate arrangement with a man who set her blood on fire and made her heart soar? How could a convenient match offering little more than occasional nights of decorous coupling compare to an arrangement with a man she loved, who wanted to hold her naked in his arms? To make love to her night and day? To reveal to her all the secrets she longed to know?

Was it so horrible to want all these things? Was it better to live out her life alone, never knowing the fulfillment hinted at by Sedge's kisses? Even if that fulfillment came through an arrangement outside of marriage?

Somehow, it was no longer a matter of whether she could live with herself if she accepted such an arrangement, but whether she could live with herself if she did not.

When sleep finally overtook her, Meg had determined what she must do.

The next morning at breakfast, she announced to Gram and Terrence that she had decided to go to London for the Season.

Chapter 17

Lord Pemerton opened the door of his town carriage and stepped out. He spoke briefly to his coachman, instructing him to return the carriage home to Hanover Square rather than wait for him. These long nights with Sedge were unpredictable. He never knew how long he would need to stay. Anyway, he could take a hackney later. Or perhaps he would walk home. It was an unusually warm night for late April, and Jack enjoyed a brisk walk.

As the carriage pulled away, Jack turned and strode up the steps of Lord Sedgewick's town house. His lips pursed into a scowl as he noted the knocker was still removed. It could only mean that Sedge still sought peace at the bottom of a bottle. And, as Jack knew from personal experience, drinking alone was the worst sort of relief. No relief at all, in fact. Whatever miseries of the soul caused one to drink to excess in the first place were only amplified with each swallow.

Jack hated to see Sedge in such a state. Of the three friends who had caroused together for years, Sedge was the least likely to have taken such a turn. Jack himself had been the most likely, and had in fact hit the rock bottom of despair and debauchery not all that many months ago. The contrast of that dreadful time and the joys of today was nothing short of incredible. Seven months of marriage to his Mary had brought him a contentment he had never thought possible.

His own state of happiness made Jack ever more aware of Sedge's misery. Ever since his first visit, when Sedge had finally told him about Meg Ashburton, Jack had made a point of checking in with Sedge at least every other evening, trying desperately to lead him away from total dissipation, struggling for the right words to bring him out of his despair. So far, he had failed. Nothing he said seemed to make a difference. Jack had been able to do little more than offer Sedge a drinking companion, for it was clear he had no intention of giving up the bottle, or of venturing out into Society. So the best Jack could do was to keep him talking, for it meant he drank less.

Night after night of talking and drinking had brought Jack no closer to wrenching Sedge out of the black despair into which he had sunk. Jack had alternately suggested that Sedge either try to forget Meg Ashburton or go back to her. But his friend did not seem capable of doing either. Jack knew all too well that the more one drank the harder it became to make any sort of decision, other than to pour one more drink. But Jack had continued to stop by Mount Street regularly, hoping that at some point his friend would reach the end of his tether and begin to climb his way back out of the bottle.

Tonight he was especially optimistic, for he had some news that he thought might jolt Sedge back to reality.

Wigan answered Jack's knock with a look of relief in his eyes.

"Good evening, my lord. Please come in."

"How is he tonight, Wigan?"

The butler hunched a shoulder in resignation. "A little worse, I am afraid. He has not come downstairs since yesterday."

"Good Lord. You mean he hasn't left his bedchamber?"

"No, my lord," Wigan replied. "Pargeter has been able to get him out of bed once or twice, but only to sit in a chair by the fire."

"Has he eaten?"

"Very little."

"Well, perhaps I can coax him into sharing a tray with me," Jack said as the butler took his hat and gloves. "I will just go on up, if that is all right. Perhaps you can have a tray sent up? With a pot of hot coffee?"

"Of course, my lord. Thank you, my lord."

Jack charged up the stairs, more concerned than ever. It sounded as though Sedge's state of mind was deteriorating rapidly. If he didn't get out of that bed and out of that room soon, he might sink into a decline from which he would never recover.

As Jack reached the landing on the second floor, he stopped in his tracks. What was that smell? He lifted his nose and drew a deep breath. Good God, he thought, choking back a cough. Smoke! What the devil?

A terrible foreboding twisted Jack's stomach into a knot as he rushed toward Sedge's suite of rooms just on the left. He flung open the bedchamber door and was met by a wall of smoke and searing heat.

Oh, my God, Sedge!

Jack waved his arms about wildly to clear the smoke. "Sedge? Sedge?" he called out, unable to see much beyond the reach of his hand. When he received no response to his shout, he backed quickly out the doorway and poked his head into the corridor.

"Wigan! Pargeter!" he shouted at the top of his voice, then broke into a spasm of coughing. "Come quickly!" he added when he was able to find his voice again. "Fire! Fire!"

Turning back into the room, Jack ripped at his cravat until he was able to jerk it loose. He quickly wrapped it around his mouth and tied it behind his neck. All the while he was searching through the blinding smoke for the bed. When the cloth was in place and both hands were free, he held them out in front of him like a blind man as he moved cautiously toward the side of the room where he knew the bed to be. His eyes smarted and teared. Squinting, he was soon able to make out the shape of the bed. Good God, the bed curtains were engulfed in flames that shot up to the ceiling.

"Sedge!" he cried, the sound muffled against the cloth.

Smoke and flames were thick around the bed and Jack could see almost nothing. He reached out his arms in search for his friend. "Sedge!" Finally, his hand came into contact with a booted foot Without further thought, he tugged on the foot, found the other and began yanking hard on both of them. When he had pulled enough to reach Sedge's waist, Jack lifted his friend's inert body with a strength he had no idea he possessed. Dodging to avoid a burning length of fringe that fell from the canopy above, sending a shower of sparks raining down upon them, he hoisted Sedge over his shoulder like a sack of potatoes. Jack kept his breathing shallow and rushed through the smoke in what he hoped was the direction of the door.

After only a few labored steps, Jack collided with something soft. The sound of choked coughing was followed by the touch of a hand on his arm.

"My lord!"

The voice was Pargeter's. He was followed closely by Wigan. Jack pushed by both of them. "I have him," he rasped. "I have him."

Wigan shouted orders to footmen, who brought buckets of water. Jack did not stay to see how or even if they fought the fire. His only thought was to get his friend to safety. As he hurried, he became aware of a hacking, sputtering presence at his side. Pargeter.

"This way, my lord," the valet wheezed.

Jack followed Pargeter to a small chamber at the end of the hall. "We should be safe here," the valet said, "if they are able to contain the fire." The shouting and continuous thunder of rushing footsteps in the adjacent bedchamber indicated that a valiant attempt was being made to do so.

Jack dropped his burden onto the bed. He flexed his shoulders briefly in an attempt to return some kind of feeling to them. He had no idea how he had been able to lift his large friend so easily. He bent over Sedge's unconscious form on the bed. "Sedge?" he shouted as he roughly slapped his friend's cheek. This was no time to be gentle. Sedge must be roused. At the sound of a muffled groan, Jack dropped to the edge of the bed and gave a raspy sigh. "He's alive," he murmured. "He's alive."

"Thank God," Pargeter said.

Jack glanced up at the valet to find a stricken look on the man's face as he stared at his unconscious employer.

"I don't mind telling you, my lord," he said, turning to Jack, "I was that scared. When I saw that room of smoke, I thought he'd really done it this time." He ran a shaky hand through his hair, then moved toward the foot of the bed and began to remove Sedge's boots. "Lord Sedgewick is one of the kindest, most considerate employers I have had the pleasure of serving," he continued as he worked one boot heel gently back and forth. Finally, after one good yank, the boot came sliding off, sending Pargeter flying backward. Recovering, he began to work on the second boot. "But, if you don't mind my saying so, my lord," he said, "these accidents of his are giving me a weak heart."

"Accidents?"

"Yes," Pargeter said while tugging on the second boot. "I've never known anyone so unlucky. He—"

His words were interrupted by a low groan followed by a hacking cough as Sedge appeared to revive. Completely at a loss to understand Pargeter's strange words, Jack would have to leave the explanation for another time. The valet dropped the boot and seemed almost magically to produce a glass of water—Jack marveled momentarily at the resourcefulness of the fellow—which he held against Sedge's lips.

After a few sips, Sedge opened his eyes and looked about the room with a dazed expression. "Wha—" he began before succumbing to another fit of coughing.

Jack took the glass of water from Pargeter and placed an arm around his friend's shoulder as he helped him sit up. He whispered a few words to the valet, who nodded and left the room. After helping Sedge to another sip of water. Jack allowed him to sink back against the bed pillows and catch his breath.

"Jack?" he whispered.

"I'm right here, Sedge."

"Wh-what happened?"

"I'm not sure," Jack said. "I can only tell you that when I came to your room your bed curtains had caught fire and you were passed out on the bed."

"Oh, God." Sedge's eyes widened with a look of alarm. "You mean . . . you mean I could have . . . that I almost ... Oh, God, Jack. What have I done?"

Before Jack could answer, a knock sounded on the door followed by the appearance of a bedraggled-looking Wigan.

"Oh, thank goodness, my lord," he said as he entered. "You were not harmed, I trust?"

"No," Sedge said, shaking his head. He seemed to experience a moment of dizziness, and reached a hand up to his head. "No," he repeated in a soft voice. "I am not harmed. Is everything under control, Wigan?"

"Yes, my lord," the butler replied, masterfully maintaining an air of dignity despite his soot-smeared face and damp clothing. "The fire has been put out."

"Could you tell how it might have started, Wigan?" Jack asked.

Wigan looked at Jack with furrowed brows, then turned to Sedge with an expression of incredible sadness. "I cannot be sure, my lord," he said, "but it appears most likely that a... a candle on the bedside table was ... was overturned somehow... setting the bed curtains on fire."

Jack felt the same sadness he read in Wigan's eyes and heard in the butler's halting voice. That Sedge—carefree, easy-going, ever-smiling Sedge—should have come to this. It was an unthinkable outrage. It should never have happened. Jack felt helpless and angry that he had not somehow been a better friend to Sedge, been able to talk him out of his despair, to help him stop drinking.

Jack turned his gaze to Sedge, only to find him staring back with an equal amount of shame and misery. Jack knew in that moment, as their eyes locked, that Sedge felt the same outrage that he felt. An understanding passed between them with that look. An understanding that Sedge had sunk as far as he could go, and must now begin the climb back to reason and sanity.

"We are fortunate that Lord Pemerton arrived when he did," Wigan said, shattering the tense moment. "Otherwise ..."

The butler left the thought unspoken, but it was clearly understood. Sedge might have been killed.

Pargeter entered at that moment, bearing a tray of food and a pot of coffee. Wigan cleared a space on the bedside table, where Pargeter then deposited the tray. The butler poured coffee for each gentleman into small straight-sided porcelain coffee cups that seemed incongruously delicate for a masculine household. They must have come from Sedge's mother.

Jack signaled for the two servants to leave.

"Drink it, Sedge," Jack said when they were alone. "If you refuse, be prepared to have it forced down your throat."

Sedge glared at Jack, then took a small sip. His mouth puckered up like a drawstring bag and a shudder shook his shoulders.

"Drink it!" Jack ordered.

And Sedge drank it. His hands shook so that the coffee sloshed about in the porcelain cup, threatening to spill over the sides. After the first sip, the next few swallows seemed to come more easily. Jack reached for the tray and spread a slice of bread with a generous dollop of jam. "Here," he said, handing the bread to Sedge. "You'll need something sweet to help keep the coffee down."

Sedge took a bite of the bread and another swallow of coffee. Finally, he sank back against the headboard, balancing the bread and coffee on his lap. "Thank you, Jack," he said quietly. "Thank you."

* * *

Jack stayed with Sedge through most of the night, making him eat and walk and drink coffee and talk. When they finally came back to what had happened here tonight, Sedge was full of shame. Though grateful for his friend's timely intervention, he was nevertheless chagrined that Jack should have been witness to such a thing.

Without a word from Sedge, Jack seemed to understand his shame. He suggested that they keep tonight's events confidential. No one need know what had occurred, he promised. Jack believed the servants could be trusted, but agreed to have a word with Wigan when he left. He would himself never mention the incident, although he admitted he would probably tell Mary, since he had no secrets from her and she would wish to know where he had been all night. And Mary could be trusted. Sedge could be sure that neither of them would ever mention it again.

Sedge had no desire to spread the tale of his ultimate shame, so he agreed with Jack that the incident would be kept secret. The fire had done what Jack had been unable to do: it had forced Sedge to face the truth. It seemed that he was forever having to be reminded of the truth. At Thornhill, he had been forced by his cousin to admit that not only had he been malingering and had long overstayed his welcome, but that he was weaving foolish dreams about Meg. Dreams spun out of loneliness and boredom. Not based in truth. Never in truth.

And then Jack, good old Jack, had tried to make him see that he was avoiding the truth through drink. And Jack should know. For that matter, so should Sedge. Was he not the one who had cajoled and berated Jack for behaving like a fool when Mary left him practically at the altar? For not handling it all in a more mature and sensible manner? And God knows Jack had more reason to despair than Sedge. Meg had never agreed to marry him, after all. And yet here he was, behaving in the same idiotic manner as Jack had done.

"Is our sex doomed to behave like idiots over women?" he asked.

Jack laughed. "Probably. But I can promise you, my friend, that once those moments of madness are past and differences resolved, they are really quite pleasant creatures. I would no more trade my Mary for my old life of debauchery for all the treasures of the world. Such a woman is worth waiting for."

Sedge heaved a sigh. He was more than willing to wait for Meg, but he had no confidence that she would ever come to him.

"Speaking of treasures," Jack said, "thought you might be interested in the latest Incomparable to hit Town."

"There's a new one every year," Sedge said. "What's different about this one? Are you trying to tempt me with a tasty diversion, hoping I'll forget about Meg?"

"Not exactly," Jack said, slanting a glance at Sedge from his position near the window, silhouetted against the rosy glow of sunrise. The smell of smoke still permeated the air, and the window had been thrown open some hours ago. A soft breeze now ruffled the edges of the draperies that framed the window. "I just thought," Jack continued, "that this particular one might pique your interest."

"Why? Who is she?"

"Don't know, precisely." Jack propped a hip against the broad windowsill and stretched one thigh along it. Leaning his back against the open shutter, he crossed his arms over his chest and idly swung the raised foot back and forth. "Never have heard her name. Mary told me about her." He smiled. "You know, as much as Mary loves Pemworth, she still adores all the bustle and fuss of the Season. Knows everyone. Goes everywhere. Hears everything. You know Mary."

"Yes," Sedge said, wishing Jack would get to the point. "Delightful woman, Mary."

"Isn't she, though?" Jack grinned. "I simply adore her. But, as I was saying, she has told me of the latest Incomparable. Seems she is quite an Original. Has a court of dozens of young swains eager to earn her pleasure."

"Like I said before, there's a new one every year. What makes this one different?"

"Let's see if I can remember all the details," Jack said, tapping his chin and staring at the ceiling until Sedge wanted to shake him. "She has red hair, I believe. And a sort of amber- colored eyes. Or maybe it was more like sherry."

Sedge sat up straight in his chair, as sober as a Methodist for the first time in weeks. Red hair and sherry-colored eyes?

"The interesting thing is," Jack continued, "she is apparently no green girl straight out of the schoolroom. A mature woman, Mary says. Very poised and elegant."

Sedge swallowed with difficulty. Could it be? Had she come to Town? What did it all mean?"

"Oh, and I almost forgot the best part of all," Jack said as a grin split his face. "The lady is six feet tall if she's an inch."

Sedge bolted out of his chair. "She's here! Meg's in London!"

Jack smiled. "Apparently, so, my friend."

Chapter 18

Meg opened and closed the sticks of her fan and wondered if this would be the night. She had looked for Sedge at every function she had attended and had yet to see him. As their carriage sat in the line of traffic queued up for the reception at Grosvenor House, Meg craned her head out the window to see how large a crowd tonight's function would boast. The line of carriages and link boys stretched as far down Park Lane as she could see.

"Meg!" Gram scolded. "Close that window and turn around, my girl. You will have people thinking we are bumpkins straight from the country."

Meg laughed. "Aren't we?" Catching her brother's eye as he sat facing her on the seat opposite, he grinned and winked.

"Hardly bumpkins," Gram replied. "No one would dare call you a bumpkin in that gown," she added with a sniff of disapproval.

Meg grinned and turned her head to peer out the carriage window. She was really quite pleased with tonight's gown. French gauze over a sea green crepe slip, it was cut deep in the front, showing a wide expanse of bosom. The rich green chenille embroidery at the neckline, matching that along the hem, set off Meg's fair skin to perfection. Or so the modiste had said. Meg had no eye for such things and simply trusted Madame Yolande to provide her with the sort of wardrobe she required.

"I think her dress is fine," Terrence said. "You look beautiful, Meggie."

Meg felt her cheeks color up at her brother's uncharacteristic compliment. "Thank you, Terrence." The fact was, she did feel beautiful. Ever since she had arrived in London, all snugly wrapped up in her secret purpose, she had felt like a new person. Like a woman. Nothing like the gawky hoyden of six years ago. She faced London this time with all the confidence of a mature woman who knows what she's about.

Gram had disapproved of much of the new wardrobe. But she had been so thrilled that Meg wanted to come to Town at all that she had acquiesced in the end. Meg had wished for a wardrobe more suitable for a worldly, mature woman, and had hinted as much to Madame Yolande, who had been happy to oblige. Gram had soon admitted that Meg's new gowns were no more daring than almost every other gown they had seen at *ton* affairs. And she had finally agreed that Meg should not have to dress in the whites and pastels of a young miss in her first Season. Even Meg realized that such pale colors did not suit her. Madame Yolande had agreed.

"Do you suppose Lord Bellingham will be there tonight?" Gram asked. "Such a nice young man."

"I do not know," Meg replied. Nor did she care. There was only one gentleman whose presence would make any difference to her.

"Well, if he is there," Gram continued, smiling contentedly, "I have no doubt he will seek you out. He always does."

"Yes," Meg said. "He does."

"And not only Bellingham," Terrence added. "You

seem to have gathered quite a court, Meggie."

Meg smiled at her brother and shrugged as if it all meant nothing. But, in fact, she was secretly pleased and surprised at all the attention she had received. She continued to be astonished at the attitude of people, gentlemen in particular, during this Season. It was such a marked contrast to what she had experienced six years ago. Then, she had been ignored. This year, she was fawned over, flirted with, and received more attention than she could ever have imagined. She was seldom without a dance partner, and there was much competition to escort her to supper.

"Well, I, for one, am exceedingly pleased to see Meg's popularity this year," Gram said. She reached over and squeezed Meg's hand. "Only good will come of it, just you wait and see."

Meg knew that Gram expected her to find some gentleman to make her forget Lord Sedgewick. She had said as much while they had planned their trip to Town. And Meg was almost certain she had dropped such hints to Terrence as well. It was the only explanation for the strange looks he sometimes gave her lately. And for the new solicitous way he treated her. Between Gram and Terrence, the way they coddled her, Meg often felt as if she had just recovered from a serious illness. Perhaps she had not done such a good job after all of concealing her broken heart. In any case, Meg had allowed Gram and Terrence to believe that she wanted to have another Season after all these years as a means to repair that broken heart. It was true, after all. No one need know what she really intended.

"Quite a change this time out, eh, Meggie?" Terrence said.

"Indeed. It is all quite extraordinary. I do not understand it at all." Meg could not be sure what precisely had wrought such a change. Other than a new wardrobe and a few extra pounds, there was nothing so very different about her. She was the same old Meg.

Terrence chuckled and waved a gloved hand at her gown. "I don't suppose the new dresses have anything to do with it?"

"Perhaps." Sharing a grin with Terrence, she knew they were both thinking of those horrible, girlish dresses Gram had made her wear six years ago. "But, after all," Meg continued, "I am still unfashionably red-haired and too tall by half. Same as before."

"Ah, but you are not the same as before," Terrence said. "That's just it. Oh, you are still tall, to be sure. But you don't try to hide it anymore. No more slouching or bent knees."

"I suppose it is just a matter of getting older and accepting things as they are," Meg said. "No sense in hiding it. I am what I am."

"And there you have hit on the very thing that sets you apart this Season," Terrence said. "You are more comfortable with yourself, and it shows. You no longer enter a room all hunched over, glaring at your toes. You walk in tall and proud, with your head held high, commanding attention. It makes all the difference, Meggie. You force everyone to notice you and appreciate how beautiful you are." He reached over, took Meg's hand, and brought her fingers to his lips. "I am very proud of you, my dear."

Meg was overwhelmed by her brother's words, and squeezed his hand before relinquishing it. He had never said such things to her in all her life.

She supposed there was a certain amount of truth in what he said. It was true, she was more comfortable with herself and her height. But there was also the fact that she cared so little about what Society thought of her. They could take her or leave her. She did not care. So long as she found Lord Sedgewick, the rest of them did not matter in the least. Perhaps by not trying to impress them, she had done just that. Or perhaps her secret motive for coming to Town had given her a certain air. The fact that she was ready and willing to enter into a sophisticated, clandestine affair made her feel like a mature woman of the world. It was possible that new confidence showed in her face or in her bearing or in her manner. Whatever the reason, she was certainly treated with a great deal more respect this Season than six years ago.

While their carriage inched its way to Grosvenor House, conversation turned to Thornhill. Terrence, who had been coerced by Gram's incessant badgering into accompanying them to Town, had reluctantly left Seamus Coogan in charge of the stables. It was breeding time, and he worried aloud about which stallions would be allowed to cover which mares, until Gram put a halt to such indelicate conversation.

Meg's mind wandered as Terrence fretted. She watched the congestion of carriages along Park Lane and thought how lucky they were to have received an invitation to Lord Grosvenor's reception. Somehow, though, they seemed to receive invitations to all the right places. As Gram had anticipated, Terrence's school friends, hunting cronies, and business associates had been the source of a continual stream of invitations. Gram still had many acquaintances in Town as well, having kept up a lively correspondence with several old friends throughout the years. And these, too, sent invitations. At any other time, Meg would have been terrified at the prospect of attending all the functions represented by the stacks of invitations lining the drawing room mantel. This time, though, any one of those functions could be the means to locating Sedge, and letting him know she had reconsidered his offer.

And so each evening had been filled with parties, balls, routs, concerts, and every other sort of entertainment *ton* hostesses could dream up. Though she had not yet located Sedge, which was a puzzle to her, Meg had nevertheless managed to enjoy herself. It was much more fun to be accepted than to be ignored, to dance than to be a wallflower. After her last experience, Meg could never have imagined a Season could be so enjoyable.

And she used every opportunity to listen for news of Sedge. Twice, she had heard his name mentioned. It certainly sounded as though he was in Town. But why had she not seen him? Six years ago, he had been everywhere. She had understood from their conversations at Thornhill that he was a very sociable person who truly enjoyed all the frantic activity of the Season. Could he still be incapacitated by the broken leg? It seemed unlikely. His recovery at Thornhill had gone remarkably well. He should be out of the splint and walking fairly normally by now. So, where was he?

As the carriage finally reached the entrance to Grosvenor House and she mounted the steps on Terrence's arm, Meg thought—as she always thought upon first entering a ball or party—this could be the night.

* * *

Sedge grabbed a glass of chilled champagne from the tray of a passing footman. He moved behind a large potted plant and downed the glass in a single gulp. His shoulders sagged in relief. He had needed a drink to steady his nerves, but had promised Jack, and himself, that he would practice a little temperance on his first formal evening of the Season. But what harm could a bit of champagne do?

Sedge hid the empty glass in the leaves of the plant, then edged out from behind it. He placed his hands behind his back and strolled casually into the main ballroom, nodding and smiling at various acquaintances along the way. Lady Montrose's ball looked to be a rousing success. If Meg was there, it was going to be difficult to find her in the crush of people.

And he did indeed want to find her.

The fire in his bedchamber and the news of Meg's appearance in Town had the combined effect of knocking some sense into Sedge's hard head at long last. He came to realize how ridiculous his behavior had been, allowing himself to wallow in self-pity over Meg's rejection. And Jack was right. If he really felt that strongly about her—and he did—then he should not give up so easily. If only he could see her again, talk to her again, maybe he could turn her around. Or at least understand better why she had turned him down in the first place. Surely she owed him an explanation.

Sedge skirted the edge of the ballroom, keeping his eyes on the dance floor. No tall, red-haired woman in sight. He moved toward every cluster of gentlemen he saw, using his height to peer over shoulders in order to locate the woman who claimed their attention. None of the women was Meg.

"Looking for someone?"

Sedge turned to find the smiling face of Sir Gerald Hathaway, one of the young men who had joined him in carousing and gaming during his first days back in London.

"Hullo, Ger. Just looking around to see who's here."

"Thought you had left Town," Sir Gerald said. "Haven't seen you around. Noticed your knocker was removed."

"I am in Town, as you see."

"How's the leg?"

"Much better," Sedge said, looking down and flexing the limb in question. "No cane tonight. Don't think I'm quite ready to dance, though."

Just then a chorus of laughter floated up from a nearby group of gentlemen surrounding a dark-haired beauty. When Sedge turned back to Sir Gerald, the young man's eyes were fixed on the woman with open admiration. Sedge smiled. "So, why are you not a part of that beauty's court, Ger? Too much competition?"

Sir Gerald tore his eyes away and heaved a sigh. "I suppose so."

"Who is she?"

"Miss Sybil Danforth," Sir Gerald replied, pronouncing each syllable with reverence. "Old Perriton's granddaughter. Beautiful, ain't she?"

"She is," Sedge replied. He decided to probe a bit. "This Season's Incomparable, eh?"

"One of them," Sir Gerald replied.

"Only one of them? 'Tis a bountiful Season, then?"

"Oh, yes. Quite a few interesting new faces. There's Lady Susan Endicott, for example, just over there. See? The tall blond, all in pink?"

Sedge located Lady Susan and nodded. "Pretty," he said. "But not so very tall, I think."

Sir Gerald looked up at Sedge and laughed. "From your vantage, I suppose she does not seem so very tall. Oh! But there is one new incomparable who is quite tall indeed."

Sedge's heart began to hammer in his chest. Attempting to mask his excitement, he flicked a nonexistent piece of lint off his sleeve. "Oh?" he said in a bored voice.

"Yes," Sir Gerald said. "A Titian-haired giantess who must be almost as tall as you."

"Indeed?" Sedge said in a disinterested tone as he examined his fingernails. "How unusual. You must point her out to me at once."

"Oh, she ain't here," Sir Gerald said. "At least, I haven't seen her tonight."

"What a pity," Sedge said before stifling a yawn. Damn. He would have to seek her out somewhere else. But there was one thing he had to ask. Just to be sure. "What did you say her name was? This red-haired Amazon?"

"Oh. It is Miss Meg Ashburton. Her brother is Sir Terrence Ashburton. Owns Thornhill stables. You are sure to see her about. She seems to be everywhere." He laughed. "Can't miss her, you know."

Oh, but I can. And I do. Meg, where are you?

* * *

Meg strolled through one of the galleries at Grosvenor House accompanied by the Misses Willoughby, two young ladies who were nieces of Gram's friend Lady Stanton. The elder Miss Willoughby, Eugenia, was of an age with Meg and the two had struck up a comfortable friendship. While Eugenia chattered away about the questionable taste of the red-covered walls, Meg glanced about the room, as she always did, seeking a particular tall, blond gentleman. Suddenly, her gaze landed upon a familiar face in the adjacent gallery.

She laid a hand upon Eugenia Willoughby's arm. "I am sorry to interrupt you," she said, "but I see an old friend in the next room. I simply must go say hello. I hope you will excuse me."

"Of course," Miss Willoughby said.

Meg made her way to the adjacent gallery as quickly as possible, hoping she had not lost him. She soon located him in a far corner, his back to her as he spoke to a group of gentlemen. She stepped up quietly behind him.

"Mr. Herriot?"

He spun around too quickly and almost lost his balance. It was clear that Mr. Albert Herriot was foxed. His eyes bulged in astonishment when he saw her. His bleary gaze then traveled slowly up from her toes to her neckline, where it lingered too long before moving up to her face. Meg's cheeks flared and she would have liked nothing more than to whack him across the face with her fan. He made her feel as if she stood naked before him, and she wished now she had not spoken to him at all. But her only thought had been that he might lead her to Sedge.

"Miz Ashbur'n," Mr. Herriot said as he sketched a wobbly bow. He had moved slightly away from the group of gentlemen, and his eyes darted left and right, as though making sure they could not be overheard. "What on earth brings you t' Lunnon?" he said in a thick-tongued voice. "I never thought t' see you here."

Meg could not tell if he was surprised or angry, but he made her very uncomfortable in any case. She shrugged off his question. "My family simply decided to come to Town for the Season. That is all." Meg did not have the stomach for small talk with Mr. Herriot, particularly in his present condition. She determined to get straight to the point. "And how is your cousin?" she asked. "Lord Sedgewick?"

He snorted loudly and flung his hand as if he were shooing away a fly. "That idiot! Wha'd' you care 'bout him for? He's a fool. Shootin' at people. Throwin' people outa his house. Drinkin' alone. Bloody fool."

Though she could make no sense of his words, a tremor of fear ran down her spine. "Mr. Herriot? What are you talking about? What shooting? What has happened? Is Sedge all right?"

Mr. Herriot threw back his head and laughed, causing eyes to turn in their direction. " 'Course he's awright. He's always awright." He shook his head and laughed mirthlessly.

"But the shooting?" Meg prompted, her hands aching to slap the man silly.

"Oh, he blew a hole in a highwayman's shoulder, tha's all. Almos' blew my head off. Cork-brained idiot."

"You were held up by a highwayman?"

"Oh, yes. But good ol' Sedge saved the day," Mr. Herriot said with a limp wave of his arm.

"Well, thank goodness for that," Meg said.

"Yes. Good ol' Sedge."

"But he is back in Town now?" Meg asked, hoping she could get some sort of coherent information out of the man.

"Sure, ever since we lef' your place." Mr. Herriot's eyes bored into Meg's as he continued. "But he's a sorry mess,

Miz Ashbur'n. You don' wanna see him now." He lowered his voice conspiratorially. "He's taken to drink, y' see. Pretends he ain't home, but he's there awright. Drinkin' hisse'f int' a stupor. All alone. Drunk as can be. 'Tis a pit'ful thing, Miz Ashbur'n. A pit'ful thing."

"Oh, dear." Meg's heart wrenched to think that what Mr. Herriot said might be true. What had happened? Sedge was not a drunkard. What on earth had happened?

Mr. Herriot reached over and placed a hand on Meg's arm and bent closer, the liquor fumes from his breath almost knocking her backward. She tried to wriggle away, but he kept hold of her arm as he whispered close to her ear. "I'll tell you the worst," he said. "Almos' killed hisse'f, Sedge did. Set his own bed curt'ns on fire. Knocked over a candle or somethin'. Got saved, tho'." He absently dropped her arm and his eyes seemed to glass over as he gazed into the distance. When he spoke again, he seemed to speak almost to himself. "Di'nt die aft'r all. Bad business."

Feeling awkward and uneasy, Meg watched as Mr. Herriot shook his head slowly back and forth and appeared to have forgotten all about her. "Bad business," he repeated as he turned away from her, slowly weaving his way across the room. "Bad business."

Meg stared slack-jawed at Mr. Herriot's retreating back. It had been one of the strangest encounters she'd ever had. Though he had been completely foxed himself, she suspected that the things he had said about his cousin were true. What reason would he have to make up such tales?

She turned to walk through the other gallery in hopes of finding Gram or Terrence. She felt like going home early. The thought of Sedge sinking into a debauch tore at her heart. It simply did not sound like the Sedge she had come to know— and love—at Thornhill. What could have pushed him to such limits? Drinking so heavily that he had almost killed himself?

She stopped up short, causing a couple walking close

behind her to crash into her back. The woman gave Meg a baleful glance as they walked around her, but Meg paid them no attention. She stood in the middle of the gallery floor with her hand to her mouth, oblivious to all the activity around her.

Almost killed. Sedge had been almost killed. Again. Good heavens, the man was forever being almost killed. And not only the fire, but also this new business with the highwayman. What sort of man was he, to bring about such a string of bad luck? Meg covered her mouth to hide a grin as she considered that she must find him quickly before he tripped and fell in the path of a speeding carriage. Otherwise, all her plans would be for naught. She must find him quickly and protect the foolish man against himself.

Meg stood still as a statue in the center of the gallery, grinning to herself, as images raced through her mind— images of Sedge clasped to her breast, her arms protecting him from any further mishap. Her reverie was interrupted by the voice of Gram, hailing her from the opposite doorway. She looked to find her grandmother waving for Meg to join her. Meg finally stirred herself to move toward the door. As she nudged her way through the crowd, a raucous laugh rose above the din of conversations. She recognized the laugh as Mr. Herriot's, and all the sad implications of her strange encounter with him came crashing back to her. Poor Sedge. What had happened to him? But there was something disturbing about that conversation. What was it?

When she reached Gram's side at last, the old woman began to chatter about the next party they were scheduled to attend and what Mrs. Hamlin-Lacy had just told her about Lady Bowditch, and Meg lost the train of thought completely.

Although she could not put her finger on what had really troubled her about the conversation with Mr. Herriot, the real problem was Sedge and this new drunkenness. Meg considered this situation as they retrieved their wraps and waited in line for their carriage. She was normally impatient with all the waiting. But just now she appreciated the time to think. If only Gram would quit chattering. Meg wondered if she had miscalculated in coming to Town after all. Perhaps Sedge would never show up at one of the Season's events. Perhaps he would simply stay at home getting drunk.

Or perhaps Mr. Herriot had exaggerated.

By the time their carriage was brought round and she was handed inside, Med had determined to continue her search at each new affair. He was bound to show up eventually. She would find him. That was, after all, the point of this trip to Town. She would not lose him again. Not through her prudishness or through his drunkenness. Or through another silly accident. Yes, she would find him. If she had to go marching up to the door of his Mount Street town house, by God, she would find him.

Chapter 19

Meg's search continued that evening without success at Lady Erskine's rout. A success of a different sort, though, seemed to be hers all evening, as she found herself almost constantly surrounded by a group of attentive young gentlemen. The same held true when she and Gram moved on to the Montrose ball. Within five minutes of greeting their host and hostess, Meg had promised a half-dozen dances.

She danced a waltz with Lord Bellingham, who stood a good half foot shorter than Meg but did not seem to mind. The way his eyes darted to her bosom with alarming frequency, she began to understand why her height mattered so little. She danced a cotillion with Mr. Soames, a gentleman closer to her own height but who stuttered and stammered through the most vacuous conversation. She was partnered in a country dance with Sir John Cunningham, who used each movement that brought them together to whisper words of flattery in her ears.

She found herself breathless after the lively country dance, and determined to sit out the next one. Lord Edmund Foote begged her company during the set, and she sent him to procure a glass of punch. As he left, Meg looked about for an empty bench, and caught a glimpse of Eugenia Willoughby talking with a group of ladies. Guilty for having abandoned Eugenia at the Grosvenor House reception, Meg went straight to her side. Eugenia was happy to see her and pulled her into the circle of conversation, which centered around the latest fashions.

After a moment, a tiny brown-haired woman came forward to greet Eugenia. Everyone seemed to know her, except Meg, who was introduced to the Marchioness of Pemerton.

"Oh!" Meg said as she bobbed a curtsy. "I have heard much about you, my lady."

"Indeed?" The largest hazel eyes Meg had ever seen smiled up at her. "And though I did not know your name, I believe I have heard much about you, Miss Ashburton. You are, of course, the tall red-haired beauty who has taken the *ton* by storm."

Meg shrugged and felt her cheeks color.

"Perhaps you would care to stroll with me for a bit," Lady Pemerton said, "and tell me what it is you have heard about me."

Meg smiled down at the diminutive marchioness. "I would love to." She nodded to the group of women as she stepped away with Lady Pemerton.

As they walked side by side, the marchioness began to chuckle. "My, what a pair we must make," she said. "The shortest lady in the room with the tallest." She laughed again. "Well, let them all stare and wonder what on earth we have in common."

"We have a friend in common, I think," Meg said. "Lord Sedgewick. While he convalesced at our farm at Thornhill, he spoke often of Lord Pemerton. He also mentioned his friend's delightful new bride. I believe you were only recently married?"

"Yes, only seven months ago," Lady Pemerton said, nodding at a passing acquaintance. "And you are correct.

Sedge is one of Jack's closest friends. And now mine, too."

"Then, may I ask you something, my lady?"

"Of course," she said. She stopped and turned to face Meg. "But only if you agree to call me Mary. Since we have a close friend in common, we should be friends as well."

"Thank you, Mary. And my name is Meg."

"What was it you wanted to ask me, Meg?" the marchioness said as they began to walk again.

Meg looked down at her toes and hesitated. "I ... I heard something rather disturbing this evening. About Sedge, that is."

"Disturbing?"

"Yes. You see, I encountered his cousin, Mr. Albert Herriot, earlier at Grosvenor House. He indicated that Sedge had ... well, had become something of a ... a drunkard."

"Oh, dear," Mary said as they skirted a group of young men who were laughing boisterously and slapping one another on the back. She lowered her voice. "I hope he is not spreading that tale all over Town."

"To tell you the truth," Meg said, "he was a bit on the fly himself, so I was not sure how much to believe."

Mary placed her hand on Meg's arm and pulled her away slightly from the groups of people that clustered along the edges of the ballroom, so they could be more private. "I can only tell you that Jack had also been quite concerned about Sedge. He was apparently very depressed about ... about something, and did seek solace in drink. But Jack assures me that Sedge has come around. He seemed to be more of himself when I saw him earlier this evening."

"You saw him this evening?" Meg's heart began to beat an erratic tattoo.

"Yes, we met him leaving just as we arrived here."

"He was here?" Meg's voice rose to something close to a squeal.

Mary smiled and patted Meg's arm where her hand still rested. "I am afraid you missed him, my dear."

"Oh." Meg felt like a deflated balloon. He had been here. Damnation, she had missed him. "But, if he was here, then Mr. Herriot must have been wrong. He is not sitting home alone, with the knocker removed, drinking himself into a stupor."

"Is that what Mr. Herriot said?"

Meg nodded.

"The idiot!" Mary exclaimed. "He had no business telling you, or anyone, such things about his own cousin."

"That was not all he told me."

"Good heavens," Mary said. "What else?"

"He said that Sedge had almost killed himself by setting fire to his bed curtains."

Mary's big eyes widened in surprise. "He told you that?"

"Yes. He seemed very ... very distressed by it all."

Mary heaved a sigh. "Listen to me, Meg. You must not repeat that story to anyone. *Not to anyone.* I am surprised Mr. Herriot told you. In fact," she said, her brows puckering up in concern, "I am surprised he even knew of it. You see, Jack was there when it happened. It was ... an unfortunate incident. Best forgotten. They had agreed it would be kept secret, to save Sedge from embarrassment." She lifted her shoulders in a slight shrug. "But Mr. Herriot is Sedge's cousin, after all, so maybe he confided in him. But the point is, it must go no further. If you care for Sedge,"—her hazel eyes bored into Meg's—"then you will not repeat what you heard."

"Of course not," Meg said, her cheeks heating up again. "And anyway, Mr. Herriot—"

"There you are!"

Meg turned to find Lord Edmund Foote holding two glasses of punch. Good heavens, she had forgotten all about him. "Oh, I am sorry, Lord Edmund," she said, offering a contrite smile. "I had not meant to disappear like that. I am afraid I became engrossed in a conversation with Lady Pemerton." She took the glass of punch he held out to her.

"Lady Pemerton," he said, bowing slightly, "may I offer you a glass of punch?"

"You are most kind, Lord Edmund," she said, flashing him a huge smile, "but I really must run my husband to ground. We are expected at Lady Dunholm's." She turned to Meg. "It has been a pleasure, Meg. Please call on me one day soon. We're at Hanover Square."

"Thank you, Mary."

The marchioness nodded and turned to walk away.

Lord Edmund raised his glass to Meg in salute and smiled. "Was that Albert Herriot I heard you discussing when I approached?" he asked.

"We mentioned him," Meg said.

"A friend of yours?"

"An acquaintance," Meg replied. "He spent some time recently at our farm."

"Ah, the famous Thornhill," Lord Edmund said. "Lucky devil."

Meg hunched a shoulder and took a sip of punch.

"Or perhaps not so very lucky just now," he continued.

Meg raised her brows in question, her glass poised midway to her mouth as she prepared to take another sip of punch.

"Frightful luck at the tables," Lord Edmund said. "Bad show, I'm afraid. Oh, I say, I hope that brother of yours ain't offering Herriot credit toward a bit of horseflesh. Couldn't pay if he wanted to. Up to his ears, I hear. Dun territory and all that."

"Oh, dear." Meg began to understand why Mr. Herriot might have been drunk and angry, if his life was in fact in such disorder. Poor man. Perhaps she had misjudged him.

"So, tell me, Miss Ashburton, would you like to drive in the Park with me tomorrow?"

"I would be delighted, my lord." Meg smiled at the anxious young man as he began to chatter on about his new curricle and pair.

* * *

Sedge had not found Meg on his first night out of the Season. He had heard of her, though. Everywhere he went, there were whisperings about the glorious Miss Ashburton. Her name seemed to be on the lips of every unmarried—and some married—gentlemen of the ton. She had certainly made her mark, his beautiful wallflower. He had known she would. He only wished he had been able to present her as his own, to lead her into a ballroom on his arm, acknowledged by one and all as his intended bride. Instead, if he was really interested in pursuing her, it appeared as though he would have to insinuate his way into her circle of admirers, and compete alongside the rest of them.

The notion of competing for her made him almost angry. He had courted her for weeks at Thornhill. He had stated his intentions. Despite the fact that she had turned him down, he felt he should have some sort of precedence. And what was she doing in London anyway? She had made it abundantly clear that she hated the very idea of another Season. He was at a loss to explain her actions. But obsessed enough with her to keep searching.

And luck was with Sedge on his second night out. From the moment he entered the Portland ball, he knew she was there.

"Did you see what Miss Ashburton is wearing?"

"Have you ever seen anyone so elegant in all your life?"

"Where do you suppose she's been hiding all these years."

"I think I am in love."

"Do you suppose Miss Ashburton would dance with me?"

"I have written a sonnet on the color of her eyes."

"She is *not* too tall. She is a goddess."

"Who is she dancing with?"

"Is she wearing yellow roses? I sent her yellow roses."

"I see The Ashburton has gathered her court."

"Will she throw us a crumb, do you think?"

By the time Sedge had reached the ballroom, he was heartily sick of Miss Ashburton. Could this Incomparable possibly be the same intriguing young woman he had known at Thornhill? The one who shunned Society and convention, who dressed and behaved as she pleased? The one without artifice who seemed so unaware of her own beauty? Without having yet even laid eyes on her, he felt this new Meg Ashburton was not the same woman he had fallen in love with. Somehow, she had been transformed out of all recognition into a Society coquette, one who apparently dangled a court of admirers and caused a stir wherever she went.

Sedge wanted to turn and run and forget all about her. But he must see her first. Just one more time. Perhaps if he saw for himself what she had become, he could get her out of his system once and for all.

And then he saw her.

She towered above all the other ladies and most of the gentlemen, her red hair blazing like a beacon. She was standing in a corner of the ballroom, surrounded by a dozen young swains—Bellingham, Soames, Lamb, Cunningham, Foote, Marsden, and others he could not identify. Her profile was to him, and Sedge stared for several moments in admiration of the classic lines of her nose and jaw, the chin held high over the long curve of her neck. Her hair, burnished to a fiery glow by the candlelight of a nearby torchère, was worn higher on her head than usual, giving the impression of even greater height. He could see nothing below the tops of her shoulders, which appeared quite bare. All he could see was luminous white skin, tickled by curling coppery strands that escaped at her nape.

Sedge's heart hammered against his chest as he recalled the softness of that white skin beneath his lips, the seductive scent of wild violets lingering on that long, white neck. God, but she was beautiful. The very sight of her singed him all the way to his toes.

As Sedge watched, Sir John Cunningham's lascivious gaze slid from her delicious sherry eyes, to her full lips, and down over each shapely curve of her body. The blackguard! How dare the man denigrate his woman with such vile attentions?

But she was not *his* woman. She had rejected him.

He watched her from across the room before he began moving slowly, inexorably toward her busy corner. What would he say to her? What would she say to him? Based on their last encounter, Sedge could not be sure that she would not give him the cut direct.

I am sorry, my lord, but I cannot accept your offer.

Her words rang in his head as he came nearer to her circle. He watched as she threw back her head and laughed, then flirted with her fan with two young men standing near. How could she have rejected him so coldly, and then flirt so easily with all those young fribbles? Had she merely been toying with him at Thornhill? Practicing her wiles on him? Using him to hone her irresistible charms before descending upon London in all her glory? London, with its wider selection of willing gentlemen. Gentlemen more appealing than Sedge.

Sedge had wanted Meg Ashburton more than any other woman he had ever known. But she had made a fool of him. A thousand kinds of fool. As he watched her laugh and flirt and tease like the most accomplished coquette, he feared she might do so again. Was doing so now. Sedge suddenly felt almost sick to his stomach. He did not think he could stand to watch much longer.

* * *

Meg was enjoying herself. She had gathered quite a crowd of young men this evening. All of them were in high spirits, laughing and joking and flirting outrageously. None of them seemed the least bit serious, so she had allowed herself to join in their fun.

She turned her head to listen to something Lord Bellingham was saying, and her heart gave a sudden leap. Over a sea of heads stretching across the width of the ballroom, a shock of familiar golden hair rose above the rest and a pair of piercing blue eyes stared straight into hers.

The instant their eyes met, Meg's pulse began to race and a surge of heat coursed through her body. She experienced a giddy joy at the familiar and wonderful sight of him, more certain than ever that she had made the right decision. None of the gentlemen surrounding her now— these young men who had flirted with her, flattered her, danced with her, sent her flowers, wrote poems to her— none of them had made the tiniest dent in her heart. It belonged completely to this man who glared at her so intensely just now. And she must waste no time in telling him so.

"Sedge." She mouthed the name silently as he continued to stare at her with that strangely serious expression. She turned fully toward him and smiled, her knees ready to melt at the first sign of his own devastating smile.

But it did not come. Sedge did not smile. Meg raised her brows, beckoning him. But he did not even acknowledge her presence. Meg's heart began to pound with uncertainty and she clutched her fan tightly in trembling hands. What was the matter? Why did he just stare and stare like that, his forehead creased with a frown? Had her rejection of his offer of *carte blanche* angered him somehow? Or perhaps it was embarrassment? Or even disappointment that she should be so prudish and unsophisticated? Oh, but she must tell him he was wrong, that she had changed her mind. She must tell him!

Meg lifted a hand toward Sedge in a gesture of welcome, smiling uncertainly. *Please come to me, Sedge.*

To her astonishment, he turned on his heels and quit the room.

Meg winced involuntarily, as if she had been physically struck. As she watched him walk away she heard one of the thin ivory sticks of her fan crack beneath her fingers.

Chapter 20

Sedge moved through the crowded ballroom in something of a daze. Vaguely aware that acquaintances here and there beckoned to him or greeted him, he navigated the crush of people like a nag with blinders. He would not be deterred from his single-minded purpose: escape. He desperately needed fresh air, for he was feeling very warm and the knot in his stomach had become so tight he thought he might truly become ill. He headed outside through the first set of French doors he encountered.

Sedge found himself on a large terrace. He stood still for a moment, tilted his head back, and breathed deeply of the cool night air. Hopefully, the fresh air would calm his wretched stomach, his racing heart, and his spinning head. His poor brain was not used to so many complications. He felt as confused as he had when Meg had rejected him. But this time, it was his own reaction that confused him.

He wanted her, did he not? He had behaved like a bloody fool over her, so apparently he did. And her eyes had beckoned him, had they not? Clearly and openly. Then, why had he stalked off like that?

Sedge wandered over to the balustrade overlooking the lantern-lit garden below, and considered that he was probably the world's biggest fool. A fool who could not seem to make up his mind. He wanted Meg Ashburton. But when he saw her surrounded by all those prigs and popinjays, somehow he did not want her anymore. Was that it? Or maybe he simply preferred to have her all to himself, as he had at Thornhill. Strange. He had never been afraid of a little competition before now, and he seldom suffered from jealousy. What was wrong with him? He did not seem to know whether he was coming or going.

"Sedge?"

His shoulders flinched at the sound of the achingly familiar voice. Sedge was not sure he could turn around without scooping her up in his arms. Despite everything, he still wanted to do that.

He kept his hands on the balustrade and simply turned to look over his shoulder. "Hullo, Meg." After one brief look, he whipped his head back around and fixed his gaze on the garden below. One quick glance told him she looked more beautiful than ever, wearing that shimmery, clingy blue thing, cut low at the bosom with a neckline so wide it merely skimmed the tops of her white shoulders. If he had not torn his eyes away, he might have found himself leering at her in much the same way as Cunningham had done.

Meg moved to stand next to him, her shoulder almost brushing his as she, too, gazed out into the garden. Sedge ached to touch her, but kept his hands clutched tightly around the top railing of the balustrade. She did not speak right away, and he closed his eyes, pretending she was not there. But he was not very good at pretending, and the fragrance of wild violets assaulted his nose.

"I have the next set free," Meg said.

Oh, God.

"I—I'm sorry." He turned toward her slightly, but without looking her in the eye. "It's my leg. I—I cannot dance. My leg ... is still a bit stiff. I'm sorry. I... I would have loved to dance with you, Meg." As he spoke her name, his gaze at last lifted to meet hers, and he found himself drowning once again in those sherry eyes. Oh, God, had she really wanted to dance with him? Did that mean she was willing to give him another chance?

"I am glad, at least, to see you no longer need crutches," she said, her voice soft and her eyes locked to his. "I have wondered how you were doing."

"You have?"

"Yes. Often. Are you able to walk a bit? I am not used to these overheated ballrooms. Would you stroll in the garden with me, Sedge?"

If she had asked him to jump over the moon, he could not have been more surprised. After a startled moment, the corners of his mouth twitched up, and all at once his face arranged itself in the familiar smile for the first time in weeks. He turned and held out his arm. "I would be delighted," he said, straining to curb his excitement, his impatience to be alone with her again.

Meg smiled and took Sedge's arm, and they walked down one of the twin sets of stone steps that curved into a horseshoe as they reached the garden below. Though only a sliver of moon shone in the sky, the garden was hung throughout with strategically placed paper lanterns, creating intimate pools of illumination. They walked in silence from one pool of light to the next, through a series of formal gardens bordered with clipped yew hedges taller than either one of them. They passed other strolling couples, and a few couples otherwise occupied, until the lanterns became fewer and finally disappeared altogether.

Sedge steered Meg into an arbor lit only by the crescent moon and swung her into his arms.

"Sedge, I—"

He stopped her words with his lips. Slanting his mouth across hers, first in one direction, then the other, he explored, enticed, incited. He felt her arms snake around his neck as he deepened the kiss. She was every bit as sensuous, as passionate, as sweet-tasting as he remembered. She opened her lips freely and his tongue swept inside, circling, stroking, fencing with her own. He drank in the sweet, hot taste of her, and all the doubts and concerns of a few minutes before evaporated as quickly as frost on a sun-kissed windowpane. Sedge knew without question that this was the woman he wanted for his wife.

When his lips left hers and moved to the long column of her neck and down to the irresistible expanse of white shoulders, Meg began to mutter faint protests. "Please, please," she begged, arching away from Sedge, who took advantage of the access to her exposed bosom. He trailed kisses along the soft mounds of her full breasts, above the silky neckline of midnight blue—so dark against such white skin—and dipped his tongue down into the valley between them. Her breath became labored. But still, she protested.

"Please, not here," she said in a tremulous voice. "Not now. I... I just wanted to talk to you."

Sedge continued his exploration, back up to her neck and jaw. "Talk," he said between kisses. "I'm listening."

"No. Please, Sedge. No."

Meg squirmed in Sedge's arms, and he realized he had lost his head. He had never forced a woman in his life, and certainly had no wish to force this woman. He would do nothing to dishonor Meg. He wanted her to come to him willingly, as his wife. He stepped back at once, but kept his hands on her upper arms. "I'm sorry, Meg. Blame it on that dress. You are quite irresistible."

She blushed. How could such a remark cause her to blush after the heated kiss they had just shared? Sedge grinned.

"I... I wanted to talk about... about what we discussed the day you left Thornhill."

Sedge's heart did a somersault in his chest. She had changed her mind! "Yes?" he prompted, keeping his voice as level as possible.

"Well," she continued, dropping her eyes, as if suddenly bashful, "I have been giving it a lot of thought. Your... your offer, that is."

"Is that so?" Banking his excitement, Sedge nevertheless thought he might explode with joy. But he would not rush her. Let her say what she wanted to say, what he desperately wanted to hear. Only then would he crush her soft breasts against his chest once again.

"Yes," Meg said. "I have had time to ... to reconsider." She raised her eyes to his. "If you are still interested, that is."

Sedge squeezed her arms. "Oh, Meg—"

"I am willing to be your mistress."

The earth seemed to have stopped spinning and slammed him abruptly to the ground. He dropped his hands from her arms as though stung. "What?"

"I said I am willing to be your mistress, Sedge."

"No!" He could not have heard correctly. His mistress? "No." He shook his head in disbelief. How could she think that was what he had wanted from her? How could she believe he would be willing to treat her so dishonorably? A gently bred, innocent young woman like Meg. "No." Or was she not so innocent after all? Had he been an even bigger fool than he had thought? Images of her surrounded by a circle of men formed in his mind, flirting with each of them while they ogled her bosom. What had become of the sweet, blushing, artless woman he had fallen in love with at Thornhill? Dumbfounded by her startling suggestion, he could only shake his head slowly, back and forth, refusing to believe that the woman he wanted for his wife was only interested in being his mistress. "No. No!"

Meg's hand flew to her mouth as Sedge shook his head and looked at her as if she had sprouted wings. "No," he kept repeating, as if she were feebleminded and needed to hear the word over and over before understanding.

But Meg was not feebleminded. She understood perfectly.

Mortified, she choked back tears as she turned and fled, following the trail of lanterns that wound through the gardens. She wished the earth would open up and swallow her, for she did not think she could bear the shame.

After thoughtfully and logically concluding that she could, and perhaps should, accept his offer, she had shamelessly thrown herself at him. It had never occurred to her that he might have changed his mind as well.

Sedge no longer wanted her.

He had kissed her. But only because she had been bold enough to invite him to stroll in the relative privacy of the gardens. What man would not attempt to kiss such a brazen creature? The implication of such an invitation was clear. And so he had kissed her, as any man would have done, under the circumstances.

But that was all he wanted. A stolen kiss in the garden. Nothing more. He was no longer interested in a more intimate relationship. She had had her one chance, and she had refused it. He was not giving her a second chance. Sedge was no longer interested in her in that way. He did not need her anymore, as he had thought he did at Thornhill, where she was the only young woman for miles around. He had returned to London, where the number of willing women was legion. He probably had some other doxy already set up in his love nest. Another woman whose arms would welcome him this very evening, after dallying with Meg in the garden.

It was the second time this man had mortified her beyond imagining.

Meg hurried from one pool of lantern light to the next until she had reached the horseshoe steps once again. She stood at the base of the steps, dabbed at her eyes, and pinched her cheeks so that she might appear reasonably normal when she reentered the ballroom. She lifted the skirts of her gown and slowly climbed the steps, her shoulders straight and her chin raised. She would leave this ball with her dignity, if not her heart, intact.

Upon entering the French doors, she could see several gentlemen preparing to rush to her side. Ignoring them, she turned in the other direction and began searching for her brother. Her eyes skimmed the room in a wide arc, finally resting upon Terrence's familiar auburn hair as he handed an unknown young lady through the steps of a cotillion. The set should be almost over. Meg kept her eyes fixed on Terrence while she moved along the edge of the dance floor closer to where he danced. He caught her eye as he twirled in her direction. Meg sent him an imploring look which he acknowledged with a brief nod. She kept herself buried amongst the crowd until the set ended, fobbing off anyone who attempted to engage her in conversation. She only waited for her brother to take her home, she explained, for she had developed a splitting headache.

Satisfied that Terrence would come to her, Meg began searching the clusters of older women—mothers, chaperones, dowagers—who gathered about in groups, gossiping and watching the younger set on the dance floor. Though Meg's height afforded her a clear view of the room from one end to the other, Gram was not so fortunate in her stature. Her short, plump figure was nowhere to be seen at the moment. She might be seated, which meant that Meg could be required to traverse the entire room in order to locate her.

But first she must speak to Terrence and have him bring their carriage round.

Thinking the set might never end, Meg had worked herself into quite a state by the time Terrence came to her side. She really did have a headache now, no doubt from the effort of reining in her emotions. The sting of tears began to build up behind her eyes. The last thing she wanted was to break down in public. If she did not get out of here quickly, she might do just that.

"What is it, Meggie?" Terrence asked. He laid a gentle hand on her arm and lowered his voice to a whisper. "You don't look so good."

"I do not feel so good," Meg replied. "I have a blistering headache. If I locate Gram, could you call for the carriage? I really must get home before I collapse."

"Oh, poor Meggie." He lifted a hand to stroke her cheek. "You do look a bit pinched. I'll take you home, love. But let me take you to Gram, first. She was just over here last time I saw her."

Terrence took Meg's elbow and steered her toward a group of dowagers seated near one of the fireplaces, their plumed and turbaned heads bent together in lively discussion. Gram sat in the middle of the group, pink plumes bobbing as she listened intently to one of the other ladies. "Excuse me, Gram?" At Terrence's words, feathers righted and eyes swiveled in his direction.

"Hello, my dears," Gram said, beaming with pride at her two grandchildren. "Are you acquainted with—"

"I'm sorry, ma'am," Terrence interrupted. "But Meg is feeling a bit out of curl. Would you help her to the cloakroom while I see about the carriage?"

Gram sprung up like a marionette manipulated from above. She studied Meg with concerned eyes. "Oh, my poor girl," she said, stepping to Meg's side. "You have been overdoing it, my dear. I was afraid all these busy nights would catch up with you. Come," she said, taking Meg's arm from Terrence. "Let's get you home. I will tuck you up all right and tight, and prepare you a nice tisane to help you sleep."

Terrence hurried away to send for their carriage while Gram walked Meg slowly through the ballroom. Meg kept her head bowed, avoiding the eyes of anyone who dared to approach, though Gram kept most of the interested gentlemen at bay with a stern look. They walked through to the main reception area, where Gram flagged down a footman to retrieve their cloaks.

"It is too bad that we cannot say our proper thank yous to the duke and duchess," Gram said as her eyes scanned the crowd milling about the reception area. "But I doubt they will even miss us in this squeeze. I will send a note round to Her Grace tomorrow. It was a lovely ball, was it not?"

"Yes," Meg muttered, wondering how much longer she could maintain her composure when her heart was breaking and would surely start bleeding all over the floor at any moment.

"Oh, my dear," Gram said as she gently patted Meg's arm. "You really are feeling ill, are you not? Let us hope your brother has the carriage ready. One can only hope that the traffic will have thinned out a bit from the mad crush when we arrived."

The footman returned with their cloaks, and the two ladies made their way down the sweeping marble staircase. Terrence met them at the entry and—thank God!—had the carriage waiting. He handed Meg and Gram into the coach before jumping in himself to take the seat opposite. Meg kept her eyes closed on the short trip to Duke Street, where Terrence had leased a town house for the Season. No doubt believing her asleep or ill, neither her grandmother nor her brother spoke during the trip home.

As the coach bounced along the streets of Mayfair, Meg directed her thoughts away from the full mortification of her encounter with Sedge. She concentrated on the jostling ride, the soft velvet of the squabs that cushioned each bounce, the regular clip-clop of the horses hooves on the cobblestones, and squeezed her eyes more tightly to hold back the tears that threatened to fall.

* * *

Sedge wandered aimlessly through the dark edges of the garden, feeling as though he had walked into someone else's dream. Nothing made any sense. Nothing. First, Meg coldly rejected an honorable offer of marriage. Then stunned him with this latest offer of her own. On occasion, Sedge had had to deal with mistresses who had designs on being wives. Never had he thought to find a woman he wanted as a wife who had designs on being his mistress. It did not make any sense.

These last few months did not make any sense. It had all started with that stupid carriage accident. Sedge absently reached up to finger the scar over his left temple. Perhaps that knock on the head had done more damage after all. Perhaps the brain fever had affected his reason. Dear God, perhaps he was no longer completely sane. Was that not possible? He had heard of blows to the head severe enough to result in brain damage. Is that what had happened to him?

He came upon a rustic wood bench and plopped down upon it. Still touching his scar, Sedge began to consider the very real possibility that his reasoning had been impaired by his accident. It was the only explanation. Try as he might, he could not seem to make sense of anything. Meg's behavior, now and at Thornhill, proved to be a complete enigma. His own feelings had become so jumbled he no longer even knew what he wanted. One minute he wanted her, the next minute he did not.

He felt helpless to reason through anything. He could not seem to logically consider the situation in his usual plodding but pragmatic way, because he simply did not understand it. Nothing about it seemed logical.

Sedge rose and ambled his way through the garden, determined to return to the house, fetch his cloak and hat, and take his leave. Assuming he could find his way. He no longer had any confidence in his mental faculties. Perhaps he would wander, hopelessly lost, for hours until some kind soul came to his rescue. Poor old Sedge, they would say. We have to keep an eye on him now, since he is not able to look out for himself.

But soon enough, he found himself at the base of the horseshoe steps. He had made his way after all. Somehow. Not bad, he thought, for a pitiful half-wit.

Now, if he could just get the hell out of here without further embarrassing himself.

Chapter 21

Meg maintained a stoic silence as her maid helped her out of the dark blue silk gown. She had been so proud of this gown. It had made her feel sophisticated and worldly. Now, she could not wait to be rid of it.

How she wished she were at Thornhill, where she could pull on a pair of breeches and take Bristol Blue for a brisk gallop. But there was nowhere in Town that accommodated such neck-or-nothing freedom. Or such blessed solitude. She would have to make do with the privacy of her bedchamber. If only Pansy, her maid, would hurry.

While Pansy brushed the gown and carefully hung it in the wardrobe, chattering all the while, Meg began to unpin her hair. The maid then unlaced Meg's stays, helped her out of her chemise, and dropped a fresh muslin nightgown over her head.

After dismissing Pansy, Meg dragged herself across the room. All at once, the pent-up emotions of the evening burst forth in a torrent of tears as she flung herself facedown on the bed. She cried for her broken heart, her naïveté, and her foolish pride. She let the full force of her jumbled emotions— shame, heartache, confusion—expend themselves in great wracking sobs, soaking the linen sheets beneath her face.

It was in this state of abject misery that Gram found Meg when she entered with an herbal tisane.

"Good heavens, my dear," Gram said as she rushed into the room, leaving the door slightly ajar in her haste. Quickly depositing the teacup on the nightstand, she sat down on the bed, lifted Meg's shoulders, and pulled her granddaughter into her arms. "There, there," she said in a soothing voice as she rocked Meg against her plump breast, as she had done so many times when Meg was a girl.

"Oh, G-Gr-Gram!" Meg stammered through her tears.

"Hush, now," Gram said, holding Meg's head down against her shoulder while gently stroking her hair. "Do not try to talk yet. You just have a good cry first."

And Meg did. She had no idea how long she wept in Gram's comfortable arms. But some time later, feeling drained, she pulled away and rubbed the heels of her hands against her eyes. She sat thus for several minutes, breathing deeply to combat the hiccups that followed the tears. All the while, Gram's hand massaged up and down her back in gentle circles.

"What is it, Meggie? Can you tell your old Gram what happened to upset you so?"

"Oh, Gram." Meg kept her eyes covered. "It is Lord S-Sedgewick."

The soothing hand moving on Meg's back came to an abrupt stop. "Lord Sedgewick? Have you seen him, then? What has he done?" Gram pulled Meg's hands away from her eyes and forced her to look up. "Meg, what has he done to you?"

"N-Nothing."

"Meg! You must tell me." Gram took a deep breath and her voice became less agitated. "Please, love, you must tell me. Has that young man done something to ... to hurt you?"

"No, no," Meg said, still battling hiccoughs. "It's m-me. Not h-him. It's all m-my fault. Oh, Gr-Gram! What have I d-done?"

"I do not know, love. What have you done?"

And so Meg told her. She told Gram everything. From the beginning, and leaving nothing out. She told how she had fallen in love with Sedge six years before, and how she had done so again. How that love had deepened during the times they had spent together at Thornhill. How she began to hope that he might have some feelings for her as well. How he had kissed her. How she had felt when he kissed her. And how he had offered her *carte blanche*.

*   *   *

After bringing Meg and Gram home to Duke Street, Terrence had retired to his study, where he indulged in a glass of brandy. The night was early yet, and he had plans to meet some friends later at Boodle's. But he did not wish to leave without first making sure that Meg was all right.

Poor girl. She had looked so down-pin. Meg was seldom ill. She enjoyed the vigorous, blooming health of a girl raised in the country who got more than her share of exercise. It was likely the fast pace and late hours of life in Town had finally had its effect on her. That, and the wretched air, and the rich food, and too much drink, and not enough exercise. It was a wonder anyone could remain healthy in such circumstances. Though he enjoyed coming to Town on occasion, Terrence always looked forward to his return to Thornhill. He supposed he was a country gentleman at heart, and always would be.

He took the last swallow of brandy and rose from his comfortable leather chair. He should check on Meg. She had had enough time to change clothes and crawl into bed. He would just peek in to see that she was all right.

As he approached the landing on the second floor, he could hear Meg's sobs. Horrible, gut-wrenching sobs that tore at his heart. As he neared her bedchamber, he heard his grandmother's soft voice through the partially open door. "There, there," she was saying.

Unwilling to intrude, Terrence entered his own bedchamber, just across the hall. He had never heard his sister cry like that. He had never heard anyone cry like that. What on earth had happened? He must ask Gram later. He did not imagine Meg would appreciate his barging in to see what was the matter. Besides, he was not very good with crying women. He never knew what to do or say, and always felt awkward and embarrassed. He would let Gram comfort her. Poor Meggie, she sounded so miserable.

He puttered around his bedchamber for some minutes, hoping Meg's tears would have ended by the time he entered the hallway again. He examined his cravat and decided it looked limp from the exertions of the Portland ball. He pulled out a fresh stack of neckcloths, untangled the one from his neck, and began the task of arranging a perfect Mathematical.

Satisfied, after three tries, that the folds were flawless, Terrence surveyed the rest of his attire in the cheval glass. After dusting a piece of lint from his sleeve, he was ready to go. Entering the hallway outside his bedchamber door, he heard the voices of Gram and Meg. At least his sister seemed to have stopped crying. Thank goodness. Meg was not the crying sort, and it gave him a twinge of concern to think what might have caused such wretched sobs.

As he closed his own bedchamber door and turned to head down the hall to the landing, an overheard snippet of conversation in Meg's room stopped him up short.

"He asked you to be his mistress?" Gram said, her voice rising on the last word.

"Yes," Meg replied in a soft, quavering voice. "He offered me *carte blanche*. He even mentioned a house, jewels, and carriages."

Terrence stood unmoving in the middle of the hallway, his hands balled into fists at his side. Someone had offered

Meg a slip on the shoulder? Who, by God? What scoundrel had so insulted his only sister?

"Good heavens," Gram said. "I am afraid I truly misjudged that young man. He seemed so amiable. I would never have expected Lord Sedgewick to suggest such a sordid arrangement."

Sedgewick! Good God. How dare he!

Terrence moved away from the door, afraid to hear any more details. Afraid to vent his anger in front of Meg, in case she might misconstrue it as directed at her. He hurried down the two flights of stairs to the entry hall. Sedgewick must have been at the Portland ball. That is why poor Meggie was so upset that she had to leave. How dare he insult her so!

As Terrence entered the carriage that had waited on the street in front of the town house, he suffered an anger stronger than any he had felt in his life. Dear, sweet, beautiful Meg. Innocent Meg. How could any man presume to make her such an offer? And Sedgewick, of all people. A man who had accepted Terrence's own hospitality. Who had been rescued and nursed back to health in Terrence's home. Who had spent hours and hours alone under the same roof with his sister.

Oh, God. How far had he taken his insults? Had he attempted to seduce Meg at Thornhill?

Terrence recollected the warnings of Sedgewick's cousin Albert Herriot. He had thought them ridiculous at the time. It had never occurred to him, never once, that Herriot might be right. Even worse, it had never occurred to him that Meg would inspire that sort of attention.

How could he have been so blind? She had grown into a beautiful woman. He knew that. He had recognized that for some time now, especially when some of the stablehands ogled her long legs clad in a pair of his own breeches. But she had always seemed like such a... a tomboy. He had simply never imagined she would willingly receive any man's particular attentions.

What a fool he had been. Since coming to London—and for the first time he thought he understood why she had wanted to come—he had seen her for the beautiful young woman she was. He had seen men drawn to her like bumblebees to red clover. And he had watched her handle her circle of admirers with ease. When had she grown up so?

But he had known about Sedgewick. Herriot had warned him. He had known, and had done nothing to stop it. My God, what had he done? How could he have allowed such a thing to happen to his sister?

Oh, Meg. Please forgive me.

The more he thought about Sedgewick, the angrier he became. The man had seduced the entire family. Gram doted on him. Terrence himself had liked him immensely. He had used that dammit-all smile to twist them all around his finger.

By Jove, he would have satisfaction from that blackhearted scoundrel. The man would be exposed for what he was: a charlatan and seducer of innocent young women. Terrence would see Sedgewick dead or exiled, he cared not which, so long as he never laid eyes on the bastard again.

Terrence had never felt a hatred of such pagan intensity. His preference would be to kill the rascal with his bare hands. To put his fingers around his throat and throttle him until the last breath was squeezed from his body.

But he could not do that. Justified as he was, he could not do that. Like all gentlemen, he was bound by the rigid rules of honor. But he would get satisfaction. By God, he would.

As the carriage wound its way through the traffic outside the Portland ball, Terrence pulled off his right glove and began absently slapping its fingers against his left palm.

* * *

Meg sat up in her bed, pillows propped up high behind her. Gram sat at her side, holding her hand, legs stretched out next to Meg's. Two sets of bare toes peeked out from beneath white muslin nightgowns.

Gram had been so wonderful. Meg did not know why she had kept all her worries to herself for so long. Sharing them with Gram was akin to purging her soul of shame and heartache. She felt so much better, so much less stupid. For Gram had understood. She had not scolded or lectured or belittled the matter. She had understood.

"I remember the first time my Henry kissed me," Gram said.

"Grandpa?"

"Yes, though he was no one's grandpa yet, of course. He was not even my husband." Gram smiled as her eyes gazed off into some private distance. "He was so handsome. I think I loved him from the moment I clapped eyes on him. One day he took me for a walk in my father's garden. He took me into the shell grotto—you know the one, Meggie—and kissed me." She chuckled softly and squeezed Meg's hand. "I had never been kissed before, and I thought it was the most wonderful thing in the world. I actually thought my knees would buckle and send me sprawling."

"Yes!" Meg said. "That's exactly it. That's how Sedge made me feel when he kissed me. That and ... well, that and more."

"Suddenly warm and tingly all over? Especially here?" Gram laid her free hand just below her belly.

Meg felt her cheeks flush. "Yes."

"Sweetheart, don't be embarrassed. All women feel that way. With the right man."

"But don't you see?" Meg said. "That is precisely why I

thought Sedge was the right man. Why I so shamelessly threw myself at him. He made me feel that way. He made me tingle from head to toe." Meg blushed again, embarrassed to be speaking of such things. And with her own grandmother! But there was so much she wanted to know. "Gram, does that mean he *is* the right man?"

"Not necessarily," Gram said. "I do not like to believe that a man who would make such a dishonest offer to you could be anyone's right man. It just means that he is the first man to stir something in you. That special something that makes you a woman. Someday, dear, another man will come along who sets your senses on fire. A good man who will treat you right."

"Oh, Gram, I don't know. Look how long it took me to find this one!"

Meg turned her head to catch Gram's eye, and they both burst into laughter.

"But look at ail the young men chasing after you this Season," Gram said when their laughter had subsided. "Why, the drawing room is filled to bursting with flowers. None of them, as I recall, from your precious Lord Sedgewick. Now that you have come to Town again—as I have begged you to for years—you see how popular you are with the gentlemen. Any one of them could be the right man, if only you gave him the chance."

"But none of them makes me feel the way Sedge does," Meg said. "I knew the moment I saw him tonight that none of the other gentlemen would ever affect me the way he does. None of their hand-kissing and poetry and flattery and flowers has touched me in any way. And yet, only looking at Sedge across a crowded ballroom made me weak in the knees. No other man can do that to me."

"But one will," Gram said. "Someday. If you continue to go out socially—and not keep yourself secluded so much at Thornhill—more and more gentlemen will come to your notice. And someday, I promise you, my dear, someday one of them will cause your knees to buckle, just like this unfortunate young man has done."

"Oh, but, Gram. I loved him so!"

"Yes, I know, dear." Gram stretched a plump arm around Meg's shoulders and pulled her closer. "And there is nothing more painful than love."

"I think I would like to return to Thornhill," Meg said, resting her head against her grandmother's.

"I think it best that you not decide just now," Gram said. "You are too heartsore to be thinking clearly. Besides, it may be wiser to remain in Town. I would hate to see you run away."

"Is that what I am doing? Running away?"

"Perhaps," Gram said. "Not only from Lord Sedgewick, but also I think, from yourself. I have never known you to run away from difficulty, Meggie. Look how resolute you are with the horses. You set your mind to something, and you do it."

"You always said I had a stubborn streak as long as my legs."

Gram laughed. "And so you always have. So, set your mind to mending your poor heart and getting on with your life."

"But what if I should run into him again?" Meg asked. "I do not think I could bear it. What should I do?"

"After what he has done, I recommend the cut direct."

Meg curled up against Gram's neck and chuckled.

Chapter 22

"**S**top laughing. Jack. It ain't funny."

"Lord Pemerton waved a dismissive hand, unable to speak through convulsive laughter. Rocking back in his chair in the subscription room at White's, his feet danced a spirited jig against the hardwood floor, while one hand slapped his thigh again and again as he hooted with laughter.

"Jack, please!" Sedge pleaded.

But still his friend laughed. A few other gentlemen were drawn to the merriment and wandered over to see what was the joke.

"What's with Pemerton?" Lord Alvanley asked Sedge, cocking a thumb in Jack's direction. "Seems to have lost a screw, what?"

Jack howled at Alvanley's words and doubled over in renewed peals of laughter.

"I say, Sedgewick," said Poodle Byng, who had sauntered up along with Alvanley, "you really must tell Pemerton to control himself. Not quite the thing, don't you know. Bad *ton*, and all that. Very bad *ton*. What set him off, dear boy?"

"If you don't mind," Sedge replied, irritated to have

gathered a crowd, "it is a private matter."

"Private joke, eh?" Alvanley asked.

"Quite," Sedge said.

"Then, why ain't you laughin'?" Poodle asked in his most practiced drawl while deftly flicking open a snuffbox and delicately lifting a pinch to his nostril.

"I b-beg your pardon, gentlemen," Jack sputtered as he appeared to gain control of himself. "Hope I haven't disturbed your play. It's just that... that..." Another whoop of laughter burst forth before he could continue.

Sedge sincerely wished he had never met up with Jack as he left the Portland ball, that he had never agreed to accompany him to White's, and, most of all, that he had never confessed his fears to him. Up until this very moment, Jack had been the best of friends. But just now, Sedge wanted to plant the man a facer.

"You see, gentlemen," Jack continued when he was able, still grinning from ear to ear like some jackass, "our friend Sedgewick suffered a blow to the head recently."

"Ah, yes," Poodle drawled. "Thought I detected a new scar. Quite ... provocative, Sedgewick."

"And now," Jack went on, a wicked gleam in his eye, "poor Sedge thinks he may have ... may have suffered brain damage. You see, he believes he has lost his mind!" Jack succumbed once again to laughter, wiping tears from his eyes with the edge of a tablecloth.

"What's this about Sedge losing his mind?" Albert Herriot said as he joined the group.

Oh, Lord, Sedge groaned to himself. Not Albert, too. This was all he needed.

"And what, my dear boy, makes you think you've lost your mind?" Alvanley asked, one side of his mouth lifted in a cockeyed grin.

"Wait!" Poodle cried. "Don't tell me. Let me guess." He removed his quizzing glass from the buttonhole of his waistcoat, and tapped it against his chin while he narrowed his eyes in mock contemplation. "I have it!" he announced after a suitably dramatic moment. He raised his chin and lowered his voice. "A woman."

Sedge dropped his head into his hands and groaned while all the gentlemen gathered around him guffawed boisterously.

"Is that it, Sedgewick?" Alvanley asked. "Has one of the fairer sex set your head to spinning?"

Sedge looked up and glared at the portly man but did not respond. God, but he wished he had never come here tonight. He could have just as easily gone home alone to wallow in misery in peace. He did not need all this.

"He has discovered that he doesn't understand women," Jack said, "and believes that means he's lost his mind."

"Ha!" Alvanley exclaimed. "If that were the case, then we'd all be bleedin' idiots."

More general laughter followed, and Sedge felt the corners of his mouth begin to twitch upward into a smile.

"So I have tried to tell him," Jack said. He turned to Sedge and laid a hand on his shoulder. "'Tis the nature of the beast, Sedge. They are trained from the cradle to make a man forget if he's coming or going. It has nothing to do with your powers of reasoning. When a woman enters your life, you might as well throw reason out the window."

"Here, here," Alvanley said, raising a glass in salute.

"So, who's the lucky lady?" Albert asked.

Just then, Poodle was nudged aside by a newcomer. "I say!" he said in an offended tone as he applied the quizzing glass to his eye and raked the man from head to toe.

Sedge looked up to find Meg's brother glaring down at him. Good Lord, this could be awkward, considering the direction the conversation had taken.

"Sir Terrence," he said, nodding a greeting. Sedge turned toward Jack to begin introductions when he heard someone gasp and the room grow suddenly silent. Turning back, he recoiled at the sting of gloves slapped purposefully across his face.

What the devil!

Sedge sprung from his seat and stood facing Sir Terrence Ashburton in the tense silence that followed his assault. The rage emanating from the young man was palpable in its intensity. What on earth was going on?

"Name your seconds, Sedgewick." Without another word, Meg's brother spun on his heels and left the room.

For a few heartbeats, the group of gentlemen did nothing but stare at the retreating back of the angry young man. In the next moment, the room was abuzz with the din of a thousand questions, all directed at Sedge. But he did not hear them. He sank back into his chair, once again experiencing the strange sensation of walking through a dream. This could not be happening. It was not possible. It did not make any sense.

Finally, Jack held up an imperative hand to quiet the group. When he had obtained silence, he turned toward Sedge.

"Sedge," he began in a quiet voice, "who the devil was that and why the devil did he challenge you?"

Sedge swallowed convulsively and stared straight ahead. Though still not completely certain this was not a dream—a nightmare—he reluctantly proceeded to play the part he had been assigned. "It was Sir Terrence Ashburton," he said in a steady voice.

"Ashburton?" Jack's voice rose in surprise. He would know the significance of that name.

"Yes," Albert piped in. "Sedge and I were guests of his recently. At Thornhill. You know, the stud farm."

"Thornhill!" Poodle exclaimed dramatically. "*That* Ashburton. Good heavens, Sedgewick, is this all over some nag?"

"No," Sedge replied, still stunned and confused. "No. I do not know what it is over."

"You don't know why he challenged you?" Alvanley

asked.

"Sedge," Jack said in a conspiratorial whisper, "you saw his sister tonight. Could she have—"

"I don't know! I just don't know."

Jack's eyes darted around the interested group that had now grown two- or threefold. His eyes signaled to Sedge that they would speak of it later, in private.

"There is nothing for it now, old boy," Alvanley said. "He has challenged you. You must fight him. He is not required to state his offense, you know. Unless your seconds can convince his seconds to divulge it."

"I will second you, cuz," Albert said with unexpected enthusiasm, considering their recent disagreements. "In fact, I have a new pair of Mantons you may use. Recessed breech, elevated rib, trigger spring—the best. It's your choice of weapons, after all."

"Thank you, Bertie. But I... I have my own set."

"But, Sedge—"

"You know you can count on me as well," Jack said. "It is the least I can do. As the challenged, you choose the ground as well as the weapons. May I suggest that we repair to either my house or yours to discuss the terms in private."

"Mine," Sedge muttered.

"Good," Jack said as he rose from his chair. "Herriot, you will join us, please. Gentlemen." He nodded at the assembled group as he led Sedge and Albert through the crowded subscription room.

As they descended the brief steps to St. James's Street, Sedge's stomach knotted up once again, as it had earlier in the evening. He was so confused he could not think straight. He had no idea how he managed to put one foot in front of the other. His legs seemed to move of their own accord, like some lifeless automaton. Though the night was clear, he might as well have been walking through a thick fog. Or a nightmare.

How had it come to this? All he ever wanted was to marry Meg, and here he was, about to meet her brother in some secret place at dawn. It was now an affair of honor, whether or not he understood the cause.

And he most certainly did not understand it.

* * *

After Gram left her room, Meg felt decidedly better, though still somewhat overwrought. There was no possibility of sleep. Too many thoughts raced through her head. She sunk deep into the stack of pillows, reviewed all her encounters with Sedge, and considered what she might have said or done in each instance so things might have come out differently.

She appreciated Gram's encouraging and comforting words, but it was not as simple as all that. Gram had never lost the man she loved. Until Grandpa died, that is. She had enjoyed a long, happy life with the only man who had ever kissed her, who made her feel warm and tingly all over. She could not know how hard it was to forget a man like that. Meg did not know how she could ever forget Sedge, how she could ever stop loving him.

She rolled onto her side and flipped a pillow over, savoring its coolness against her cheek. She listened to the sounds of the street below. It was hard to get used to the constant noise of London. It never stopped, even in the wee hours of the morning, she listened to the rhythmic clip-clop of horses and the grating of carriage wheels on the cobblestones and then realized the carriage had stopped in front of their house. She heard muffled voices, footsteps, and then the sound of the front door opening.

Terrence must be home. The sound of someone bounding up the stairs like a Hessian soldier proved her correct. She heard her brother shout for Droggett, his valet, and close his bedchamber door. In that moment, Meg wanted very much to talk to her brother. Needed to talk to him. It had been a long time since they had shared a nice coze. She could not, of course, tell him all she had told Gram. She could not tell about Sedge's offer, or about her offer to Sedge. He was her brother, after all. He would not be at all understanding about such things. But perhaps she could talk to him about returning to Thornhill.

Meg threw back the covers and swung her legs over the side of the bed. She poked her toes around until she had located her slippers, and slid her cold feet into them. Grabbing her wrapper, she tied it about her waist as she opened the door into the hallway.

The sound of Terrence's raised voice gave her a start. Terrence seldom shouted, and almost never at servants. She crept quietly across the hall as the shouting continued, indistinct but obviously angry. Only a word here and there penetrated the thick wooden door. "Insult." "Seconds." "Never." "Pistols." "Sedgewick."

What?

Terrified, Meg shamelessly swung open the door to Terrence's bedchamber.

"... blow a hole through the bastard's—Meg! What are you doing here?"

"Dear God, Terrence, what is going on?"

"Go to bed, Meggie," Terrence snapped. "It is none of your affair."

"Oh, but, Terrence, I think it is."

Terrence handed a wooden box to Droggett. "Take this and do as I asked."

"Yes, sir." The valet cast an uncertain glance at Meg, and then scurried out the door.

"Terrence," Meg said, her voice barely above a whisper, "are you ... are you fighting a ... a duel? With Lord Sedgewick?"

"Stay out of it, Meggie."

"Oh, God!" She began to tremble uncontrollably and

took several steadying breaths to slow her racing heart. "Terrence, how could you! How could you? Why, *why* are you doing this?"

"I have told you to stay out of it, and I mean it."

He shrugged into a plain, dark jacket with fabric-covered buttons, a sharp contrast to the claret-jacket with brass buttons he had worn earlier. Meg had heard that shiny buttons made clear targets in a duel, and the thought made bile rise to her throat. Terrence pushed past Meg and strode toward the door, but she stopped him with a hand on his arm.

"Is it because of me, Terrence? Is it something to do with me?"

"I have to go, Meg. Please, let me go."

"You must call it off! Please, *please* call it off."

"It is too late for that."

The tears gathering on her lashes finally began to fall. "Oh, God," she wailed, "You might be killed."

Terrence pulled her into his arms and rested his cheek against her hair. "I won't be killed, love. I promise you."

"B-But, you might kill him."

Terrence abruptly wrenched away and turned his back on her.

"Is that what you want, Terrence?" she asked, her voice barely above a whisper. "To kill a man whose life we fought so hard to save only a few months ago?"

Without a word, Terrence stormed out the door, down the hallway, and out of the house.

Meg covered her face with her hands and choked back sobs. Crying was useless now. She must think. She must act. She must do something.

She returned to her room and rang for Pansy. The poor girl was probably asleep, but she might be able to help. While she waited for the maid, Meg wore a path in the carpet as she paced nervously. The two people she loved most in the world were about to face one another with pistols. One of them might die. She did not believe she could bear it.

She must put a stop to it. Somehow, she must stop it.

A soft knock was followed by the entrance of Pansy, wide-eyed and clutching a shabby woolen wrapper.

"I am sorry to wake you. Pansy, but—"

"Oh, I weren't asleep, miss. I been restitching that flounce in your lilac silk."

"Good, good. Now, Pansy, I need your help."

Meg told Pansy everything she knew about the duel and asked her to ferret out as much information from Droggett as she could. Especially the time and place. "And, please hurry, Pansy. There is no time to waste."

"Yes, miss." The excited little maid dashed out the door and headed toward the back stairs.

The next half hour was almost unendurable. Meg paced and fretted and cried and wrung her hands until she was in a more agitated state than ever. What would she do if Sedge was killed? What would she do if Terrence was killed? Dear God, it was all her fault. Somehow, her brother must have found out about Sedge's offer. It was the only explanation. How he discovered it, she had not a clue. But it did not matter. He had found out and had challenged Sedge to a duel. And it was all her fault.

When Pansy returned, Meg literally pounced on the startled girl. "What did you find out? Tell me. Tell me!"

"It's a duel, all right," Pansy began. "Sir Terrence, he challenged Lord Sedgewick on account of some insult to you, miss."

Meg groaned. "Oh, God. I knew it. I *knew* it."

"His seconds are Lord Skeffington and Mr. Hawksworthy," Pansy continued, as if reciting a memorized verse. "Lord Sedgewick's seconds are Lord Pemerton and Mr. Herriot. The same Mr. Herriot what stayed at Thornhill, miss. Lord Sedgewick chose pistols. Sir Terrence will be usin' his own set. The viscount will be usin' Mr. Herriot's set. Lord Pemerton told Lord Skeffington that Mr. Herriot was set on usin' his own pistols. Real pushy, like. Lord Sedgewick didn't care one way or t'other, but Lord Pemerton thought it queer."

"But *where*, Pansy?" Meg wanted to shake the girl. Who cared about pistols and seconds? "Where is it to take place, and when?"

"Droggett don't know, miss."

Meg threw her head back and gave an inarticulate wail.

"We must find out, Pansy. How can I stop it if I don't know where it is?"

"But how, miss? How can I find out?"

"I don't know." Meg clutched her elbows and pressed her crossed arms tight against her abdomen. "I don't know. But we must do something. We cannot just sit here and wait until—Oh, God."

Pansy's face crumpled as she watched Meg's distress. "Lemme think," she murmured and began pacing the same path worn by Meg. After several trips across the room, she came to a stop and her head tilted up like a baby bird. "James," she said quietly to herself.

"James?" He was one of their footmen. "What about James?"

"He has a friend over to Mr. Hawksworthy's," Pansy said. "A footman. Thomas, from home in Suffolk, same as us. Maybe James could find out somethin' from Thomas."

"Yes!" Meg exclaimed. "James can find out something. Pansy, go find him at once and send him over to the Hawksworthy house. Now, hurry!"

"Yes, miss!"

A glimmer of hope began to flicker through the dark despair of the evening. James was a wily fellow. He would find out where this unspeakable outrage was to take place. And then maybe she could do some good for a change, and save two lives.

Charged with new energy, Meg tore off her wrapper

and gown and rummaged through her wardrobe. She pulled out a heavy merino carriage dress—sensible and warm—and kid half boots, and began to change.

It was five o'clock when Pansy finally returned, bursting with news. The duel was to be held at six o'clock at Tothill Fields, near Willow Walk. Six o'clock? Meg had less than an hour to get there, and she had a vague notion that Tothill Fields was some distance away.

"Yes, miss, it's in lower Westminster, practically to Chelsea."

"Dear God, I'll never make it," Meg said. "And I don't know exactly where it is."

"Not to worry, miss," Pansy said with a smile. "Thomas wrote out directions. Here."

She held out a crumpled piece of foolscap that Meg grabbed and took to the nearest branch of candles. The directions were clear, but it was indeed some distance.

She began to rip off the merino dress. "Get my breeches, Pansy. I'll have to ride. And ride fast."

Chapter 23

Sedge arrived at Tothill Fields with Jack and Albert several minutes ahead of schedule. He had not slept—how could he?—but was not weary. Heartsore, but not tired. He was too nervous to be tired.

Jack had learned from Skeffington and Hawksworthy that Ashburton had issued the challenge as a result of an insult to Meg. An insult to Meg! What could be more ludicrous? No only had Sedge made her an honorable offer of marriage which she had baldly rejected, but had refused her own less honorable offer. What had he done that could possibly be construed as an insult? Dammit all, if anyone had been insulted it was *him*.

He could not apologize for what he had not done, so this duel was to proceed. Sedge had never before been involved in a duel, except once as a spectator, and was thoroughly unnerved by the situation.

"Don't worry, old chap," Jack had told him. "I've fought my share of duels, in my former dissolute life. I will get you through this one."

Sedge almost did not care how or if he got through this one. His life had been turned topsy-turvy ever since that carriage accident. The broken leg had left him with a permanently stiff limb. The knock on the head had left him prone to headaches and very possibly had affected his sanity. He had sunk into drunkenness. The woman he wanted to marry did not want to marry him. And he was accused of an insult he had not made. It all added up to a less than perfect life. If Ashburton killed him, so be it.

Sedge was a fairly good shot, having hunted game every year since he was a boy. But he was uncertain about how well he could do with a dueling pistol. He kept a pair, of course. Every gentleman did. And he had practiced with them on occasion. But it was almost impossible to shoot straight with the damned things. And that concerned Sedge just now. He did not mean to harm Ashburton. It was dishonorable to fire in the air, though, God knows, that is what he would prefer to do. Instead, he hoped to take aim and miss. But with the vagaries of a dueling pistol, he might just as easily kill the man.

After all, he had hit that blasted highwayman with a single shot, from an awkward position in a carriage.

Thoughts of that episode sent a shudder down his back. He would most definitely aim to miss. Miss wide.

On top of the general concerns, he would be using an unfamiliar gun. Bertie had been adamant. He seemed so proud of his new Mantons that Sedge hadn't the heart to refuse him. But it concerned him that he would not know how to compensate in his aim.

Ashburton and his seconds arrived a few minutes later, with the doctor following close behind. The carriages were lined up along Willow Walk like black crows against the pink sky of early dawn. The field dipped down a bit from the road, and then flattened. It was at this area that the men congregated.

The seconds came together to formalize, in the presence of the principals, the terms and the distance. Sedge listened with half an ear while he studied his opponent's face. Ashburton's mouth was set in a grim line, and he seemed to

have acquired a permanent pair of creases between his
brows. His anger was still very much in evidence. Sedge
shuddered with a premonition that this man would kill him.

After terms were agreed upon, and the doctor took his
place in the distance, the seconds brought out the gun cases
and began to load.

* * *

Meg memorized Thomas's directions before setting out,
for it would be too dark to read them along the way. As she
galloped through Green Park and the Queen's Garden
toward Pimlico, she was haunted by alternate visions of
either Sedge or Terrence, bleeding and dying on some
distant green. Please God, let her be in time to stop it.

She did not wish to be the cause of yet another of
Sedge's unfortunate misadventures. Strange how he seemed
to attract misfortune. Who would have thought that a
private, though highly improper, discussion weeks ago at
Thornhill would result in this? Pistols at dawn. Meg had
never mentioned Sedge's offer to a single soul before
telling Gram last evening. How on earth such private
information could have reached he brother's ears, she might
never know. Blame it on Sedge's run of bad luck.

Meg rode hell for leather through the parks, but had to
dodge morning traffic as she reached James Street. The
slower pace that took her through the less than savory area
old almshouses and taverns made her glad she had dressed
as she did. She would surely be taken for a young man, and
hopefully left alone. At this hour the streets were filled with
peddlers and draymen and vendors of all kind, getting
ready for the day's business. She was likely in no danger.
And if she was she was in too much of a hurry to care.

The plodding pace made her jumpy and anxious as she
wound her way to ward Rochester Row. She must not be
too late. She must not.

Consideration of all the possible impediments to a timely arrival sent her thoughts back to Sedge and his bad luck. First there had been the curricle accident. But Seamus had been certain it was no accident. Then there had been Gram's mix-up with the monkshood. Surely an accident, though Gram had never believed that. Then there had been the time when Sedge had almost fallen down the stairs. Another accident? Or had someone deliberately spilled the oil of vitriol? She had almost thought so at the time but had dismissed it.

If they had not been accidents, then who had planned them? And why? Meg had never liked the valet Pargeter. Could he have been responsible? He had not been in the curricle with Sedge at the time of the accident, but had been with him the night before. As she recalled, he had stayed behind with a mysterious illness. He had certainly had access to the still-room, for Gram had showed him herself where to find the herbal mixture for her infusion. And he admitted spilling the oil of vitriol.

Good Lord, could Pargeter be trying to kill Sedge? Or was her mind overly agitated by this morning's urgency? What cause would Pargeter have to kill his employer?

And then there was the highwayman. Meg knew little about that episode, but Pargeter had certainly been there. She would wager he had also been present at the time of the fire in Sedge's bedchamber. Dear heaven, could he have had something to do with this duel?

Meg spurred her horse to greater speed down Rochester Row to Willow Walk. She saw the line of carriages and reined in. From her vantage point above she saw Mr. Hawksworthy and Mr. Herriot loading the guns. Thank God, she had made it in time! She dismounted and prepared to dash down to the field when something made her pause.

She watched as Mr. Herriot poured a measure of powder into the muzzle of his long-barreled pistol, followed by a linen-wrapped bullet which he tamped down with the ramrod. But there was something wrong. Meg had been around guns enough to know that Mr. Herriot held this one strangely, as if it were out of balance. But if the gun was not balanced, he, as the second, should not allow it to be used. And yet she watched as he handed it to Sedge, who seemed too dazed to notice anything out of the ordinary.

A shadow of a smile crossed Mr. Herriot's face as he handed the gun to his cousin. It was that smile, that mere flicker, that brought all the pieces of the puzzle together for Meg.

It was not Pargeter after all. It was Mr. Herriot. He was trying to kill his cousin.

* * *

Just as the men had finished pacing off and were taking aim, Sedge became distracted by a figure running headlong down the slope.

Meg!

"Stop! Don't shoot!" she shouted, running pell-mell between them, arms flailing, straight toward Sedge. Just as she knocked the gun out of Sedge's hands, a shot from Terrence struck him in the shoulder. Sedge crumpled to the ground with a groan.

Damnation!

Meg dropped to his side and flung her arms around him, sobbing all over his good shoulder. Sedge began to assess the situation. If he thought he was confused before, it was nothing to what he felt now. What the devil was going on? Perhaps he was, in fact, the only sane person while everyone else had gone crazy.

"Oh, Sedge," Meg said in a shaky voice. "He almost killed you."

Sedge lifted his good arm without thinking and wrapped it around Meg, pulling her close. "No, he only winged me," he said.

In the next moment, Ashburton grabbed Meg by the arms, jerked her upright, and actually began to shake her. The quick movement sent a stab of pain through Sedge's shoulder. He winced and just then the doctor knelt by his side. He quickly removed Sedge's jacket, waistcoat, and cravat in a most painful manner, and began examining the wound.

"You fool!" Ashburton scolded, shaking Meg by the shoulders. "I told you this was none of your affair. Why couldn't you have stayed away?"

"Because if I had, Sedge would be dead."

"Not dead," the doctor calmly interjected while applying an alum poultice to the wound. "'Tis only a flesh wound. The bullet struck the muscle, just here. Went clean through. Missed the bone, thank God. Messy, but not serious." He returned his attention to his patient and began winding a bandage tightly around Sedge's shoulder and under the armpit.

Ignoring the doctor, Ashburton returned his fulminating glare to his sister. "If you had not distracted me," he snapped, "I might have done more damage. But, what makes you so sure I would have killed him?"

"Not you," Meg said. Sedge watched in total astonishment as she turned and pointed to Albert. "Him." While all eyes turned to Sedge's cousin, Meg walked over to where the gun had been thrown and picked it up. She handed it to Lord Pemerton. "I think you will find this gun has been tampered with in some way."

Jack gently bounced the gun in his hand as a frown puckered his brow. "It's out of balance," he said. "Too heavy at the stock. Something's wrong here." He turned the gun over and unscrewed the base of the stock. "Good God," he exclaimed. "Look at this." Jack turned the gun upright over his palm, and black powder trickled out. And out. And out. When he held a sizable mound in his hand, he turned a furious glare on Albert. "What is the meaning of this, Herriot? A special chamber where the flint holder should be? A chamber filled with enough gunpowder to blow Sedge's head off?"

Skeffington and Hawksworthy were instantly at Albert's side, each grasping an arm so he could not escape. He looked down at the ground and said nothing.

"Good thing it wasn't cocked," Jack continued. "You might have jarred the hair trigger, Sedge, and been killed before the first shot was fired."

"Bertie? Is this true?" Sedge shrugged away the doctor's final ministrations while he studied his young cousin. His cousin who apparently wanted to kill him. "Bertie?"

The young man pursed his lips and refused to look up or to speak.

"How did you know, Meggie?"

At the sound of Ashburton's voice, Sedge wrenched his gaze from Albert.

"It all came to me in a moment," she said. "I was contemplating all of Sedge's accidents and began to suspect they might be related."

"That's the second time I've heard someone refer to Sedge's accidents," Jack said. "Would someone please tell me what is going on?"

"There are five incidents, that I know of," Meg said. "And I suddenly realized Mr. Herriot had opportunities in each case to orchestrate the so-called accident." She turned to look at Sedge. "He had been at the inn where the axle on your curricle had been sawn almost clean through. And I remembered Gram saying Mr. Herriot had come by the stillroom, pleasing her with his praise and recollections of his mother. He would have had access to the monkshood." She turned to Jack "He almost drank an infusion laced with monkshood, you see."

"Good Lord," Jack said, slanting a disgusted glance at Albert.

"And then there was the time he slipped and almost tumbled down the stairs." Turning back to Sedge, she continued. "Pargeter admitted spilling the oil of vitriol in the hallway, but swore he was not responsible for the oil at the edge of the landing. But, remember? He mentioned your cousin had been there and seen him spill the oil. It must have given him the idea."

"I never heard about that, Meggie," Ashburton said.

"Sorry, Terrence," she said. "I guess I had other things on my mind." She smiled at Sedge and his heart skipped a beat.

"The next thing, so far as I know, was the incident with the highwaymen."

"Highwaymen?" Jack said.

"What highwaymen?" Ashburton said.

"We were held up on our way back to London," Sedge explained. "I shot at the bounders and they fled. Winged one of 'em."

"Sedge!" Jack said. "You didn't?"

Sedge grinned. "I did." He sobered and looked at Albert. "Was that your doing, too, Bertie? Did you set that up?"

But Albert refused to speak.

"Then there was the fire," Jack said.

"And Mr. Herriot had told me all about it, you see," Meg said. "When I learned from Lady Pemerton that he should not have even known about it, I began to grow suspicious. But I did not put it all together until this morning."

Jack fixed Albert with a furious glare. "I suppose you just happened to visit Sedge before I arrived, eh, Herriot? Or did you break in, like some petty sneak thief?" Jack bared his teeth and looked like he might actually lunge at the fellow. "And now this," he hissed. "You miserable—"

"Why, Bertie?" Sedge asked, his voice and his heart full of sadness. "Why did you do it? Do you hate me so?"

A moment of tense silence ensued during which all eyes were turned on Albert. No one spoke. Finally, he raised his eyes.

"Bloody hell!" he said, lifting his chin defiantly. "All right. All right. I did it." His disdainful gaze raked them all as his upper lip twitched into a supercilious curl. "No sense in denying it now. Yes, I did it!"

"But why, Bertie? Why?"

"Dammit, Sedge," Albert said, "I was at my wit's end. Creditors on my tail. Vowels all over town. I needed your inheritance."

"But... I would have given you money, Bertie. You had only to ask."

"It was worse than that," Albert continued, his face flushed with belated embarrassment. "I've been living off my expectations as your heir for years. Then, suddenly, you up and start talking about marriage. Clear out of the blue." His voice took on a despondent tone. "I had counted on you remaining a bachelor. You had never hinted at marriage before. Never! What was I supposed to do if you married and produced an heir? Then where would I be?"

"You have two choices as to where you will be," Jack said, planting himself in front of Albert, arms akimbo. "These gentlemen can take you straight to Bow Street and charge you with attempted murder. Or you can leave the country and never show your miserable face in England again as long as you live."

"Oh, God," Albert choked. He turned a plaintive look on his cousin. "Sedge?"

"I'll take him, Sedge," Jack said, grabbing Albert's arm from Lord Skeffmgton. "I do not trust the cur. I will see that he is on his way to Portsmouth within the hour. I will even escort the blackguard. Hell, I will even pay for his bloody passage to ... to wherever the next ship sails. Come on, you despicable bastard."

Jack tugged Albert up the slope toward the line of

carriages. Halfway there, he stopped and turned around. "Oh, and, Sedge," he shouted across the distance, "you were right. She looks magnificent in breeches."

Chapter 24

Meg blushed to the roots of her hair at Lord Pemerton's words. She looked uncertainly at Sedge, who grinned, then turned her gaze to her brother, who scowled.

"I commend your clever reasoning in unmasking that scoundrel, Meggie," Ashburton said. "But why couldn't you have told me about your suspicions? Why did you have to come barreling straight into the middle of a duel, for God's sake?"

"I couldn't have told you before, Terrence. I only just put it all together this morning."

"But what were you thinking, girl?" Ashburton's voice rose in consternation. "Charging onto the field like that. You might have been killed yourself. Why would you do such an idiot thing?"

Meg's eyes moved to Sedge, then to Ashburton, then back to Sedge. "Because I love you both," she said.

Sedge's breath caught in his throat as he gazed into those beautiful eyes. She loved him. By God, she loved him! He reached out a hand and she placed hers in it. He tried to convey with his eyes all the things he would have said had they been alone. Elated by her bold declaration, Sedge was still confused by all that had happened between them. "Meg? Why?"

She squeezed his hand and he knew she understood his

question. "I thought that—"

Ashburton interrupted her by pushing himself between them. He turned his back to his sister and glared menacingly at Sedge. "I am sorry about the villainy of your cousin, Sedgewick, but there is still this other matter between us. I will have your apology, sirrah. How dare you offer my sister *carte blanche*!"

"But, Terrence—"

"*Carte blanche?* But I never—"

"She is a gently bred female," Ashburton went on, ignoring both their protests, "and you have dishonored her. I will not allow my sister to be so grossly insulted. Perhaps you ought to join your cousin and leave the country for a time. It would be most unfortunate if news of her dishonor were to spread."

And so the puzzling nightmare was not yet over. Sedge dragged a hand through his hair in confusion, wondering if he might have suffered another blow to the head when he fell. It was the only explanation for such incredible events and outrageous accusations. He shook his head slowly back and forth, wondering how things had ever gone so wrong. "I only wanted to marry her," he muttered.

"You what?" Ashburton said.

"Marry me?" Meg squeaked.

"Well, yes," Sedge said, looking at each of them with a bewildered expression on his face. "Of course. Don't you see? That is why Albert was so upset. He knew I wanted to marry you, Meg."

"Marry me?" she repeated, suddenly dumbfounded at this unexpected turn of events.

"Of course," Sedge said, his eyes narrowed in surprise at her reaction. "Did I not ask you that day at Thornhill?"

"No!"

His head jerked back on his neck. "What do you mean, no?"

"You never said anything about marriage," Meg said.

"But I must have," Sedge said, thoroughly confused. "I must have. What else would I have been talking about?"

All at once, Meg realized that she had somehow misunderstood his intentions from the beginning. She burst into laughter at the comedy of errors that had resulted from that single, misinterpreted conversation.

"I thought you offered me *carte blanche*," she said, still chuckling.

"Yes. That's what I heard you tell Gram," Terrence said.

Meg smiled at Sedge. "You talked about houses and jewels and carriages and"— she could not mention the part about making love to her day and night—"all the other. But you never mentioned marriage."

"Good Lord," Sedge said, eyes wide with astonishment, "is that true?" He reached up and ran his fingers through his hail again. "But I'm sure I mentioned marriage. Didn't I? I must have mentioned it." When Meg shook her head, he looked thoroughly flabbergasted. "I certainly intended to mention it. Truly, I did. That was my sole purpose, after all. I... I must have been overcome by ... by the moment." He looked straight into Meg's eyes, and she knew he referred to the passion of their kiss. "No wonder you rejected me out of hand," he said.

He smiled at her, and Meg's knees began to quiver. She had forgot all about Terrence and his seconds standing only a few feet away.

"But I finally decided that you were the only man I would ever love," she said in a soft voice. "I could not bear to be without you."

"Ah, Meg." Sedge's voice held a note of such tenderness Meg thought her knees might truly buckle this time. He reached out and took both her hands in his.

"I... I was ready to accept you on any terms," Meg continued, discomfited by the warm look in his eyes. "Even *carte blanche*. That is why I so brazenly threw myself at you."

"You did what?" Terrence's angry voice brought Meg back to the situation at hand.

Still holding Sedge's hands, she tilted her head over her shoulder in her brother's direction. Smiling broadly, she said, "I offered to be his mistress."

"You what!" Terrence's voice had become a roar.

Meg looked at Sedge and they both began to laugh. Terrence looked at them and clapped a hand to his head in apparent disgust. "Good Lord."

"And he actually had the temerity to refuse my offer!" Meg said in mock outrage before collapsing in laughter against Sedge's good shoulder. She felt a gentle hand stroke the back of her head and knew in that moment that everything would be all right.

"Of course I refused," Sedge said as she ran his fingers against her silky hair, warm from the morning sun and smelling of wild violets. "I am a gentleman, after all. I would never dream of treating a woman so dishonorably." He nudged Meg away from his shoulder and held her out so he could look into her eyes. "Especially the woman I love."

"Oh, Sedge."

Their mouths moved inexorably toward each other, but were interrupted by the sound of a clearing throat. Sedge smiled at Meg and shrugged in resignation, then moved her to his side, keeping an arm around her shoulders as they faced her brother.

"It seems I owe you an apology, Sedgewick," Terrence said.

"That is not necessary," Sedge said. "I understand completely. I would have done the same for my sister, if I thought some bounder had offered her a slip on the shoulder."

"Sorry about *your* shoulder," Terrence said.

Sedge laughed. "Just another one of those unfortunate mishaps on the road to happiness," he said, tightening his good arm around Meg.

"Well," Terrence said, "I suppose we had better arrange a meeting of a different sort. Am I right, Sedgewick?"

"Absolutely." He removed his arm from Meg's shoulders, and held out his hand to her brother. Terrence grasped it without hesitation and pumped it vigorously.

"I shall look forward to that conversation, Sedgewick," Terrence said, smiling for the first time. "I trust you will take good care of her. I am quite fond of her, you know."

"Thank you, Terrence," Meg said as she threw her arms around her startled brother and kissed him on the cheek. "Thank you for defending my honor. And," she said, her eyes darting to Sedge, "for everything else."

"Come along, Ashburton," Lord Skeffington said, taking his friend by the arm. "I believe we are decidedly *de trop*."

"You will see Meg home, Sedgewick?" Terrence asked as both his friends tugged him up the slope.

"Of course," Sedge replied, taking Meg's hands once again and pulling her close.

"Don't be long, Meggie."

"No, Terrence," she said absently as she lost herself in the deep blue of Sedge's eyes.

Sedge and Meg stared silently at one another—studying, admiring, loving—until they heard the sound of the carriages leaving. Only then did Sedge pull her into his arms. He crushed her to his chest and set his mouth to hers. She gave a small sigh of pleasure beneath his lips as the kiss became deep, lush, and resonant with new understanding and love.

When they separated at last, Sedge leaned his forehead against Meg's and smiled into her eyes. "What a pair of prize fools we've been, Meg," he said.

"Yes."

"All those ridiculous misunderstandings."

"Yes."

"And senseless heartache."

"Yes."

"Let me see if I can get it right this time," he said. He stroked her jaw with his thumb, the gentle caress causing Meg's heart to quicken with impatience. Finally, he tilted her chin up. "I love you, Meg. Will you marry me?"

"Yes," she said, and then covered his mouth with her own.

###

More Regency Romances from Candice Hern

The following traditional Regency Romances are available in both print and digital formats:

The Regency Rakes Trilogy:
A PROPER COMPANION
A CHANGE OF HEART
AN AFFAIR OF HONOR

The Country House Party Duo:
A GARDEN FOLLY
THE BEST INTENTIONS

MISS LACEY'S LAST FLING
"DESPERATE MEASURES" (a Regency short story)

Here's an excerpt from **A GARDEN FOLLY**:

Oh, but it was grand to be back in the country again! To smell clean air, fragrant of summer blossoms and wood smoke. To enjoy clear, blue skies unblemished with coal soot, and sweeping expanses of brilliant green parklands. To have so much space to oneself.

Catherine had not realized how much she missed the country. She had not been out of Chelsea since going there to live with Aunt Hetty after her father's death. Dorland, the small Forsythe estate in Wiltshire, had been lost along with everything else when their father died. All her young life she had longed for a Season in Town, but Sir Benjamin Forsythe's precarious finances had never allowed it. More than two years of scraping to make ends meet in Chelsea, however, had shattered any romantical notions she might have once held regarding the glories of London. Oh, there were glories to be seen in Town, to be sure; but not for the likes of impoverished single ladies in Flood Street.

Perhaps if—when!—she and Susannah contrived to find rich husbands at Chissingworth, she would not mind so much going back to London. In style, this time.

At the moment, she was simply happy to be back in the country. Chissingworth was famous for its gardens and Catherine was anxious to see as much of them as possible. She loved flowers of all kinds, especially wildflowers. At Dorland, one of her greatest pleasures had been painting detailed watercolors of her favorite blossoms. She still kept a portfolio of her paintings of which she was really quite proud.

It had been a long time since she had been able to afford paints and brushes and decent parchment. But she had brought along to Chissingworth a few rolls of foolscap and two or three pencils, one of which was tucked in her pocket at the moment. She harbored secret hopes of finding new and unusual specimens to sketch while in residence at the famous estate.

With this in mind, she wandered through the surprisingly informal arrangement of gardens. In the dressed grounds nearest the house, high, clipped shrubbery hedges of sweetbrier, box, and hawthorn surrounded each garden. Moving through the enclosed hedges was akin to walking through the various rooms of a house, each room different from the last. One was awash in the bright colors of summer, the gravel paths bordered with stocks, pinks, double rocket, sweet Williams, and asters. The morning sun fell upon spires of delphinium sparkling with dew. Her artist's eye was drawn to the glitter of moisture on the indigo and royal peaks, and she paused to seat herself on a nearby stone bench. She pulled a pencil and a scrap of paper from her pocket and roughly sketched the familiar blossoms.

After a few moments, Catherine moved on to the next garden, which was devoted to roses of all shades. She tilted her head back, closed her eyes, and breathed in the heady fragrance of so many blossoms. She did not, though, stop to draw any of the roses. She instead wandered through a break in the hedge to another garden, this one laid out in a large circle. The plantings graduated in height, from tiny candytuft and sweet mignonette, to lupin, poppies, mallows, and sweet peas. Towering above them all in the center were enormous sunflowers. Catherine was much taken with the harmonious arrangement of such humble varieties as she slowly skirted the circular path, looking for a specimen that she might want to capture on paper.

"Oh! How wonderful!" she exclaimed as she came upon a patch of sweet violets flourishing in the shade of the larger plants. Kneeling down, she carefully caressed the dark purple blossoms of what could only be a pure *viola odorata*. She had never actually seen one before, most common violets being hybrids of other *violaceae*. But she recognized the pure ancestor of the ordinary sweet violet from pictures in one of the illustrated flower books she had once owned. She really must sketch this one. Perhaps if she made a detailed-enough sketch, she would one day be able to paint it in color, from memory.

Leaning in closer, she began to carefully examine the soft, fragile petals, holding the blossom ever so gently between her fingers.

And suddenly, she was knocked backward with a thud.

What on earth?

"Damnation!" muttered the man who had apparently come careening around the garden path directly into her. He grabbed at Catherine's shoulders in an attempt to balance himself.

Instead, he knocked her flat on her back and fell directly on top of her.

Catherine gasped, her face crushed against a dirt-covered smock. "Get off me, you oaf!" she sputtered, pushing against the man's chest.

Muttering something unintelligible, he raised himself slightly and looked down at her. His hat had been knocked away and a curl of dark brown hair fell over his furrowed brow. Green eyes flickered with annoyance and his mouth was a thin line of irritation. But the most noticeable thing about the man at the moment was his weight, which was crushing the breath right out of her.

"Get off!" she repeated.

* * *

Stephen gazed down into the flashing eyes of a very pretty little termagant. Bloody hell! He was in for it now, for she was no doubt one of his mother's guests. He hadn't expected anyone in the gardens this early. He had not been paying much attention to the path, his eyes surveying the center garden as he hurried past. He had not seen the girl as she knelt down at the edge of the gravel walk. And here he was sprawled atop her in a most improper manner.

If it wasn't so awkward, he might be tempted to enjoy it for a moment. She really was very pretty. Dark blond curls were revealed beneath the bonnet that had been knocked askew. Her brows and eyelashes were a much darker color, providing a striking contrast to her fair hair. Her eyes, framed by the long, dark lashes, appeared to be gray.

She really was *very* pretty.

"Get off me!" she repeated in a choked voice.

Coming to his senses, he realized he must be practically smothering her, so he quickly rolled to the side. "I beg your pardon," he said as he struggled ungracefully to his feet. He extended a hand to help her up. "I am terribly sorry. Are you quite all right?"

She grabbed his hand and allowed him to pull her to a sitting position. She neither looked at him nor answered him, but adjusted her bonnet. "You might have looked where you were going!" she said in a petulant tone. She sat up on her knees and Stephen offered his hand again. She took it, pulled herself upright, then immediately dropped it to shake out her skirts.

"I am terribly sorry," he repeated, brushing himself off and searching the area for his hat. He did not know what else to say. He was reluctant to get into a conversation with the young woman, attractive though she may be. If she recognized him as the duke—which she had thankfully not yet done—there was no telling what sort of fuss she would make. He must get away as quickly as possible before the chit realized who he was and went squealing off to the other guests that she had sighted the elusive duke.

Damn his mother and her parties, anyway. Why couldn't they leave him in peace to putter in his gardens?

"I am so sorry," he said again, trying to keep the annoyance out of his voice as he retrieved his broad-brimmed straw hat from beneath a patch of blue gentian. He slapped it against his thigh a few times and plopped it back upon his head. "It was my fault completely. I trust you are uninjured?"

"I am fine," she said, still straightening her skirts and not looking at him. Stephen's stomach seized up with the notion that she had not yet got a good look at him. There was still a chance she might recognize him. "No thanks to you," she continued in that irritated tone. "And *of course* it was your fault. I was simply minding my own business, admiring the—" She stopped as she looked down at her hand. "Oh, dear."

Stephen moved closer, thinking she might have injured her hand and cursing himself for his own carelessness. "What is it? Have you—" He paused as he saw that she was not injured, but was holding on to a crushed purple blossom.

Good God! It was one of his violets.

His prized, rare, pure-bred violets.

Forgetting for a moment his own culpability, he raged at the girl. "How *dare* you pick my flowers without asking! Do you think these are placed here for anyone to pluck at will? Don't you know—"

"*Your* flowers?" she said, her eyes widening in surprise.

Good Lord. He had given himself away. What an idiot! He was in for it, now.

But his poor violets.

"Oh! You must be the gardener," she said.

The gardener? Looking down at himself, he realized that no one would take his scruffy appearance for that of a duke. He experienced an almost uncontrollable urge to laugh. "Yes," was all he could say. They were his gardens, after all. And he did design them and work in them. So in a sense, he *was* the gardener.

"Well, you still might try to watch where you are going next time," the girl said.

By God, she was looking him straight in the eye and truly believed he was the gardener. It was too good.

"I am sure you are quite busy and all," she continued, "with such a large estate to care for. But you must know that the duchess has a house full of guests who might be wandering the gardens at any time. You really must be more careful."

The petulant tone had disappeared and she seemed less offended. Interesting. He would have expected most young women of her station—for she must be aristocratic to have been invited by his mother—to disdain the working staff. He would have expected her to rail against his clumsiness, to threaten to report him to his employer, to exert all the superiority of her station. Instead, she looked wistfully down at the crushed blossom in her palm.

"And I was not picking your flowers, if you must know," she continued. "I was simply admiring them. I must have accidentally grabbed at it when you fell over me."

"Yes. Yes, of course," Stephen muttered. His cheeks felt warm and he knew he must be blushing as he recalled how he had been sprawled atop her. "I should not have shouted at you. It is just that..." He paused and looked down at the remains of the tiny purple flower. "Well, you cannot know how precious that little plant is."

"Oh, but I can," she replied. "It is a pure *viola odorata*, is it not?"

"Why, yes," he said, completely taken aback that this young girl would know such a thing. "Yes, it is. How did you know?"

"Oh, I have never actually seen one before," she said, "not really, anyway. But I have seen many pictures of them. I love flowers, you see and have— had—many books on the subject. Some with lovely colored prints of various blossoms. Violets have always been my favorites, the simple *viola odorata* most of all. When I saw this patch of them," she said, gesturing to the clump of purple blossoms at the edge of the path, "I could not resist examining them up close. You must have cultivated them especially to bloom so long into summer, did you not? I thought to sketch one, you see. Oh, and I had also considered drawing this one, too," she added, bending to admire the fringed gentian. "Very unusual. The dark blue coloring and the fringed edges are a combination I have never before seen. Are they a special hybrid?"

Stephen's breath was almost knocked out of him as he listened to this extraordinary speech. Here was a very pretty young woman, with dark blond curls spilling out of her bonnet and huge gray eyes peering at him guilelessly, who knew about rare flowers and special hybrids—his favorite subjects—and wasn't fawning all over him. And she actually had no idea who he was.

It was delicious.

It was too perfect.

He could not keep from smiling.

"Yes," he said at last. "How clever of you to notice. They are indeed a special hybrid. I developed the strain myself."

"How wonderful," she exclaimed. "You must be very proud. Of everything here at Chissingworth."

"I am indeed," he said, strangely affected by her genuine interest and admiration for the one thing in his life of which he was truly proud. "You must feel free to sketch or paint all you want while at Chissingworth. I promise you will not be so rudely accosted again."

She smiled at him, and he almost forgot to breathe. "Thank you," she said. "I imagine there are many other rare specimens besides *viola odorata*. It would be lovely to sketch them."

"I would be pleased to show you the gardens myself, and point out the most unusual specimens and such." He could have bitten his tongue off the moment the words were spoken. What on earth had made him say such a thing? He was trying to hide from his mother's guests. He had no business encouraging this young woman, this very pretty young woman, to fraternize with him. What if she discovered his true identity?"

"How kind of you," she said, flashing a brilliant smile. "I would enjoy that. What better tour guide could I possibly ask for than Chissingworth's gardener? By the way, I am Miss Catherine Forsythe."

Good Lord. What was he to do now? Introduce himself as the owner of Chissingworth, not merely the gardener? How would she treat him, then? Her open, artless conversation would change to egregious fawning and preening, and that inevitable predatory glint would brighten her eyes. He did not believe he could bear it.

And so, how should he introduce himself? Give his name as Stephen Archibald Frederick Charles Godfrey Manwaring? Would she recognize that moniker as belonging to the Duke of Carlisle?

Perhaps not. Perhaps if he just shortened it, did not give her all the important bits, he might get away with it. "I am Stephen Archibald," he blurted, without further thought.

"I am pleased to meet you, Mr. Archibald."

By God, it had worked. She believed it. Miss Forsythe truly believed him to be Mr. Archibald, the gardener at Chissingworth. He bit back a grin. It was almost too perfect.

"And I must tell you how much I have enjoyed your gardens," she continued. "I have only just arrived, though, and look forward to seeing the rest of the grounds during my stay."

"Shall we meet again tomorrow morning, then?" In for a penny, in for a pound. "I could show you the botanical gardens where the more exotic plants are kept." It was the least frequented area of the estate and they were unlikely to run into any other wandering guests.

"That would be lovely."

"The same time tomorrow morning, then? But some other place, please. I would not have you reminded of our ignominious introduction here. Through those hedges and a bit beyond is the Chinese garden. There is a small pavilion in the center. I could meet you there."

"Assuming the duchess or my aunt have no other plans for me," she said, "I shall be there. Thank you so very much, Mr. Archibald. I look forward to it."

With a wave and a smile, she was off, disappearing through the entrance to the rose garden. Stephen watched her go and gave a wistful sigh.

And wondered what on earth he had got himself into.

* * *

Historical Romances by Candice Hern

You might also enjoy these sexier historical romances, all set during the Regency period, and available as ebooks at most e-retailers

The Merry Widows:
IN THE THRILL OF THE NIGHT
JUST ONE OF THOSE FLINGS
LADY BE BAD

The Ladies' Fashionable Cabinet:
ONCE A DREAMER
ONCE A SCONDREL
ONCE A GENTLEMAN

THE BRIDE SALE
HER SCANDALOUS AFFAIR

Here's an excerpt from **IN THE THRILL OF THE NIGHT**:

"You want me to help you find a lover?"

Put so bluntly, it did sound rather ridiculous. Marianne suddenly felt very foolish for even mentioning the idea. What had possessed her to do such a thing? She still could hardly believe she'd decided on this course. But in her mind's eye she had seen Penelope's glowing face on one side and Lavinia's dark martyrdom on the other. There was no question about which of the two faces she wanted to wear.

"Forgive me, Adam. I should not have asked. I just thought ..."

What had she thought? That he'd do exactly what he teased her about? That he would step in and do the job, providing her with "all the pleasure she could possibly imagine?" She was quite sure he could have followed through on such a promise. One had only to look in those green eyes to know it. She was almost glad his betrothal precluded such an arrangement. He knew her well enough to realize she would never seek intimacy with another woman's man.

"You thought I was your friend and would help you, as friends do. So, how can I help you?"

She was not entirely sure. But since the last meeting of the Fund trustees, she realized she was not as experienced in the bedroom as she had thought. She did not even know what she did not know. And that was what excited her about this whole business. What would it be like to be physically intimate with a man again, intimate in ways she could not even imagine? It sometimes thrilled her to think of it, but just as often frightened her.

"Well." How to begin? How to say what she wanted to say without dying of mortification? "You see, David is the only man I ... well, you know. I never ..." She felt her cheeks flame with embarrassment. She could not believe she was having this conversation. "Oh, Adam, I just don't know how to go about this. I don't know who would be a good ... who would know how ..." She pounded a fist against the chair arm. "Damn it all, I don't know anything. I don't know how to find the right man."

Adam shook his head. "If you expect me to tell you which man would make the best lover, then you're out, Marianne. I'm sorry, but that is asking too much. How should I know something like that? You'd be better off asking another woman." He grinned. "The duchess, for example."

She had thought about talking to Wilhelmina, but became too tongue-tied to do so. And yet here she was, having just such a conversation with Adam.

"You are right. I shouldn't be bothering you. It's just ... well, it's not all about what a man does in the bedroom."

He quirked an eyebrow. "Is it not? I thought that was the whole point."

"Yes, but I also need a man who will be discreet. I don't want my name bandied about at the clubs or, God forbid, mentioned in the betting books. I would like my privacy respected."

"A gentleman of honor, then," he said. "I would expect nothing less. And what else?"

"I do not want a man with an eye to marriage, or an eye on my fortune. It must be someone willing to accept me on my own terms."

"A physical relationship only?"

"For the most part. No entanglements."

"A man of the world, one who covets your body but not your fortune." His hooded gaze followed the line of her hips and thighs, sending a sudden flush of heat through her veins. "That should not be difficult. And what else?"

Damn the man for looking at her like that. She had become much more aware lately of the words and looks and touches that passed between men and women. She had known Adam most of her life, knew him to be a seducer of women, but he had never turned those bedroom eyes on her in such a provocative way.

Or had she just never noticed?

She gathered her composure and smiled at his feigned insolence. "Well, it would be nice if he was handsome, of course."

He laughed. "Of course. A handsome gentleman of honor with some skill between the sheets who is content with an uncomplicated affair. The field narrows. And what else? A man of fashion?"

"I do not think that is important. He should be presentable and clean, naturally, but I doubt a man overly concerned with his wardrobe would be an appropriate candidate."

"Quite right. No pinks of the *ton*. Too absorbed in themselves to do right by a woman. What about fortune?"

"That should not be a consideration."

"And age?"

"Hmm. I had not thought of it. I suppose it would not serve the purpose for him to be in his dotage."

"Certainly not. The fellow must be able to perform, after all. And an old roué would not suit you." He gave an exaggerated shudder. "So, we are looking for a gentleman who is handsome, discreet, and not given to dandified ways, who offers no entanglements, and is still vigorous enough to satisfy a woman's needs. Have I got it right so far?"

She grinned and realized that he had put her entirely at ease by making a game of the whole business. "Yes, that sounds about right to me. And also —"

"Egad, there's more? My dear, if you become too particular in your tastes, you risk narrowing the field to the point where there is no man left standing."

"But, Adam, this hypothetical man and I will spend a great deal of time together, and not just in the bedroom. There ought to be more than just ... *that*, shouldn't there? I would like a man I can talk to, a man who has a way with women, a man I can enjoy being with."

A man like you.

"A gentleman with both conversation and charm." She nodded. "Yes, that's it."

"A tall order, my dear. And, of course, none of it matters if the chap is not also a skillful lovemaker. Correct?"

"Yes, I suppose that's true. Oh, Adam, I know it sounds foolish and you are merely teasing me, but I just want ..."

She could not admit it aloud, not to Adam, but she wanted that excitement and passion Penelope talked about. She wanted what her friends had experienced. Just once in her life.

* * *

Adam knew what she wanted, probably better than she did. And yet, out of sheer perversity, he seemed determined she should not have it. What man could possibly be worthy of her? And how could any man hope to measure up to David Nesbitt, who was no doubt as talented and skillful in the bedroom as he was at everything else he did?

Poor Marianne was doomed to disappointment.

Adam did not lack confidence in his own sexual prowess, and thought he just might be able to best the memory of David in that particular arena. Now that it was impossible to put that confidence to the test, he was strangely loath to see any other man make the attempt.

"All teasing aside," she said, "would you be willing to advise me on whether certain men would ... meet my needs?"

"You have someone in mind?"

"Actually, I have a list."

"Good God, a list? Damnation, Marianne, this will require more wine. Do you by chance have another bottle at hand?"

"You know where to find it."

He did indeed. She still kept it in the deep bottom drawer of the kneehole desk in the corner, where David had always kept a ready supply. Adam retrieved a bottle and uncorked it. Without bothering to decant it — this business of a list of potential lovers could not wait for such niceties — he carried the bottle with him and set it on the candlestand between them. He topped off her glass before refilling his own.

After taking a restorative swallow of claret, he said, "You have a list."

She reached for the book she'd tucked beside the seat cushion and retrieved a folded sheet of paper from between the pages. "I jotted down a few names. What do you think of Lord Peter Bentham?"

Devil take it, he was going to have to think fast. "Bentham? Younger son of Worthing? Big, strapping chap with yellow hair?"

"Yes, that's him."

"I would steer clear of that one if I were you."

"Why?"

"I've heard the fellow has a hot temper and a violent streak."

"Lord Peter? I can hardly believe it. He seems like such a kind gentleman."

"Appearances can be deceiving. Most fellows are on their best behavior in public, especially around females. But one hears talk in the clubs. I would be uneasy if I thought you were involved with a man like Bentham. For my peace of mind, may we cross him off the list?"

"All right." Her voice was tinged with disappointment. Had she really been attracted to that great hulking oaf?

"Who's next?"

"Sir Dudley Wainfleet."

He chuckled softly. "You'll have no success there, my dear."

"Why not?"

"Just between you and me, the man is not particularly interested in women."

Her eyes widened. "You mean ..."

"Precisely. Cross him off. Who's next?"

"Robert Plimsoll."

He shook his head and laughed. "It is a good thing you sought my advice on this list of yours."

She lifted her chin at a challenging angle. "Is there some objection to Mr. Plimsoll?"

"Only that he keeps a mistress and their five children in a house in Hampstead."

She gave a little gasp of surprise. "You're joking? I never heard such a thing about him."

"Women never do. Sometimes not even wives know about their husbands' second families. Trust me, my dear. Every man of the *ton* knows about that house in Hampstead."

"Oh dear. How very frustrating. It is indeed fortunate that I asked your advice." She sighed and took a sip of wine as she looked down at her list. "Harry Shackleford?"

Adam frowned, but said nothing. This exercise was becoming more distasteful. The thought of any of these men with Marianne was intolerable.

"What? Is there something wrong about him, too?"

He shrugged. "Nothing specific. Just a gut feeling."

"And what does your gut say?"

"It may sound odd, but I don't like the way the man treats his horses."

A puzzled frown marked her brow. "His horses?"

"Yes. He shows no care at all for them, and is a tad too free with the whip and the spur. He is downright cruel to the poor beasts, running them until they're lame. And I have observed that a man who mistreats his cattle often shows the same disregard for his women. I don't trust him."

A suspicious glint lit her eyes. "You think I should cross him off the list?"

"It is entirely up to you, my dear. I am only offering an observation."

"Hmm. All right then. Lord Rochdale."

Adam almost choked on his wine. "Rochdale?" he sputtered. The fellow was one of his closest friends and a notorious libertine. The very idea of Marianne and Rochdale together was simply not to be borne. The man would use her and toss her aside without a second thought. Surely she knew that. "You're not serious?"

She smiled. "No, I'm not."

He heaved a sigh of relief. *Thank God.*

"I only wanted to get back at you for objecting to every other man on my list."

"Wretch! You almost gave me an apoplexy."

"Serves you right."

Her dimples flashed and she looked adorable, all curled up and cozy in her shawl with her feet tucked underneath her like a girl. Funny. He'd never noticed what dainty feet she had. Despite Adam's best efforts, it seemed some lucky fellow was going to tuck those pretty feet in a very different posture and wrap himself around her better than any shawl. Damn.

"Now," she said, "shall we continue?"

"There's more?"

"Lots more. It's quite an extensive list, you see."

She held up the paper and it did indeed look like there were twenty or more names on it. Adam poured another glass of wine. It was going to be a long night.

* * *

About the Author

Candice Hern is the award-winning, bestselling author of historical romance novels set during the English Regency, a period she knows well through years of collecting antiques and fashion prints of the period. She travels to England regularly, always in search of more historical and local color to bring her stories and characters to life.

Her books have won praise for the "intelligence and elegant romantic sensibility" (*Romantic Times*) as well as "delicious wit and luscious sensuality (*Booklist*).

Candice's award-winning website (www.candicehern.com) is often cited for its Regency World pages, where readers interested in the era will find an illustrated glossary, a detailed timeline, illustrated digests of Regency people and places, articles on Regency fashion, research links, and much more. It is the only author website listed among the online resources for the Jane Austen Centre in England.

Visit www.candicehern.com for more information on all Candice's books, including excerpts and a look "behind the scenes" of each novel.

Made in the USA
San Bernardino, CA
03 January 2018